The Weaving

A Tyler Cunningham Collection

Jamie Sheffield

2014

"The Weaving"
A Tyler Cunningham Collection
© Jamie Sheffield, 2014

"Mickey Slips" Original E-book publication 2013
Cover photo "Cold Whiskey" by Yekophotostudio, used with
permission through Dreamstime.com

"Bound for Home" Original E-book publication 2013

"Promises to Keep" Original E-book publication 2014

"Fair Play" Original E-book publication 2014

Published by SmartPig through CreateSpace and Amazon.com KDP.
This is a work of fiction. Names, characters, places and incidents are
either products of the author's imagination or are used fictitiously.
While the descriptions are based on real locations in the Adirondack
Park, any resemblance to actual events or persons, living or dead, is
entirely coincidental.

ISBN-10 1500295078
ISBN-13 -978-1500295073

Randy Lewis joined the SmartPig team after a discussion one morning about "Here Be Monsters" at the Airport Cafe, in Lake Clear. She saw through the errors and shortcomings of an independent author's first work, to the story inside, and said that she wanted to be a part of helping me to tell stories. The work that she did to help Gail and I prepare "Caretakers" for publication was nothing short of miraculous. Beyond her technical prowess, though, Randy showered us, and me, and Tyler with love and support that made me glad and proud to have known her, and I wish that I had gotten to know her better and earlier in my writing, and in my life.

This collection, and everything I write from here on out, is for you, Randy … thank you for everything.

CONTENTS

"… warp well the long threads,
The bright threads, the strong threads;
Woof well the cross threads,
To make the colours shine."

So weave well the bright threads,
The red threads, the green threads.
Woof well the strong threads
That bind their hearts to thine.

The Weaving of the Tartan
Alice Macdonell of Keppoch – 1894

INTRODUCTION

If you want to get straight to the stories, and skip through my explanations of the thinking and process behind the novellas, I promise my feelings won't be hurt (I'll never even know), but if you have wondered about the shorts, then this may be of interest to you.

I started writing Tyler Cunningham novellas as the result of a discussion with my wife, Gail, one night while we were out enjoying dinner at Liquids and Solids in Lake Placid, SmartPigging. She asked me about some event mentioned, but not broken out in any detail, in "Here Be Monsters", and was surprised when I knew all of the details. We kept enjoying our dinner, and it came up that Gail would be interested in knowing the backstories of some of the key characters in Tyler's world; I thought about it for a minute, and decided that I would have fun telling those stories.

I think that these characters, and their stories enrich the world in which Tyler operates because he has difficulty forming connections with people, so each of those connections must trace back to an interesting formative event. I like knowing the origin of Tyler's relationships with Mickey and Maurice and John and Dorothy and Frank because they all play significant roles in the way that he moves through his world in the Tri-Lakes, as well as through the mysteries that he finds himself involved in up in the Adirondacks. I have always enjoyed the idea of peeking behind the curtain in books that I read, and comments from readers who have enjoyed the stories in this collection would seem to support the idea that other people do as well.

The process of writing the novellas is radically different than the one I employ when working on the novel. The novels are written during a month-long writing session every summer, during which I try to write 3,000 words each and every day. The shorts are written during the school year (my day job is as a Special Education Teacher in the Lake Placid Central School District), when I can find time to write … sometimes at the end of the day, sometimes early in the morning, sometimes during a weekend when my family is doing something else. I am happy when I am able to write a few hundred words on the shorts. I do lots of planning and note-taking before I ever start writing the novels, whereas with the novellas I just start writing. My novels are planned and written around Tyler's approach to a central conflict/challenge, while the novellas are conceived from the perspective of the supporting characters, and how Tyler will become involved to help them weather their particular fire.

The order of publication of the novellas was based on the importance of the subject to Tyler's world, not the chronology of events. Mickey played an important role in Tyler becoming Tyler, long before we got to know him, so "Mickey Slips" needed to be first. Tyler's 'homelessness' needed to be explained, as did the process of his slipping into the role of consulting detective; I knew about Maurice and the story of "Bound for Home" before I started writing, while John's existence was a complete surprise to me. Dorothy is a major part of Tyler's world, and so "Promises to Keep" was a logical next story to tell. Tyler's interface with local law enforcement, most notably in the personage of Frank Gibson, is important to maintain believability, and so it made sense to focus on Frank for the fourth novella.

For the purposes of this collection, these stories are presented in chronological order, rather than the order of publication. Chronologically, the first published novel, "Here Be Monsters" comes after "Fair Play" and before "Mickey Slips". The second novel, "Caretakers" comes after "Mickey Slips" and before "Promises to Keep".

The title of this collection grew from the idea that we all weave the disparate, and often messy threads of the relationships and people in our lives together to make the tapestry that our world will become ...

... this is Tyler's weaving

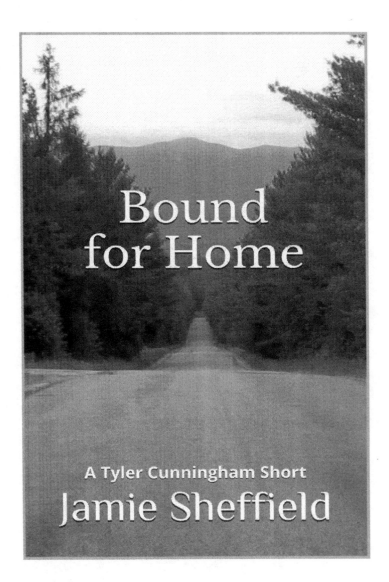

Bound
for Home

A Tyler Cunningham Short

Jamie Sheffield

Bound for Home

SmartPig Office, Saranac Lake, NY
Tuesday, 6/4/2002, 3:48 p.m.

When Maurice broke into my office and found me asleep on the couch, he pointed a narrow finger dramatically in my direction and actually said, "Aha!" (*like a policeman revealing the guilty party on an old TV show*). I struggled my way up into the world, and wondered some combination of 'now what?', 'get out!', and 'lunch? … maybe donuts'. He must have tiptoed up, putting his weight on the sides of the old wooden stairs in the old wooden building (*or I would have heard the creaking which normally alerts me to people approaching*). Since he owns the whole building and I'm never behind on my rent, it occurred to me that he had no need to sneak around, so he must have wanted something in particular.

"Maurice, come in," I offered, although he was already in. Social conventions are hard enough for me to learn and follow when people follow them, but I had no idea how to treat someone who entered my locked office without my permission; so I ignored it.

My greeting seemed to take the wind out of his

accusatory sails; he lowered his pointing finger, and jingled his keys with an apologetic tilt of his head and arching of eyebrows.

My landlord Maurice communicates largely through gestures, and in the nearly seven months that I've been renting this office space, it has become abundantly clear that he finds my manner of human-to-human interactions equally off-putting and confusing. He dragged one of the chairs around my work-table (*really a kitchen table, but there's no kitchen, so …*) and moved it close to the couch, then settled himself slowly down onto the seat as I shook myself free of the last of my nap.

"What do you want?" I asked, in a manner much too direct for Maurice, who prefers to circle the subject for discussion sometimes for an hour or more before getting down to business.

Maurice looked at me blankly, patted the chest pocket of his worn-thin flannel shirt, pulled out a mostly crushed pack of Lucky Strikes (*the short filterless ones, I noticed*), and looked around (*as he always does*) for an ashtray. I hate the smell of cigarettes, and have to air out SmartPig for hours after each visit from Maurice. He knows this, but it's (*probably*) better than him lifting his leg to claim dominance/territory like the dogs at the shelter.

I fished an empty Coke can out of the recycling bin, and passed it to him. He looked at the can with a mixture of deep sadness and disappointment (*at me … the can … both … I'll never know*), shook it, and tapped the half-inch of ash already accumulated into the can (*which gave off a sour little hiss as the hot ash fell into the few stray milliliters of Coke at its bottom*).

I don't want to repeat my question, but Maurice seemed either not to have heard it the first time, or was waiting for reasons known only to him to respond. He nodded and smoked and tapped and sighed, then whistled through his teeth and asked, "So it was cold last night, yes?"

It's been coming for months, but I saw it in a flash of conversational (*and gestural*) images now; the next ninety seconds of this conversation could leave me actually (*as opposed to only virtually*) homeless. When I settled into my new life in the Adirondacks, and found how much I loved camping and sleeping outdoors, I let the lease on my apartment in town lapse, keeping the office-space for my few belongings and to have a place to get out of the rain. Maurice must have figured out that I no longer have an apartment (*people in small towns apparently know almost everything, about almost everyone, almost all of the time*), and became concerned that I was using the SmartPig office as a residence (*which is in violation of my lease*). I had a moment of mixed fear/anger/panic/frustration as I contemplated losing this space, but Maurice didn't see it; I don't emote like other people do, and unless I'm trying, I don't generally have facial expressions … or blush … or cry.

"Yes, it was … surprisingly so," I responded, ready to talk about the weather for hours, if called upon to do so. "It was record-breaking if I'm not mistaken." (*I'm not.*) "Twenty-six this morning when I woke up next to Little Green Pond, and it hit seventy this afternoon just before I lay down for my nap."

Maurice squinted at me through his smoke, and dropped the tiny butt of his cigarette down into the can, giving it a shake before putting it down purposefully on my table.

"And tonight … where will you sleep tonight Tyler?" He looked around the room as he asked, taking in the neat piles of gear, the slightly less neat piles of books and magazines, and the messy piles of clothes that a slightly open closet door has failed to hide. He got up, shook the butt out into my garbage, rinsed the can in the sink, and returned it to the recycling container; looking uncomfortable and angry and worried, all at once. (*I love watching his face, for the emotions that play across it … I may be horrible at reading and/or portraying emotions, but his are fun to watch.*)

"I was thinking about one of the campsites around Follensby Clear Pond for tonight. Have you ever been out there? It's beautiful, and so …" I was ready to continue extolling the virtues of Follensby Clear Pond, but he cut me off.

"Acgh! No, I sleep in a bed. Every night, in a bed," his French-Canadian accent, often missing completely (*although the structure of his sentences always suggested a Gallic influence*), flared when he felt strongly about something (*which was quite often with Maurice*). "This is what I am talking about Tyler. It's no good."

"What's no good Maurice?" I was pretty sure that I could see where he was going, but it was important to the favorable flow (*and outcome*) of the conversation that he get there on his own, before we could fix it together.

"I cannot rent my building to a man with no home. When it gets cold again, you will live all the time in here … sleeping on the couch. And you will burn my building down." This all came out in an explosion of words and spit and gasps and hand gestures and eyebrow wiggles, and at the end … a hand slapped down loudly on the coffee-table for emphasis.

"You must find a place to live … a home. I like you Tyler. You are a good tenant, always neat, always paying the rent on time, help out with the garbage and recycling for all the renters …"

"… and that's why you want to kick me out? Because I'm a good tenant?" I asked.

"No. I like you. I don't want to kick you out, but I can't have a man in my building with no home. Home is like family, and family is everything." This last phrase clanged oddly in my mind and brought me back fully to the conversation, wresting me from thoughts of heading down the 23 steps and to the right for 87 paces to get some Chinese food for an early dinner.

"Maurice, what's the matter?" I asked. "You know my family is gone, but what does that have to do with my office-space?"

Maurice literally crossed himself, thinking of my parents dying in the Twin Towers almost nine months previously (*I have seen his near-mystic response to my orphan-hood before, and I tried, perhaps clumsily, to cash in on some guilt to keep a roof over my gear, if not my head*).

"My family is gone too, Tyler. My granddaughter, Sophia, my princess, her things are gone from the house, and she's beyond my reach." From the initial obfuscation, Maurice shifted gears so quickly that my nap-dumb head couldn't keep up.

"Wait, what, when … granddaughter? Maurice, what are you talking about? Did someone take your granddaughter?"

"She has been taken, yes, but of her own free will," he said, as though that made sense. He moved over to sit next to me on the couch when the topic of conversation changed from my office lease to his missing family. He leaned forward a bit and paused, waiting for pity/clarity/comfort … something. I ran through the most likely options, based on what I had seen people do in similar situations, and reached out tentatively to pat his shoulder … four times. I must have guessed correctly, or at least acceptably, because he breathed out … relaxed a bit.

"Tell me about it," I said, hoping that more information/background would help me understand what had happened that resulted in the derailing of first my nap, and then my verbal eviction notice.

"Sophia's classes at North Country (*Community College, the SUNY college campus in Saranac Lake, NY*) finished over a month ago, and she was lookin' for some kinda job with her friends. She found a hippie farm out in Gabriels ... fell in love with the people, the lil' goats, the LAND, doing 'honest' work, she says. Room and board and a small stipend, she says. She can stay for free in my house 'til the end of time I say, but she wants this. We argued, she said okay, but she moved out a month ago ... she must have waited until I went out ... she took some-a her clothes from my house and left everything else. I haven't heard from her since. I went out to the farm yesterday, my birthday, which she never misses, and the guy at the gate by the road won't let me in, says she don't wanna talk to me." He finished, and went through the cigarette ritual again (*patting for them in all of his pockets, pulling out the crumpled pack, looking around for an ashtray*). This time when I grabbed his empty can from the recycling, I also grabbed a pair of Cokes from the tiny student fridge, and sat back down ... opening the first can as he lit up.

The Cokes were both for me. Maurice apparently only drinks coffee and wine, so after his first few visits, I ceased all attempts at playing host (*as I don't do hot drinks or alcohol*). I had the tiny fridge turned as cold as it would go, but it couldn't chill the Cokes quite enough for my liking ... they were still good, and helped bring me fully awake.

"Do you think they took her, or that they're holding her against her will?" I asked, not really knowing what to do regardless of his answers to either of my questions ... hoping that more information would bring things into focus, and allow me to see through the static of people and emotions to the clarity of an answer. I live in a godless world, but worship information and patterns and clarity and answers.

"Nah, she wanted to go ... she wants to be there," he answered simply ... no clarity for me yet.

"Did you have an idea that I could help, Maurice?" One of the useful things about not understanding human artifice is that I tend to cut through the awkward waiting and misdirection that most humans seem to thrive on (*or at least need in order to communicate*).

Maurice looked pained at the direct route I had taken. He must have had an elaborate back and forth in mind, involving cigarettes and Gallic shrugs and grunts and both of us observing the niceties of conversational rules which I had never understood. He sighed and nodded at me through a cloud of smoke and skipped ahead to rejoin the conversation.

"Yah, I was hoping that you could go out and talk to this guy at the gate, to these people, to my Sophia ... to make sure that she's okay, and ... also ... to talk her out of living out at that hippie farm."

"Why do you imagine that I could do that if you couldn't Maurice? She's not my granddaughter, I'm not a cop, why would she listen to me, even if I could get passed the guy (*guard? Why have a guard for a hippie farm ... more on that later ... maybe*) at the gate." I passed the conversational ball gently, but firmly, back to him.

Maurice puffed on the tiny remainder of his cigarette hurriedly, three times, before responding. I could see him thinking about how to answer ... and also how to answer without a fifteen minute preamble.

"I lost my head a little bit at the farm ... yelled at the gate-guy a little. I grabbed the tire-iron out of my trunk and tol' him that I was gonna talk to Sophia, and nobody gonna stop me. He reached out and took the tire-iron from my hand, so quick and gentle I almost didn't see it or feel it. An ol' man like me, you think maybe it's easy … " as he spoke, Maurice's right hand darted up, flicked my left ear, and was back in his lap before I could flinch or say 'ouch'.

"Ouch!" I said. "Maurice! Point taken … so you're quick … quicker than me … so what could I do, except lose my tire-iron too?"

"Oh no Tyler, the gate-guy, he gave the tire-iron back to me nice as pie (*a clumsy simile if I've ever seen one, although I do find pie to be quite nice, and now found myself thinking about some apple pie to go with my Chinese dinner*). He politely asked me to leave, gave me his word that Sophia was fine, and that he'd look after her special for me."

"And so … what do you think I can do, Maurice?" I asked, trying to put a bit of impatience into my voice (*impatience is not me best faux-emotion, it mostly comes off as whiny*).

"You're smart Tyler, you're mailbox even says so." He heaved a couple of desultory coughing laughs at his little joke (*my mailbox downstairs had the name Smart Pig, a small play on words based on my last name of Cunningham*). "I see you reading alla time … books everywhere. My friend Jeanie at the library says you read more books than any other five people in town."

"So you're hoping that brains prevail where brawn (*or more accurately, speed*) failed? I don't know, Maurice. Sounds like a long shot, and a wasted drive, and I could make things worse," I countered.

"Oh, no Tyler. I don't see it like that. You head out there, see what you can do, and maybe get her to come home, away from there … it's a favor to me … a favor to a friend."

I don't have friends, never have. I tend to bother people in the long run, and miss social cues that everyone else understands from the age of five. In this instance, I felt as though I had a part of the picture, and that last focal adjustment was just out of my reach ... then Maurice tweaked it for me.

"A friend who does me a favor like that, he never needs to worry about where he spends the nights in wintertime. That's maybe the difference between a tenant and a friend, Tyler. Friends do favors for friends ... and maybe overlook their friends' shortcomings or essentricities (*which I assume are like eccentricities, but with more sibilance*)." He ended this last piece with a combination shrug/wink/head-tilt/smile/guilty-grimace that I took as his closing argument ... part threat, part promise of gratitude, all implied ... and all largely beyond my comprehension.

"I'll take a run out there tomorrow morning, if that's soon enough Maurice, and see what I can do," I said to an empty spot on the couch ... he was up and out of the room, shouting thanks back down the hall over his shoulder before I knew what had happened.

I gave up my plans for a night out at Follensby Clear in favor of a quick trip to the Saranac Lake Public Library before it closed, for a bit research about Maurice's hippies (*hopefully, I could bring something better than a tire-iron*).

I sent Cynthia an email on my way out the door, explaining in brief my wishes, knowing that she would get started, sifting and sorting data into useful and useable chunks for my digestion.

Saranac Lake Public Library, Saranac Lake, NY
Tuesday, 6/4/2002, 5:23 p.m.

Cynthia Windmere dumped another two inches of tax-maps and news articles onto the long table that I was working at as the after-school crowd emptied out of the library for their suppers (*I was long past ready for some mediocre Chinese food and apple pie, but as always, I'd been seduced by the flow of information, and made due with five nasty cans of Pepsi from the library vending machine*).

"I think that's it for now," Cynthia said as she dropped into the chair beside me. "See what you get out of that pile, and maybe we can re-direct before closing." Her leg bumped into mine as she stretched out her toes … I jumped and she gave a little grumpy noise, part surprise/anger/sadness.

"For Fuck's sake Tyler!" she hissed at me. "I'm not going to jump you. I'm pretty sure that I can control myself even though we're all alone back here, and you're wearing those sexy water-shoes."

Cynthia had been my research assistant (*her salary paid by the taxpayers of Saranac Lake, not me though*) for nearly six months, ever since I had moved to the Adirondacks from New York City in the aftermath of the devastation (*both personal and national*) wrought by the attacks of 9/11/2001. Although she was employed by the library (*as a somewhat-paid library tech*), she generally cleared her desk and calendar to help me whenever I came in with a focused research challenge for her.

We had initially connected because I needed/ requested some research help, and she was available; we had continued the relationship through the early awkward sessions because we both loved mining data, and were roughly the same age … in library terms (*she was a young-seeming 20-something, and I'm a mature, if different, almost-20-something*). The other people working in the Saranac Lake Public Library were decades older, and had no time for, patience with, or interest in my diverse and un-Adirondack-y (*-esque?*) research … not to mention the amount of printed paper, computer bandwidth, and inter-library loan requests I generated through my ongoing education/research.

We'd had a tense pause in our working relationship roughly ten weeks ago, when she had told me to ask her out (*she had been between boyfriends at the time, a rare occurrence*), and as we had been spending so much time together since my arrival in town, she mistook the tenor of my interest in her. I had 'fled the interview', and avoided her (*and worse, the library*) for weeks afterwards. I would have been hard-pressed to explain my fear/anger/disgust at her advances (*and my lack of understanding about them*), but we managed to work things out when she cornered me at SmartPig, and forced a confrontation that allowed us to recommence our working relationship. We were still settling into our improved/enhanced/defined relationship, and because of that, I was more than ever aware of her physical presence and the implicit sexual tension between two adult humans of the opposite sex working alone after most people have left a building.

"I'm sorry," I said, not sorry, or entirely understanding what I was apologizing for, but certain that she perceived the need for an apology on my part (*and to complete the work that I wanted to get done before falling on the Chinese place like an angry mob ... I could pretend*). "This looks great, thanks Cyn." (*which she had asked that I call her*).

I did the thing that Cynthia loves to watch next, sorting data into 'useful' and 'junk' piles through some higher (*or lower*) order functioning. I stood over the pile of newly deposited papers, focused on some keywords and concepts, and started shuffling the papers to one side or the other ... most went to the right, a few went to the left in a much neater sub-pile. The maps went as quickly as I could move my hands, the old newspaper and magazine articles (*some copied from microfiche*) went a bit slower, but still faster than I could have read them. Within two minutes, I had separated the wheat from the chaff, indicated which pile Cynthia could remove, and sat down to actually read through the much smaller pile left to me by the sorting process.

"Thanks Cyn," I said as she took the stuff wherever the stuff that I don't want goes. A few months ago she was still checking the discards to see if I was trying to fake her out or just missing stuff, but by now she trusted (*even if she didn't understand*) the process. She was back a minute later and started reading through the articles, taking notes on them and on the maps I'd kept in the selection process. While Cynthia couldn't replicate/understand my parlor tricks, she was on her way to becoming a top-notch research-librarian, and could process fantastic amounts of data into useful conclusions and questions for further study; our reading and thinking patterns were wonderfully complementary, and I appreciated her help on even minor jobs like this one (*the cherry on top was that she never asked why I needed to know, only what I needed to know*).

"Report?" Cynthia asked.

"Thanks Cyn, that would be great. Give me what you know, then what you think," I answered (*wondering for a moment if she could feel my using a different name for her in my head than with my mouth, then wondering why I cared*).

"The farmhouse at N44.4149 by W074.1739 sits in the middle of roughly six hundred acres of mixed woods and farmland. It had been in the McKinley family for over a hundred years until its sale in 1999, when it was purchased by a faith-based 501-C-3 based somewhere on Long Island," she paused for breath, and I cut in.

"Not a church?" I asked.

"Not exactly. The paperwork describes 'Helgafell' as a 'Gaian preserve and retreat', whatever that means."

I have admired Cynthia for her ability to emote while speaking since we first met. The disdain and sarcasm with which she said 'not-a-church' was palpable … even to me (*and I'm someone who often wishes for 'intent bubbles' over peoples' heads, clearly defining their feelings during conversations*).

"I assume that it refers to James Lovelock's 'Gaia Theory' … most likely 'Gaia: A New Look at Life on Earth', an interesting book presenting the metaphor that the entire planet Earth is a single living organism. It's a fascinating way to think about both global ecology and the nature of organisms, Cyn," I answered her.

"Whatever," Cynthia harrumphed at me. "So they're a Earth-church or commune or …"

"Hippies, like Maurice postulates … but with a twist (*thinking of the guard*) and a slick business plan that includes tax-exempt status."

I wasn't looking at the papers in front of us anymore, I was starting to see the terrain of my investigation in my head … using the maps I'd scanned, the story Maurice had told me, and pictures my brain had taken while I'd been driving past the farm over the last seven months (*since moving to the area*). There were more holes than solid ground as yet, but I could feel the shape of it in my brain, and suddenly wanted to get out there to learn about it first-hand.

"We've got time for me to dive back in for one more batch before I have to start shutting down for the night. Gimme some keywords!" Cynthia was used to my patterns, and must have recognized the shift in my attention/focus/thoughts. Working with her was nice because I never had to explain (*anymore*) the whys and hows of my research methods.

"That would be great, Cyn. I know everything about Lovelock and Gaia already … more on the parent company … where the money came from to buy the farm … 'Helgafell' is a mountain in Iceland, but I'm certain there's more than that, so dig there a bit … I know nothing about communes/cults and the like, so some prep-work on that would be nice. Grab and print what you can before you need to close, I'll read through the rest of this, and I'm buying all the crappy Chinese food that you can eat."

Cynthia and I often ate dinner together after working, taking turns buying, splitting the bill, or using separate checks as the mood took her (*I tended to follow her lead on dinners out, but often paid after a session without any advanced warning*). Recently, she's been choosing my less favored Chinese restaurant in Saranac Lake (*Crappy Chinese, as opposed to Good Chinese*), because she insisted that their dumplings were less doughy and Kung Pao more spicy. I could survive either place, so I didn't mind indulging her *(if it reinforced her desire to help me with my research projects).*

She ran upstairs to ransack various databases and websites, while I digested the information already sorted on the table. We had both finished our appointed tasks in time to help Jeanie, the librarian working the front desk, close the library down for the night after chasing the last retiree out into the still-light evening. Cynthia and I jammed her new material and a sub-set of the material I'd just been reading into my backpack for another look later this evening, and headed down the hill, walking towards the Crappy Chinese restaurant.

It was pretty crappy, but still better than any Shepard's Pie I've ever had.

Helgafell Farm, Gabriels, NY
Wednesday, 6/5/2002, 6:10 a.m.

I noted the time when I rolled off of the tarmac and onto
the rutted dirt of the driveway to Helgafell Farm ...
because I note things like that (*and then remember them
forever, like everything else that crosses the threshold of my
consciousness*), but also (*and especially*) because 610 is the
fifteenth number in the Fibonacci Sequence. I could see
the big farmhouse, and assorted barns and other
bunkhouses and sheds, about 400 yards past the gate and
gatehouse ... and gate-guard ... all of which waited for
me less than twenty yards off of the main road, Route 86.
He must have heard my Honda Element slow down and
turn onto the dirt, because he was waiting for me in the
middle of the driveway by the time I rolled up to the gate.

    "Good morning," the tall man said. "You must be the
next level, although you seem a bit young for the role ...
if you don't mind my saying so."

    I waited for him to say more, but he seemed content
to stand there, with a small upturn on both ends of his
mouth, breathing in the cool morning air. His hat and

gloves and puffy coat indicated that he had to be from downstate (*no Adirondacker would layer up like that on this 40 degree morning*). He looked comfortable standing there, waiting for me to do something … comfortable standing, comfortable with the hour, comfortable with the cold, and comfortable with himself. He carried some grey and some gut, and didn't try to hide or minimize either.

"Maurice said something," I guessed.

"When I asked him to leave, he promised that it wasn't over, and that he was bringing it to …" he gestured with his hands to indicate me, and him, and the gate, and the Adirondack Park.

"He's a sweet old man, worried about his granddaughter."

He nodded and seemed to settle, although he was still standing straight and tall, and looked into the fields and morning light behind me, towards Whiteface Mountain.

When he didn't answer my comment about Maurice, I continued, "So I guess I am the next level. Maurice is my landlord and I told him that I would come out and see what I could find out about Sophia. My name is Tyler."

"Heimdall … John Heimdall. Pleased to meet you Tyler."

He didn't offer his hand, as I hadn't. I sometimes go weeks without touching another human, and wondered if he was the same … and how (*if*) he felt about it. I aimed for amusement and a chuckle, but clearly missed.

"Is something wrong?" he asked.

"No, but someone's Norse is showing. Helgafell is one of the Norse heavens, and also a holy mountain," I said sweeping my behind me and around past John's shoulder at the mountains all around us. "Heimdall is a Norse God, a guardian who brings the gifts of the gods to mankind. He's also out of place in Helgafell, which is a

19

place for good souls who aren't warriors, which I suspect you might be."

"I live and work here as a favor to the church," he said, gesturing to the gatehouse, which couldn't have been more than a few hundred square feet in total. "My duties as guardian of Helgafell, Mr. Cunningham, include threat analysis and assessment."

He might have been hoping for a shocked/scared/amazed reaction on my face at the revelation of my last name, but my face doesn't do those (*even when I tell it to, most of the time*), and it only seemed fair that if I could research them, that he could research Maurice (*and by extension, me*).

"Did your instincts indicate that Maurice was a threat to your church?" I asked.

He chuckled and said, "No, but all the votes aren't in on you yet. You may bring more to the table than your reedy, late-teens, slept in his clothes look would suggest."

He waved me towards, and into the gatehouse, opened the door for me, and followed me in, to the smell of coffee and fresh bread.

The single room was square, twenty feet on a side, with a chunk taken out in one corner for what I assumed was a bathroom. The Gatekeeper's home smelled the way that new wooden construction smells until all of a sudden it's old … like pine and paint. This one had added olfactory layering from books (*an unbroken wall of them … twenty feet of shelving from floor to ceiling rafters*), pipes (*I could see a rack of them by an overstuffed reading chair in once corner*), fancy coffee (*there was an espresso machine on some counter-space over by the bathroom … the kind with brass and copper tubing and an eagle on top*), and guns (*none were visible, but the smell of Hoppe's and Rem-Oil was strong enough that I suspected the large armoire against the wall by the Gatekeeper's Spartan bed held more than extra shirts*). Good smells, all, but not overwhelming the smells of pine and paint and cleanliness. There were no dishes in the little sink by the coffee-maker, and no dirty clothes in piles/corners/duffels (*at least none visible*).

"Coffee?" he gestured vaguely to the machine as he took off his layers, eventually ending up in black slacks and a black polo shirt … with matching black shoes and socks (*I wondered briefly if his boxers were black as well, and dismissed the thought, toying briefly with the simplicity of his laundry sorting*).

"Thanks, but no. I don't drink hot beverages." My standard reply usually makes people give me a second look, but he moved on as if he hadn't heard.

"They bring me fresh bread from the farmhouse every morning, and it's wonderful, if you'd care for a slice; they make the butter as well."

I nodded and he cut me off a pair of thick wedges of bread, and slathered them thickly with butter before handing them to me on a plate.

"Sit." He waved to the butcher-block table, and while I went over and started in on the yummy bread, he started fiddling with the espresso machine … little squeals and jets of steam and burbling noises and a mechanical groan all came from that corner of the room before he joined me at the table with a small cup of midnight-black coffee with an oily sheen on its surface. He slurped the whole thing down in one go, gave a contented sigh, and reached across the table to break off a chunk of bread for himself, wiggling his eyebrows for permission first.

"So …" he said, chewing the crust with obvious enjoyment, "why?"

"Why what?" I replied.

"Why you? Why six a.m.? Why alone?" he pause for another round of contented chewing before continuing,

"What are you hoping for? What's your lever? What's the 'or else'?"

I looked at the Gatekeeper, reflected on his six, nearly perfect questions, and took 13 seconds composing my answers before speaking.

"Maurice asked, and I wouldn't mind him owing me a favor. I like mornings, am awake and thinking at this time of day, and most people don't, and aren't. I didn't have anyone else to bring, and even if I did, I'm not looking to outnumber or out-muscle the whole farm. I'm hoping to talk with Sophia to make sure that she's okay, here of her own free will, and knows that her grandfather is concerned for her well-being. I have no lever besides my brain and what I know about this place. There's almost no 'or else' … if you tell me to leave, I'll leave … but I might call the newspaper or the state police and tell them that you're holding a young woman here against her will … Sophia's not a minor, and it wouldn't be much hassle for you, but letting me talk to her is even less of a hassle, and I'm hoping that you'll understand that truth, and see things my way."

The Gatekeeper (*I couldn't bring myself to call him either 'John' or 'Mr. Heimdall' just yet*) tilted his head a bit like a dog, and grinned at me before saying, "I'm pretty sure that I couldn't see things your way if I tried, although I've always been a morning person too. You would seem to be more than I originally anticipated, and that sort of surprise is a nice way to begin any morning. Regardless of what you and other people might think, these people are not a cult … not kooks or Moonies … they're just living simply and want to be left alone."

"I'll be happy to be on my way if I can just talk to Sophia first," I said … not entirely true in the strictest sense. Maurice had asked me to find some way to get her to come home … I couldn't see any way to do that from my current vantage point, but hoped that if I could get a foot in the door, something might happen (*or I could make something happen*) that would bring Sophia home (*and secure my place/lease in the SmartPig office*). "Also, Heimdall's not your name, so what do I call you? I'm getting tired of thinking of you as 'The Gatekeeper'."

He smirked at that, mouthed 'The Gatekeeper' to himself, and said, "John is actually the name that my mom gave me in St. Luke's all those years ago. I've never been much on last names, Tyler, had too many of them, so you can just call me John. On the other thing, I'm not much for threats, even implied ones like you dangled in front of me a minute ago … but I'm even less keen on hassle and police or publicity, so I've got a proposal for you."

I leaned forward a bit, interested in what was going to come out of his mouth next.

"One of the kids from the farm comes down around seven each morning to pick up my dishes, and see how I feel about the options for lunch and dinner. That should be in about twenty minutes … why don't you grab a book off of my shelves, and read for a bit. If you'll excuse me, I need to make a phone call."

Without waiting for my reply, he bounced up to standing, walked over to the phone on the wall by his front-door, dialed, waited, and then spoke seven hushed words into the phone before hanging up.

John walked over to the comfy chair and sat down, picked up a book that must have been sitting on the floor beside the chair, and started reading. I walked over and strolled up and down the shelving for a minute taking in the eclectic mix of books, and trying to figure out the organizational schema. The books were not just jammed in at random, but nor were they alphabetical by title or author (*or, as I thought about John's books that I had read, by protagonist*). They were not organized by size or by Melville Dewey's system. I looked for clues by scanning for books that I knew arranged near or next to each other, eager now to crack the system.

I like my brain, but it's not always easy to live with/near/inside. I could feel it irking me that his library made sense to him and not to me. I'm generally the smartest person in most every room I visit, and over time, one gets used to the feeling, which becomes akin to a security blanket or a shield. Out of the corner of my eye, I caught him watching me stalk up and down his wall of books, smiling a bit at my body language and breathing. I was about to ask when I happened to see a copy of 'Ender's Game' sitting next to 'The Killing Floor'. I stopped, thought for a second, and smiled.

"I've been peeking," John remarked. "I like to watch how people approach the books. Most just think it's a mess. Some sorta get it, and ask for a hint. You figured it out just now ... how? What tipped you off?"

"Ender and Reacher," I replied. "Their style/viewpoint/life-strategy ... the way they approach the world. 'Get your retaliation in first' and 'Knocking him down won the first fight. I wanted to win all the next ones, too.' Massive pre-emptive violence to preserve yourself ... or those who you would protect. Your library is arranged by lessons."

He nodded, smiled, and stuck his nose back into the book he was reading ... I wondered what it was, and what lesson it offered. I picked up the worn copy of 'Ender's Game' and turned to a favorite part of mine, thinking as I always do, that I'm likely one of a very few people who sees himself in Bean.

Helgafell Farm, Gabriels, NY
Wednesday, 6/5/2002 7:04 a.m.

"Tyler. I assume Pépère put you up to this? I'm sorry you wasted your time," Sophia said when she walked in through the back door of John's cabin, the one that faced out towards the farmhouse and buildings and farmland (*and eventually Upper St. Regis Lake, according to the map in my brain*).

When she came in, Sophia recognized me. We met once before, when Maurice came around on one of his 'spot-inspections' early on in my tenure at SmartPig. He had suggested that we 'two kids hang out sometime', in the way that older people tend to do (*and that seems to have the opposite of the desired effect most of the time*). It worked especially poorly in this instance as she was/is a very attractive 20 year old, and I was/am a strange (*in both relevant senses of the word*) 18 year old who had/has trouble making eye-contact with people new to him, and doesn't know how to 'hang out'. We nodded politely/awkwardly until Maurice got uncomfortable, and left … with Sophia; I hadn't seen her since then, but she looked the same, although dirtier. She was wearing plain jeans, a drab green work shirt, and a white ball cap … it felt a bit uniform-y to me in its stiff newness, and clear lack of tailoring (*my recollection was that Sophia wore tailored clothes to highlight her female and mammalian curviness, and this outfit hid nearly all of those features*).

"Hello Sophia. Yes, Maurice asked me to come out and see you. He's concerned and doesn't understand why you're here, and why he couldn't simply walk in and talk with you yesterday." I neglected to add that I couldn't understand that myself, or why the farm had/needed more security than a gate … much less someone as serious (*and un-farmer-like*) as John Heimdall appeared to be (*try as I might, I could not dismiss the likely pseudonym, or my desire for more information about John*).

"I didn't know about Pépère's visit until I came down to grab Gatekeeper's supper plates last night."

When she said this, Sophia looked towards John, only vaguely. I searched John's eyes at the title/name that Sophia had used, and he shrugged it off … giving away none of his thoughts (*if any*) on the matter.

"The folks up at the farm call me Gatekeeper, and … it works. My job defines me up here, from time to time I switch out with one of my brothers from the City for a bit, and at any rate … we lead separate lives down here at the gate and up there at the farm … lotsa the kids go weeks at a stretch without seeing or talking to me," he offered.

I digested this information and their interaction (*or lack thereof*), and threw it into the hopper at the back of my brain, where the lizard-bits tear stuff apart and other parts reassemble things into cogent theories/questions/ideas/warnings. I got some immediate bounce-back, but decided to wait for more before proceeding … they seemed unused to being in each other's presence, and I didn't want to break the moment or garner ill will from either at this moment (*although it might turn out to be useful later*).

"I would like to speak with Sophia privately if I may John … Gatekeeper. I'd like to take her for a drive, so we can talk away from the farm." I turned up the end of each sentence, so that they were almost questions.

"I'm sure that you would, and I'm very nearly certain that it would be fine, but I wouldn't be doing my job, to the farm or to Sophia, if I permitted that. I do have a counter-proposal though, which should meet all of our needs. Help her carry the plates and cups and leftovers from breakfast back up to the house, while I remain here and wait for you to return. You can talk with her about anything you want, to make sure that she's okay, and not here against her will. This will also let you see the farm and where and how she lives. Make sure that we're not growing drugs or making porn or some such."

He looked at me, and I nodded. He hadn't spoken to Sophia, which creeped me out a bit, but she didn't seem scared or uncomfortable of him … if anything, she looked impatient at the prospect of walking me around the farm (*similar to her reaction to Maurice's suggestion at our first meeting*).

"Sounds good," I said. "I appreciate it, and will see you in a bit." With that, I helped Sophia grab the plates, bowls, mugs, silverware, and leftovers, and headed out the gatehouse's backdoor, and into Helgafell Farm with Sophia … a bit nervous and thinking of the questions that I would ask, and what my back-brain would look for in her answers.

Helgafell Farm, Gabriels, NY
Wednesday, 6/5/2002 7:23 a.m.

"Sophia, why are you here?" It was at once a stupid and brilliant question, if I do say so myself ... which I did. We were walking up the twin ruts in the dirt track running from the gate (*and gatehouse*) up to the main house and the cluster of associated buildings.

"Well ... everybody's got to be somewhere, and this seems like the right place for me right now," she offered, but the tonal upturn at the end of her sentence almost made it into a question. I knew that if I waited, she would say more ... to fill the silence if nothing else. It has been my experience that most people hate the quiet, and will fill it with anything, even things they shouldn't, if you can appear engaged and are willing to wait.

"Look, I know that Pépère wants me to do the whole college thing, and get a straight job, and live the 'American Dream', but maybe I want something different ... something for me. I like it here on the farm ... everyone's nice ... work's easy, as long as you don't mind getting up early, an' I don't ... and I ... I understand what I'm doing

… how my life works … maybe for the first time since I was a kid." She looked over at me after finishing, maybe a little embarrassed/mad/surprised at how much she'd shared with me. She also had a challenge in her eyes, daring me to laugh (*which luckily I never do, since I don't have a sense of humor in the traditional meaning of the word*).

"How does your life work?" I asked, to goad her onwards … reaching for some understanding, and a springboard to my next (*and hopefully better*) questions.

"The Church is my home and my family now. We all work together to make each day what we want it to be. We grow the food that we eat, and when we need things that we can't grow (*she pointed to her clothes and shoes*) we sell or trade with the outside world for them. It's a simple life of hard work." She wrinkled her nose at the end of her response, feeling the canned nature of what she had said.

"… And you couldn't find that somewhere else? Not at college or a job or the Peace Corps or married to a wealthy Spanish landowner?" I'd been watching my way through the Zorro movies at the video-store over the last week, and was getting a strong 'the pipples' vibe as we walked further up the hill, away from Route 86 and towards the house, seeing more young people moving out and away from the main house in the same blue/green/white garb (*uniform?*) as Sophia.

She got a little mad, assuming that I was insulting/teasing her, which was useful to me as it might bring out a genuine answer. "Fuck you! I wasn't happy at NCCC and the jobs I've had, and I am now. I don't care about money or fancy stuff. I like the way things work here."

"Take it easy Sophia, I didn't mean to insult you, or the farm. I didn't graduate from college (*or high school for that matter, but we didn't need to go into that*), don't have a job that anyone understands, and am essentially homeless (*which was, at the end of the day, why I was up here doing a favor for Maurice*). I understand wanting to direct/control/understand your life, but Maurice is concerned about why you are choosing to do it here."

"Why, because he thinks it's a cult … or crazies … or some drug thing? Because it's not. They … we … don't even go to church or pray or anything. We sometimes talk about Gaia, you know (*I nodded, having brushed up on Lovelock's writing last night*), but mostly the worship comes through working the land and respect for the Earth and plants and animals and stuff. And nobody on the farm does drugs, or even drinks … except for John … Gatekeeper. Father wants us to call him Gatekeeper," she said, almost to herself … like a reminder.

"Father?" I asked.

The guy who runs the farm and the Gaia-talks at night, an old guy from downstate. He just wants us to call him 'Father'. He says he's trying to forget his old name … his old life. Anyway, John … Gatekeeper (*she interrupted/corrected herself*) drinks coffee and has some booze in his cabin, but he's not really one of us anyhow … he keeps the boundary. That's what Father says."

While we had been walking and talking, I had been thinking about how to phrase the next question in such a way as to optimize my chances of getting an answer, and minimize my chances of getting smacked by Sophia and/or removed forcibly by 'Gatekeeper'.

"I don't want you to get mad at me, but I need to ask, to help Maurice feel better about your decision … in order to join, or since you joined, has anyone … Father or the Gatekeeper or anyone else … asked or made you do anything you didn't want to do, or weren't comfortable doing?"

Sophia stopped in her rut, turned to face me, and stared at me for a five-count, letting my uncomfortable blush creep up my neck, and bloom across my face; her eyes shifted to my ears, which were burning, and she giggled a bit. I don't understand sex or sexual coercion beyond a basic level, lacking most of the social software that most humans come pre-loaded with from birth, and Sophia (*like many people, most of them women in my experience*) sensed it at some level, and enjoyed my discomfort.

"Yes, Tyler ... yes they did. Father and a number of the other more senior members of the church forced me to do something I never would have imagined decent people doing. Sticky, messy, thrashing, screaming ... it was horrible. I'll never be the same." She let it hang in the air, hoping that I would ask (*or explode, which is what felt more likely*) before continuing, "Slaughtering the chickens, and then cleaning them. If you eat meat at Helgafell, you help to raise and butcher it." She coughed out a short laugh at my expense, and I breathed a sigh of relief.

"If this place is a whacko-cult-scam, they're doing a piss-poor job of it, Tyler. They didn't want what money and stuff I did have, it's still at Pépère's place. Hell, they even give me a tiny weekly stipend based on the sales from our farm stand and online store. If people are having sex, they're keeping private about it, and nobody's made a move on me in the nearly five weeks I've been here, and with all this clean living, hard work, fresh food, and good sleep, I'm feeling rested and ready if you know what I mean." (*I didn't, but gave a faux-knowing nod anyway*).

"I know that Pépère loves me and misses me and doesn't understand why I am choosing this life, but I am ... and it makes me happy. Now come inside and see my room. Talk to some of the other people, meet Father, and then I hope you can explain it all to Pépère." She gestured to the big house, which from this angle I could see had a newish shoebox-y addition glommed onto one side, done in competent, if not pretty/professional/matching style.

When we were still 30 yards from the porch steps, a loud honking and squawking and screaming filled the air. A mixed group of geese and ... the ugliest and noisiest birds I had ever seen ran at Sophia and me, heads down low and hissing and screaming at us. She didn't seem scared, so I pretended not to be either. There were seven birds altogether, and they surrounded us, stabbing at my legs with their bills until Sophia balanced her load of plates and such in one arm, reached into a pocket with the other hand, and scattered a handful of grain/cereal/feed behind us; at which point the birds raced each other to compete for the food.

"You would think that nobody could sneak up on this house when these guys are on duty," she said, smiling and looking back at the tiny monsters. "But, something must have though ... two of the guinea fowls were dead this morning." She was brought up short in her musing about the dead ugly-birds by the sound of a screen-door creaking open, and heavy steps on the porch above us.

"Welcome to Helgafell. I'm Father, and you're the next level." He smiled at me through a sea of wrinkles and then looked past me towards Whiteface over my shoulder. I climbed the steps and turned around to take in the view; it was essentially the same as I got from road, whenever I drove by, but he seemed to be getting more out of it than I ever had.

"That seems to be the general consensus. You and John must have talked. I'm grateful to both of you for letting me talk with Sophia this morning."

"We weren't quite sure what form 'the next level' would take, but you'll do." He sat in a suspended porch swing, and waved us back into the house. "Look around, and talk to whoever you want, but I'll ask that you keep out of my office if you don't mind ..." he paused for just a second to smile up at me over his shoulder, "... that's where we keep the orgies and heroin."

Sophia and I went inside, and I followed her (*and the smell of fresh bread and cooking eggs and bacon*) back through the house to the kitchen. She dropped off the dishes in the sink and leftover food on a big wooden table, and waved a hand at me by way of excuse when a young man with bubbles up to his elbows looked up from the sink as she walked away.

"Brother or boyfriend?" he asked Sophia, not looking at me; seeming bored, and maybe a bit angered at my presence ... a disturbance in the peace/quiet/serenity/force.

"Neither. Jay, this is Tyler ... Tyler, Jay. Tyler's here checking on me as a favor to my grandfather," Sophia said, by way of explanation.

"Got it," he said, and turned back to his dishes and pots, filtering me out of his day, having never made eye-contact or spoken to me.

We walked out another entry into the kitchen and towards a clumsy join between the old farmhouse and the new addition that I'd seen from outside. Sophia opened the door and we walked into the dormitory.

There was a long hallway with doors on both sides, evenly spaced every eight feet, ending at two doors. One of the doors was open and exposed what looked to be a plain bathroom. We continued down the hall. Sophia opened the third door on the left and walked inside. I followed her in, and almost ran into her, as the room was only eight feet on a side, and most of it was taken up by a bed and bureau and desk and Sophia ... and now me.

My eyes scanned every inch of the room, which didn't take long, and then came back to Sophia, who was glaring at me, expecting and already resenting my answer.

"Crazy right? Move out of Pépère's nice house, with closets bigger than this room, and work from sun-up to sun-down for some dirt-church … who does that, right? Crazy church people."

I took a breath, and moved to the desk (*working at not sucking in my gut as I went past her, that's how tiny it felt*), scraped out the chair, and sat down before answering.

"Nope, not in my book. Although Maurice thinks I'm a bit odd as well. I keep stuff in my office in his building, but live outside most days and nights … I cheat occasionally when the weather is horrible, and sleep on the office couch. I like simplicity … I understand simplicity. I hit the reset button after 9/11. I am trying to keep to the bare minimum of stuff I don't absolutely need, or can live without, in my life." I brought my hand across the spine of the dozen books that she had on top of her desk, "I couldn't live without books," waving to either wall I added, "and probably couldn't handle having neighbors this close; but if it works for you, I'm happy for you."

For the first time since she had recognized me in the gate-house, she smiled a real smile, and clasped my hand in both of hers, exclaiming, "You understand … I'm so happy." Then she frowned as she felt my recoil from her assertive (*albeit friendly*) human touch.

"I'm sorry," we both said at the same moment, embarrassed from both sides of the same dysfunctional human interaction.

The room felt suddenly smaller, and I stood to reach for the door, knocking the chair over backwards in my haste. Sophia gave a little yelp of fright at the big noise in the little room, and the moment of understanding that we had shared was gone as utterly as if it had never happened. I heard running feet closing on our location, and stepped back and away from Sophia (*as far as was possible in a crowded 8x8 room*), and waited for Jay to come through the door.

Sophia pre-empted the possible confrontation by walking out of her room, pointing down the hall, and saying in an only slightly too-loud voice, "and there are the bathrooms ... hot water and everything."

Jay stopped where he was, in the doorway between house and dorm, looked at both of us, turned around, and stalked back towards the kitchen, angrily shaking suds off of his hands. Sophia looked back at me, and gave a slightly sad/pitying/knowing smile. Maurice must have told her about my parents, and she guessed that I was now an island in the sea of humanity, untouched and untouching. It was a sweet and sad idea, but not true; I had been an island since long before those planes and the men flying them had taken my family from me ... I've always been an island. It was true that I hadn't touched another human in 23 days, but I had often gone longer than that as a child, while pressed in with millions of people, growing up in Manhattan.

She understood a piece of me, or thought that she did, which was the same thing (*to her*). I understood a piece of her, or thought that I did (*based on what I had seen/heard/inferred in the last hour*). Neither of us had the real picture, nobody ever does, but I knew that to be the case and could make allowances for the difference between perception and reality.

"Okay, so this works for you ... now how do I make it okay for Maurice? How can I help him understand?" I wasn't really asking Sophia so much as talking to myself, but I could feel her working towards some form of answer as we walked back out into the house-proper (*despite the show that she had put on for Jay, neither of us felt the need for me to inspect the bathroom*).

We avoided Jay and the kitchen this time, and went the other way around the interior of the downstairs of the farmhouse, through a living room and past a room with a closed door. My internal CAD software figured the room to be 10x12 feet(*ish*), most likely an office or storage space. I noted, as we drifted by, with Sophia complaining about how stuck in his ways Maurice was, that the door to the office differed from the other doors in the old part of the farmhouse; it had no panels, the frame looked to be painted metal, and the keyhole suggested a serious key (*not like the ancient and gaping keyholes at the front door and open doors throughout the house, which I suspected a bent spoon could sweet-talk*).

"Father might know," Sophia offered, as we reached the front door. "I've got to get to work in the greenhouse, but Father often spends some of the morning on the front porch, and you could talk with him before you go."

"Thanks Sophia. I'll talk with him for a bit before heading out (*I didn't want to call him 'Father', but didn't know another name to use … I hoped that I wouldn't run out of pronouns before I left*). I'll talk with Maurice later today, and tell him something (*hopefully that would prevent his attacking Gatekeeper again, and/or throwing me out of my office-space … both would be nice*). Here's a business card with my phone and email address, so you can get in touch with me if you need/want anything … anything at all."

She took the card, jammed it in her jeans pocket without looking at it, and took off down the stairs. She headed around the side of the house, presumably towards the greenhouse (*which was more useful than you might think, given that there had been a frost the previous morning*) waving me distractedly toward the man we'd met at the door on our way in. I walked over and sat in a chair near the swing he was creaking back and forth in ... and waited.

I'm quite good at waiting, as the awkwardness that most people feel at empty conversational space is missing from my programming. Good as I was though, he was better. Seven minutes later, I was beginning to assume that he either hadn't noticed that I was there on the porch with him, or he was simply willing to outwait me, when he turned abruptly and asked me, "Well?"

I was unsure of the meaning implied by his tone, so I tried a friendly/sincere/helpful smile (*my #3 smile of the eleven functional smiles I have field tested, only the first five are very convincing*) and waited....

"Well ... do you think we've kidnapped her? Are we gonna chop her up and put her in the Sunday supper? Maybe get her hooked on smack and sell her to white-slavers? Brainwash her and teach her to fly a passenger jet into one of the big buildings in downtown Saranac Lake?"

He probably saw something in my eyes when he said the last thing, because he ran down, like a wind-up toy, just when he'd gotten up a head of steam. I know that my face didn't give anything away because I didn't feel a blush, and didn't tell my face to make an expression; nevertheless, he sat back and looked at me for 37 seconds before leaning towards me again, and this time he spoke differently/diffidently.

"Do we pass muster, Tyler?" he asked, openly, honestly, confident of what my answer would be. "Are we taking good care of Maurice's granddaughter?"

"I think so," was the only quick answer that I had, so I gave it. He may have expected me to pause and think before I gave it, but I couldn't see any point in drama (*I never do/have/will*).

"Why? And why only 'think so'?" he asked.

"She seems to be here of her own free will. You and your farm/church/commune(/*cult?*) don't seem to present any direct or short-term threat to her well-being, but I haven't seen her interact with the other people here ... or listened to your sermons about Gaian theory and why you're all here ... and I don't know what happens six months from now, when you die or get voted out or change Helgafell into a bar/bordello/bingo-parlor."

He smiled, but nodded, and said, "Fair enough, young man ... fair enough. What are you going to do now though, lacking the luxury of seeing into the future?"

"I'll probably tell Maurice that his granddaughter is old enough to make her own decisions, and that she could make worse ones than living on this farm for a while," I said, carefully, not wanting to promise either more or less than I felt.

"Sounds good to me." He looked around, thinking, and then brought his eyes back to me and smiled. "Do you like bacon, Tyler?"

"I surely do ... (*I could feel the pause stretch awkwardly as I refused to call him by his assumed, and honorary, title*). Why do you ask?"

"We have some smoke-cured slab bacon hanging out back, and I'd love to send you home with a piece."

Having said that, he pushed down on his knees to stand up, groaned his way out of the swing, and tottered stiffly to the stairs and down to the yard, where he turned around to wait for me.

I joined him, and as we started around the house we ran into the noisy bird that had attacked me before. The old man ignored them and walked through the mixed flock as though they weren't there (*and he couldn't hear their squawking*). I'm not sure if they were used to him, or could sense my uncertainty/fear/reticence, but they nipped at my pants and shoes and made even more noise.

I peripherally noted a difference in one of the windows that we walked by, and turned my head from the birds to let my eyes and brain figure it out. There were two windows at one corner of the house that were newer/heavier/tougher than the others we had passed. A back portion of my brain informed me that it corresponded to the room with the closed and locked door … interesting.

The birds heard a door slam around the front of the farmhouse, and left us to go and yell at those invaders for a while, which was a welcome relief. We walked into the smokehouse, both of us enjoying the smell of wood smoke and curing fat. The old man pulled down a hefty slab, wrapped it in some butcher's paper, and handed it to me.

"Best bacon you'll ever taste!" he exclaimed. "We sell it online, along with some other comestibles and handicrafts that we make here at Helgafell. One of the kids does a website, and we sometimes set up a roadside stand or go to the local farmer's markets." His speech had lost some of the interest that it contained before, and I felt that now, bacon in hand, I was dismissed.

"Thanks for letting me talk with Sophia, and for the bacon," I said, and turned to leave.

"We're not a cult, not going to hurt Sophia, not working an angle. They all come, all came, to get their hands dirty and their souls clean; me too. Hardest job for the worst pay you've ever heard of, and we have to turn kids away; old farts like me too, but less often. A sore back at the end of a long day feels good, and we like to see our labor directly translated onto the table. A few of the kids feel they're paying dues to make up for past lives, but mostly we're just hiding from the rat-race, trying to lead good and simple lives."

"What about John 'Heimdall"? Is he up here for the simple life ... a clean soul ... low pay?" I asked, anticipating obfuscation/avoidance/misdirection.

The old man chuckled under his breath and smiled in my direction (*and/or the direction of John's gatehouse*). "Nope, and that's where it gets a bit ... different. I guess I am up here paying some dues to make up for a past life like a few of those kids think they are, and John's a remnant of that life." He looked as though he was going to continue for a moment, then thought better of it, and gestured back down the rutted drive to the gatehouse and gate and my Element, and beyond that, the rest of the world.

"Well, I hope that you'll tell Sophia's grandfather that she's here by choice, and not in any danger." His eyes and tone got just the least bit cold and hard with his final words, "And we'll not expect to see you again, unless it's during a visit to our farm stand or stall at one of the local markets."

There was more to this old man than a friendly codger watching the world from a porch-swing ... more (*and quite possibly less*) than a religious figure or cult-leader. My mind has a nearly infinite and highly varied capacity for interests and research, but this place, these people, didn't ignite the spark of interest necessary for me to commit to the task any further ... I had completed my task, so I left, stopping for some eggs at the Mobil station on the way (*to go with my bacon*).

It was likely, nearly certain, that there was more going on at Helgafell Farm, and also with 'Father' and 'Gatekeeper', but as I ran a replay of the morning in my head, I could find nothing likely to have an impact on my report to Maurice. Sophia was there by choice, and not in danger/risk so far as I could judge. Maurice might be relieved, but I had failed to get her to leave the farm (*to come home to him*), so he had no reason to overlook my homelessness.

That was a problem for another day; my immediate future seemed bright, with a case of cold Coke in the fridge, and enough bacon and eggs to feed a Mongol horde. I cooked/ate/napped like a man who hadn't wasted his time.

I woke up at 2:35 in the afternoon (*which pleased me with its Fibonacci-ness*) looking into the very angry eyes of John Heimdall sitting in my comfy chair, reading through the papers formerly located in my locked safe (*inside my locked apartment I added, if only to myself*).

SmartPig Offices, Saranac Lake, NY
Wednesday, 6/5/2002, 3:58 p.m.

"Tyler, we've got a problem … and by 'we', I mean you. You've got a big fucking problem unless you can turn my frown upside-down in the next few minutes. Tell me everything that you know about dead birds, starting … now." John said all of this casually, but punctuated it by slamming a paring knife that he must have grabbed from my sink down on the coffee table between us.

"I actually know a lot about dead birds … the reasons that they die varies tremendously, as does the possible impact their deaths can have on mankind. There were mass die-offs of flamingos in two lakes in Kenya a few years ago, that were attributed to pesticide/fertilizer misuse/overuse … Lake Begoria and Lake Nakuru … tourism is a big deal in Kenya's Rift Valley, which is probably the only reason that anything was done about it. More recently, there has been some concern in the scientific community about the possibility of a nasty variant of Avian Bird Flu jumping species and becoming a human pandemic." I started to root around the nooks and crannies of my still-sleepy head for more dead bird facts, when I noticed his face doing the thing that humans do when they are displeased and impatient.

"... But that's not what you want to talk about with me. I bet that you want to talk about your two dead guinea fowls. I'm getting a Coke to help jump-start my brain, can I offer you one?" John gestured towards a travel-mug on the coffee table, so I just grabbed two cans of Coke for myself.

When I had popped the top on the first one, and downed a third of it, he cut through my enjoyment of the cold and sweet elixir with a sharp, short, barking sentence, "Three birds, not two."

Either the Coke or his tone grabbed my attention, and I snapped more fully awake. "Sophia mentioned that two of the guinea fowls had been killed during the night ... she suggested that some animal must have snuck up on them. Do you have dogs at Helgafell?"

"Two, but neither go near the nasty things. Between the geese and the guinea fowls, the dogs are terrified," he answered in the manner of a person humoring someone obviously lying to him, and for me to pick up on it, he must have been hamming it up facially/tonally.

"You watched me leave a couple of hours ago, and I haven't been back to the farm ... also, how is anyone going to sneak up on those things without giving themselves away?" I asked.

"That's a good question, and a part of our larger problem, which we'll circle back to in a minute, but the short answer is that someone defeated the guinea fowls with technology. When Mark (*likely one of the kids on the farm that I hadn't met*) told me about another dead bird, I checked it out, and found that it had been shot; I'm assuming that the other two were as well. You walked the farm today, inside the house and out; first outsider in a couple of weeks. I'm not a large fan of coincidence, so as I said a minute ago, tell me what you know about the dead birds … and sooner would be better than later, so leave out the crap about Kenya and China." That being said, he settled back into my good reading chair, grabbing his travel-mug on the way back, and looked pointedly at me.

"Give me a minute," I said, and went back into the back rooms of my brain to root through some old recordings/pictures/maps with (*hopefully*) relevant information, in the hope that I could avoid the portion of the day when John would skip ahead to the threats and paring-knife portion of his visit.

"TYLER!" John had clapped his hands just in front of my face, and was staring into my eyes from a distance of less than a foot, "What do those numbers you just said mean?"

"2, 3, 2, 2, 3, 7, 8 are the digits in the fourth step in the juggler sequence for the integer 77 … math nerdery … never mind. I play math games in the front of my head while the real work goes on around the back."

John shook his head like a wet dog, seeming confused and entirely unsatisfied at my explanation, so I went on before he did more rattling of cutlery or shouting.

"I've got some things … not necessarily in order, but here they are. I don't want/need/know about whatever is in the secure room in the farmhouse, but someone does. The only way to get to that room is to go through those birds and that would cause a ruckus, which is likely why someone is killing them. I don't have, and have never fired, a gun of any sort. The nearest good cover for someone to shoot at the guinea fowls is from the trees on the side of the small hill to the southwest of the farmhouse, which must be nearly 400 yards away … the noise either suppressed or baffled by shooting from some distance back into the trees. Everyone up here has a gun, but very few people can hit anything beyond 100 yards. Whoever did shoot the birds will keep on doing it until all the birds are gone, but they are hoping that you'll blame the dogs or wild animals, so they're likely shooting with a small caliber round … 22 long rifle or 17. You should go to the police and let them find this person … this is exactly the sort of thing that they're good at, and the reason that we pay their salaries … but you won't, or you wouldn't be here."

"How do you know all of that … how did you put all of that together in the two minutes you were doing your 'Rainman' thing?" he asked, this time with a tone different than he had used before, much less hostile/angry/accusatory … I was relieved that some corner had been turned in this encounter.

"I read and watch and listen and remember … everything. Detective novels, crime TV, I have a good eye for landscape topography and distances and directionality," I offered him, by way of an answer.

"So, allowing that it wasn't you who shot the birds, which I am doing … conditionally … what's next?" John looked at me as I popped the second Coke and started working on it.

I tried to sculpt my face into an expression of surprise (*and must have failed to some degree, as his face became quizzical*) when I responded, "What's next? I splash my face, head downstairs for some Chinese food, and figure out where to go camping tonight. It's a problem, to be sure, but the best thing about it is that it's your problem, not mine."

One of the upsides to my lack of emotional expression, is that I don't have to worry often about giving my thoughts away; in addition to the things I'd shared with John a minute ago, I had also gamed out this exchange through the next couple of moves (*on both of our parts*) and had an idea that might help both of us get what we wanted.

"A minute ago, you suggested that the police would be good at figuring this sort of thing out, and that it would make sense to talk with them, but you assumed that I wouldn't. You're right that we don't want to bring the police in unless it's absolutely necessary…" I cut him off.

"We're both in agreement that there is most likely someone shooting in the direction of your farmhouse, admittedly they're aiming at birds, but people could get in the way of one of those bullets … many people would argue that it was already necessary to bring the police all the way in."

He looked almost to be in some degree of physical pain when he replied, "Agreed, but the shooter has so far gone to great lengths, it would appear, to avoid hurting anyone, and as long as that's the case, Father would like me to avoid bringing outsiders into, onto, Helgafell."

"I'm having trouble calling him Father … it feels a little Papal to me … does he have a name we can use for the purposes of this conversation?" I asked.

"The one his mother gave him, but Helgafell was created for sanctuary and privacy; I've called him lots of names over the years, and if you need a name for the purpose of our conversations, call him Nick, but that's not for anyone or anywhere else." John gave me a look that I assume was meant to convey trust and gravitas and some small degree of warning, so I nodded.

"In addition to reading lots of stories, John, I make up stories … about people and places and things I see or read or hear about; I make up stories and then poke holes in them, and fix the holes and poke new holes, and fix those … and so on, until it feels right. The story that I have made up about you and 'Nick' and Helgafell has been poked and patched through a couple of generations, and while I'm not fully confident of the particulars, I would bet you a plate of the passable Chinese food downstairs that I'm pretty close."

"I'm listening."

"You were both in an extra-legal import/export business on the lengthy island/drumlin deposited by the last ice-age at the southern end of this state. Nick accumulated a mixed pile of loot and guilt, and decided to retire to the country, and the simple life, like in 'Green Acres', and you got stuck playing the role of Zsa Zsa, except when you get too tired of babysitting the old man, when one of your brothers comes up to man the gate for a while." I looked over to see how he had followed my story so far.

"I don't know whether to be proud or insulted that you didn't cast me as Eb in your story," John replied, smiling and nodding for me to go on.

"It mostly makes sense to me, except for the Gaian talk/preaching ... why bother with the church/cult/eco-farmer business if he doesn't have to?"

"He believes it, and likes talking about it with the kids. We've discussed it at length during some long winter nights, when the sun goes down at four and doesn't come up again until nine the next morning, and everyone else in the farmhouse is asleep after a long, hard, cold day working outside. I see it as an interesting metaphor, and a way to look at a series of interconnected systems, but he's talked himself into taking it to the next level, and really thinks of the Earth as an immense and incredibly complex organism. Anyway, enough about that Tyler, why do you care, and why should that matter to me?"

"A couple of reasons. I find the whole situation interesting/stimulating ... crime, murder, sniping, fugitives (*from justice, commerce, big-city life ... something*). My life has been spent exploring patterns in the world around me, and mapping them so that I can function somewhat like other people; and this unknown/disruption/newness is uncomfortable to me. I'm not a big fan of cruelty to animals, even to ugly birds, and would like to stop it. As far as that goes, I would also like to help you avoid a 'Soprano'-like conclusion to this if/when you find the guy who has been shooting the birds; doing so would help protect Sophia and her new life, which was my original reason for getting involved with you and Nick and Helgafell at all."

"Jeez, anything else?" he asked jokingly.

"Well, since you asked … I enjoyed the bacon, and wouldn't mind getting some more of it in the future … it's pretty expensive on the farm's website."

I grinned at this last reason, but meant it at least as much as the other reasons I had given (*more, really*). I had one other reason for wanting to get involved, but there was no need to share it with John, as it likely ran counter to his role at the farm.

"Well, you came close enough with your story about Father and me for me to buy you a plate of the passable Chinese food; we can talk about whether or not I can trust you enough to let you help me stop the 'Great Guinea Fowl Slaughter of Ought-Two', and why I should."

With that said, he stood up, put my paring knife back in the drawer it belonged in by the sink, put the papers back in my safe (*giving the dial a twirl after closing the door, and muttering "cheap safe" under his breath, which it was*), unlocked the door (*even the chain and deadbolt, which I never use, and which gave me a nasty few seconds while I thought about why he might have wanted that level of privacy with me*), and then headed out/down/around and into the Chinese place, presumably assuming that I would follow … I did.

SmartPig Offices, Saranac Lake, NY
Wednesday, 6/5/2002, 4:37 p.m.

Being that it was between the usual hours for lunch and
dinner, there wasn't anyone else in the Chinese restaurant
beside John and me, so we placed our order, paid, and
went over to the table farthest away from the guy cooking
to talk while we waited. It has been my experience that
the smells of Chinese food cooking are nearly always the
same, regardless of the way that the final product tastes,
which was/is/will be a mystery to me, but not one that I
had/have a burning desire to solve.

"So, if it's not you ..." John let his statement hang in
the air for a moment, possibly hoping to see me squirm
or try to prove myself innocent to him.

"Then we wouldn't be here, waiting for our food to
come, and trying to figure out how to work together for
maximum benefit ... so it must not be me," I finished for
him.

"I can make a list of people who might think that they
have a reason to break into the farmhouse," John offered,
as an opening volley.

"That's probably a waste of time. I bet that Nick or you paid cash with a big bill or four once too often, or someone doing work on the farm saw a safe or cash box, (*or Marsellus Wallace's briefcase?*) back in Nick's office. The trouble is that the list wouldn't have to be restricted to whoever he/you spoke to … it could include anyone that they spoke to as well."

"So should I start asking people on the street if they shot the birds, or will you?" he asked me, as the cook brought our plates over.

"I think that if we take motive off the table, and assume opportunity for the moment, then we can focus on the most interesting and selective determinant … means. There can't be many people in this part of the world who can confidently take a shot at a moving chicken-sized bird from 400 yards. If we can find/identify this subset of people, we should be able to eliminate the wheat from the chaff with motive and opportunity in short order."

"Sounds good Tyler, but how do we get a list of people who can make that sort of shot. I know a guy in the State Police, and WE know some people in the armed forces." (*I could feel the emphasis on the 'WE', and assumed that he meant 'Nick'*)

"You could also spend some time at the fish and game club, trying to see who can shoot, although I don't think they have a range longer than 200 yards (*and why would they, as wooded as it is up here in the Adirondacks?*), but I think I've got an easier way to find out what we need to know that should pay off by noon tomorrow," I said, as I started feeding the hot and fatty goodness into my mouth.

John had a superb perplexed face, which I took a mental snapshot of for later practice.

"How are you gonna do it?"

"It's so much more impressive if you don't know … you can imagine all sorts of computer hacking, back-alley meetings, and high-level government contacts. I'll call you tomorrow, once I know, and you can buy me lunch … again … while I share what I know and suggest a possible solution."

"Suggest?" John asked. "You're not just going to tell me what I'm going to do?" Even I could tell that he was using sarcasm (*although it's possible that he had noted my difficulty in picking up on social cues, and leaned on the sarcasm extra-hard*).

"Nope, they're your birds, and your money/loot/alien corpses … whatever. I'm working for you in this matter, and I'll be content to suggest a possible course of action that avoids bloodshed, as well as a legal hassle for Sophia or you or the farm."

I finished my food, and half of his, and said goodbye to Helgafell's Gatekeeper until the next day.

The woods near Middle Saranac Lake, NY
Wednesday, 6/5/2002 6:43 p.m.

I had hurried upstairs from my late lunch with John, grabbed a minimalist pack and stuffed it with what I'd need for an overnight (*it was only supposed to get down into the 40s, so I wasn't worried*): camping hammock, sleeping bag, my current reading-book, snacks/drinks, bathing suit/towel, fleece for my head and feet and hands, a tiny first-aid kit, and some rope. There's a nice beach roughly forty percent of the way from Saranac Lake to Tupper Lake, along Route 3, opposite the trailhead for Ampersand Mountain, and that was my goal for the night.

In my new home, the Adirondacks, you can camp anywhere on State Forest Preserve, as long as you are back 150 feet from water/trails. I had been having fun since spring's arrival exploring/mapping my new environment ... building a list of places to camp, and categorizing them by view/hike/bugs/beasts/swim. I was enjoying the feeling of my new world expanding day by day.

I parked my Honda Element alongside six other vehicles, but instead of crossing the road and climbing Ampersand to the south, I went back into the woods and headed north to the beach. Three minutes later, I stripped and changed into my suit for a swim before the sun disappeared behind the trees along the shore at the western end of Middle Saranac Lake. I set up camp in bare feet (*perhaps only 100 feet back from the water, but it was a nice spot*), enjoying the pricking and pinching of pine-needles and pinecones and sticks and stones while I found the perfect trees to hang my hammock from for the night; it's a Hennessy, which has built-in bug-netting, to protect me from the black flies and mosquitoes overnight.

With my hammock hung, and sleeping bag stuffed up into the chamber, I grabbed my book, slammed a granola bar and a bottle of Gatorade, and walked out into the water (*up to my waist*) to read in the remaining sunlight, out of reach of most of the bugs. I was currently enjoying "Sleeping Dogs" by Thomas Perry. As I read, I could feel my brain shaping some ideas and responses to my current situation, and new acquaintance John, based on Perry's interesting storyline. I eventually found myself squinting in the near-dark, and swatting at a cloud of blackflies that had braved the crossing from shore to drink my blood ... time to go and hide in my hammock.

I secured a length of rope to my backpack, threw the free end over a tree branch about 20 feet overhead (*with the help of a perfectly chosen stick*), hoisted the pack (*with my food and toothpaste and other smelly stuff in it*) up and out of reach of bears and raccoons, and tied it off. I climbed into the hammock through the entry-flap in the underside with my book and headlamp, a sports bottle of Gatorade and some Reese's Peanut Butter Cups, meaning to read and snack a bit, but falling asleep almost instantly instead ... listening to the water and wind and feeling the gentle rocking motion of the hammock under/around me.

Middle Saranac Lake, NY
Wednesday, 6/5/2002, 10:23 p.m.

I woke up four hours later, in the pitch black you only
find 100 feet inside thick forest. I could hear and smell
the water off to my left, and it helped me get
oriented/placed in the map in my head. I felt around for
my headlamp and sat up, sliding my legs back out (*through
what I couldn't help thinking of as my hammock's birth canal*) to
stand on the needles in my lightweight sleeping bag. I
shed the sleeping bag leaving it puddled at my feet,
stepped out gingerly onto the cold and slightly damp
ground, and started to pick my way down to the shore …
hearing a beaver slap its tail on the water in warning as
my feet felt the dirt and needles give way to sand and
shells.

I turned off the headlamp about three feet from the
water and stripped, leaving my clothes in the sand, and
walked out into the water … warmer than the air, but not
warm. I remembered the feeling of being in the middle of
the lake and not knowing where to swim to retrieve my
clothes and headlamp from my first night swim. I looked
back over my shoulder before I got too far into the lake,

and confirmed that I could, in fact, see the gentle glowing of my watch face (*it always glowed, and/ but I always checked*). I dove under, gasping at the full-body cold upon breaking surface again, and flipped over onto my back to swim out further into the nighttime lake.

A minute later, I could feel that the bottom had fallen away from my feet, and I used the bright stars overhead to grab onto my sense of place in the universe again ... Polaris (*North Star*) was easy to find, and I knew that my clothes were in the opposite direction. I floated face up on the lake for a half hour, feeling the lake both move around me, and move me around. When I started shivering, after 34 minutes in the water, I found Polaris, oriented myself away from it, and did my imitation of an Olympic freestyle back into shore to warm up.

While swimming into shore, getting dressed, by headlamp, creeping back up to my campsite, and climbing back up into the hammock, I thought about my current state of quasi-homelessness, and decided that although I liked it most nights, it might be nice to have Maurice's blessing to spend the occasional night in the SmartPig offices. I had 73 percent of an idea about how to bring this about while also doing what I had told John that I would do ... I knew from books that I had read, and discussions that I had had with Mickey, one of my childhood parent/teachers, that my solution wasn't socially or morally acceptable, but it would meet my needs, and not unduly injure or inconvenience anyone else.

I settled back down into my sleeping back, seduced into another four hours of sleep by the wind rocking my hammock, the smell of the water and moss, and the sound of the wind through the tops of the white pines 100 feet over my head.

SmartPig Offices Saranac Lake, NY
Thursday, 6/6/2002, 11:46 a.m.

I had woken in the failing darkness that signals the coming
of morning, and slid down and out of my hammock and
sleeping bag for a round of input/output management (*the
body's needs are troubling and tiresome, but I had tried to stop output
by eliminating input once, when nine, and was rushed to the hospital
three days later by my parents. I promised never to try it again*). I
read by headlamp until the first mosquito found me, as
night warmed into day. Then I headed back up the trail to
my Element, and eventually to the SmartPig offices … by
way of Dunkin' Donuts.

Eight donuts, four Cokes, and 273 pages later (*159 in
"Sleeping Dogs", and 114 of the newest of John Sandford's Prey
books*), I could hear the tromp of work shoes, and
slip/slide/shuffle of cardboard boxes coming up the stairs.
I let the UPS guy, Pete, in before he could knock.

"Hey Tyler, I've got a couple of things for you today …
nothing to sign."

"Hi Pete, can I get you a Coke?" Pete had something
for me on most days, and had gotten into the habit of

occasionally stopping for a few minutes to check out some new piece of camping gear (*he was an avid camper, and seemed to enjoy living vicariously through me gear-wise ... he loved hearing reviews of gear he had delivered that I'd just used*).

"Cold one two nights ago, huh? Were you out in that, Tyler? Didja try the new stove yet?"

"It was ... I was ... I did. The stove (*a nice, if heavy Optimus*) worked well enough, but was a bit too noisy for my taste ... like a little helicopter under my pot. I just read an article about a DIY alcohol stove that might be just the thing for warm-weather camping."

At this point I ran out of things to say to Pete, and had no idea of how to bridge the gap to my next desired topic of conversation ... this is one of the tough things about not having the standard installation of social/emotional software that most humans get. Pete thought for a few seconds, presumably about the potential of alcohol stoves, and then seemed to start getting ready to move on ... up and out of my comfy couch, and towards the next delivery on his route.

"PETE!" I almost shouted, more from forcing it out through my social reluctance than any depth of feeling, but Pete looked a bit worried nonetheless. "I've got a question that I'm pretty certain that you can help me with ... it's important."

"Sure, Tyler, but if it's about that spot down near Old Forge, I forgot the map again, so no joy on that front ..." he trailed off by the end of that thought, seeing the shake of my head (*I'm good at basic positive/negative gestures, having learned them early in life ... it's the complex social communication that is beyond me*).

"I definitely want more info about that pond up north of Old Forge sometime, but I've got a question about UPS."

This was delicate territory for both of us now; I knew that people didn't always want to talk about some aspects of their jobs, especially with people (*like me*) entirely lacking in cool/calm/stealth.

Pete looked warily at me, and nodded as he spoke, "Yup … what's on your mind, Tyler? What can I tell you about Big Brown?"

"A month ago, when I got that huge shipment of beeswax from Texas (*I had wanted SmartPig to branch out and start making lip balm and candles, and found a guy to ship me 80 pounds of wax from his hives*) … I felt bad about making you carry those heavy boxes up here, and you said something about it not being as bad as the ORM-D shipments. I looked it up after you left, and lots of ORM-D shipments are ammo, and UPS is the only shipper in most cases. Is that right?"

"Yes." Pete said nothing else, perhaps sensing where I was headed (*which was a good thing, as I could feel that I might have trouble getting there*).

"What I'm going to ask you to do for me is almost certainly against UPS policies, but it is also completely moral, and entirely the right thing to do."

He looked at me nervously, but nodded, and took a sip of the Coke I'd given him. I'd laid the foundation for his cooperation, and thought that I had a final touch that would close the deal … I wasn't sure, as I've said before, I'm not any kind of judge of character among humans.

"Who do you deliver the most ammunition to, not counting the Blue Line (*Saranac Lake's sporting goods store … only steps from my front door*)? I want a list of the top five or ten, and I'll tell you why before you decide if you want to help me … okay?"

Pete hadn't run from room, so I continued. "Someone has shot a couple of dogs, family pets, at extreme range …

300 to 500 yards. Shooting like that needs daily, or near daily practice, and that translates to ammo shipments, which you deliver."

I could see that I nearly had him, "Shit, Tyler, I could get fired for even talking about stuff like that ... but ... pets?" I'd helped Pete grab boxes out of the back of the truck for SmartPig before, and seen pictures of his family members, including pictures (*with studio backdrops*) of his three dogs. If I was the kind of person who felt guilty about manipulating people, this would be a good moment for it ... but I'm not.

"Yes, inside-dogs, playing next to their houses, in one case with kids nearby."

Another falsehood, but I could see from the flush creeping up his neck, and the wetness of his eyes, that he was picturing the tiny blond girl in one of the pictures on the dashboard losing her dog, or being shot at/adjacent/near to ... and he was mine.

"Should we go to the cops?" popped out of his mouth, and these were six words I had not planned on. I tried to think about books that I had read, and how people talk/act/react in these situations ... I didn't have more than a second to formulate my reply, so I hoped it would suffice.

"No, definitely not. There won't be enough evidence for an arrest or a warrant, and it will just make him careful. I know one of the dads (*I hit the word "dads" with more emphasis than I ordinarily would, to hammer the point home*), and he wants to go and have a talk with the shooter ... a talk. Nobody is looking to channel Marsellus Wallace, after the basement with Zed (*I noted that it was the second time in as many days that I'd reached for a "Pulp Fiction" reference, and wondered briefly if I should be bothered that my life seemed to be developing some parallels ... I decided not*), just a talk to let him know that we know, and that it has to stop, now."

Pete mulled all of that over for a few seconds ... we'd talked movies and books a few times, when he'd see them on the table in SmartPig, and I refused to rise to any other conversational gambits (*this was back before he had shared word of his love for camping*); then he rolled his eyes up and to the left, perhaps trying to recall/redraw a map of ORM-D deliveries.

"Robert Everson, Brent Martin, Mark LaFleur, Tony Allen. Those four. Nobody else is even close. Those guys get monthly or better shipments of serious quantities of ammo from multiple vendors ... they must shoot a thousand rounds a month, or better, each."

"Thanks Pete ... want a Coke for the road?" I had other plans for the remaining donuts, or I would have offered him a cruller. He looked at me as though he had more to say, but didn't know where to start, so I did it for him (*leading off my #7 smile, 'knowing and sly', which was still awkward and untested*), "I trust that you won't talk about this with anyone."

He nodded.

"... and I'll let you know what I can, when I can ... if I can." I hoped that this was sufficiently cryptic, and dismissive, to bring this encounter to a close, so that he would leave, and I could eat my donuts and figure out the last few moves.

It was.

Donnelly's Ice Cream, Saranac Lake, NY
Thursday, 6/6/2002, 12:39 p.m.

I had a large Black-Raspberry cone in hand, and once
John came out with his, more modest, baby cone, we
moved off some distance to talk about what I had found
out, my ideas for getting to checkmate, and … hopefully,
setting up a schedule for future payments in bacon.

I had called John as soon as Pete clumped down the
stairs and out to finish his route, suggesting Donnelly's as
a meeting place for a number of reasons: it was
approximately equidistant from both, and they serve
fantastic ice cream with the best view (*that I've yet seen*) in
the Adirondacks. They also don't force me to choose my
flavor (*I have trouble making choices without sufficient evidence to
make a considered judgment … growing up in NYC with Baskin
Robbins was torturously stressful … Donnelly's has one flavor
everyday … you just have to choose the size*). I sat down on the
grass and found the castle on top of Whiteface in the
distance.

"Tony Allen, Robert Everson, Mark LaFleur, and
Brent Martin," I said while handing him a folded sheet of

paper. "Their names and home/work addresses and phone numbers are on that." I tapped the paper, at the same time doing some speedy repair work on my dripping cone. Donnelly's has been using the same soft ice-cream machine since 1953, and while it is a marvel of mechanical endurance, it can deliver overly soft treats when they get busy ... as they were today.

"What, all four of them killed the birds?" John asked, unbelieving.

"Of course not, but I don't know which of them it is," I answered, getting ready for his next question.

"So why the fuck are we sharing this pleasant, if runny, dairy treat, Tyler?" He gestured dramatically with his cone, and three drops of light-purple goo spattered my t-shirt like thick blood. "You said that you'd get the information I needed to stop the bird-icide (*avicide, I thought, but didn't interrupt*), and here we are ... you just gave me a random list of names ... these guys could owe you money or steal your morning paper for Christ's sake!"

"Yes, possibly, but they don't and didn't. One of these four heard or saw something directly or indirectly that makes them think something in your not-so-secure office is worth stealing. I don't know what it is, or which one it is ... nor do I really care. I have a plan to end/head-off your problems without having to do the last bit of legwork ... do you want to hear it or not?"

He perked up at this, and I leaned/dodged/ducked out of the way of some more black-raspberry spatter-evidence. "Do tell."

"I've identified four possibles. We don't want to stake them out for days/weeks to find the guilty party; we just want the slaughter of innocents (*I gave him a bit of my #4, playful, but could tell that it, to some degree, flopped*) to stop. Our advantage is that we don't need to establish guilt beyond reasonable doubt … that, coupled with a comfortable disregard for the rights and property of others."

I could see that he had a glimmer, so I continued.

"Allen has a sugarbush not far from Helgafell, and it feeds into a sugar shack."

John looked at me as though I was speaking Dutch.

"A stand of sugar maple trees and a house that he uses to boil the sap down into maple syrup, " I explained.

He nodded.

"We burn the sugar shack … it's insured and nobody's ever in it at this time of year. Everson owns a store in town that sells formal-wear and other clothes … we break the front display windows. LaFleur drives a new Escalade … we flatten all four tires. Martin has an attached garage at his home, and no dog (*or guinea fowls*) to raise the alarm … we can hose it down with blood-red paint."

John looked at me like I was crazy.

"Four different forms of vandalism won't seem connected/related to anyone who doesn't have my list already in their head (*especially the police*), but the guilty party will definitely take it as a message … the one who actually killed the birds and wants to rob you will get the message, and stop … the rest will collect insurance and feel unlucky for a day or two."

He tilted his head at me, like a dog trying to get a fix on a mysterious whistle, "You're an odd duck, Tyler Cunningham, no shit." John smiled at me, and did some clean-up work on his ice-cream which had started running down his wrist. "Afterwards, how do we find out which one it was?"

"We don't. We don't care. I think that it's most likely Allen, and is least likely to be Everson, but it doesn't really matter … nobody gets hurt … just stuff," I said.

John looked at me like I was from Mars, but nodding slightly, as if he could live with knowing this particular Martian.

"It meets our/your needs, stops the birds dying, protects Nick's secrets and '*loot*', and avoids you having to run any bodies through the wood-chipper."

I felt confident now that I could see my way through the next minute or so of conversation to the twist that, if it came off, would end my day even better than a large cone from Donnelly's.

"I like it ... not least because it's not at all my style, and Nick won't tumble to my having had to fix anything."

This fed into my twist so perfectly, that I couldn't wait for my planned opening, 30 seconds from now, "There's just one remaining loose end, John. My source also indicates that there was likely someone inside feeding information to the shooter."

I paused here to give him time to jump to a conclusion that I would reinforce a second later, "It's critically important to me that nothing happen to Sophia." I let that hang, while John crunched things around in his head, and ate his soggy cone, before pulling out a napkin and wiping his hands.

He swallowed my baited prompt, "She'll have to leave the farm, Tyler. Nothing bad's gonna happen to her, but she can't live there anymore ... she's out this afternoon. After I have a talk with her." He leaned on the last sentence in a way that I wasn't crazy about, so I reiterated my earlier position.

"The important thing is that nothing bad happens to her ... you can't make her talk about her involvement in this without tipping that we don't know which one it is, so it's best to just make her leave. She'll report back to whichever guy is the guilty party, and that will convince him that you know he did the shooting. He'd be crazy not to walk away from it, and think himself lucky."

This was one of those instances in which my lack of emotional response/display comes in handy; now I just had to get out of here cleanly before he thought about it too much.

"Funny how it's working out, isn't it? We met because Sophia's grandfather wanted her out of Helgafell, and here it is ... happening ... just a few days later."

"She's the newest '*recruit*', which is logically when a family member is most likely to want a relative out of a set-up like the farm, and also the likeliest person to be a plant/scout for someone wanting to steal from you." This was sketchy, but could hang together if John wanted the symmetry to work.

"I guess. So, how should I work it? Sooner is better than later, and I want Sophia gone ASAP," John offered.

"I can take care of the tires and the storefront in town, if you can manage the sugar shack and the garage," I offered, both to sweeten the deal, and to move things along, past Sophia.

"Just because they're closer to you, doesn't mean they're easier for you ... I've got some experience with things like the in-town 'accidents' you suggested. Let me handle them, and you can wander the backwoods of the rural Adirondacks for the maple-shack and what's-his-name's garage. Wear gloves, be quiet, and get gone as quickly as you can afterwards."

"Better ... thanks John." It would be best to let him help in planning, to shift some of the plan over to him in his mind.

"Sounds good Tyler ... we should do them all within twenty-four hours of Sophia getting bounced ... I'll take care of that this afternoon, deal with Everson and

LaFleur tonight. I'll bring some eggs along with another slab of bacon tomorrow sometime. Can I bring them by your home?"

"I'll be in and out, but there's a key under ... never mind ... you can leave it in the fridge, assuming that you can get in as easily as you did last time," I said.

"I could shout at those locks of yours and get through the door in less time than you can with your keys," he said in a tone devoid of boast/pride ... almost concern (*I would have to get some better locks when all of this was done ... assuming that it worked out as planned, and I still had the SmartPig offices*).

Tony Allen's Sugar Shack, Gabriels, NY
Friday, 6/7/2002, 3:37 a.m.

There's an island of forest and wilderness bounded by
routes 86, 186, and 30 ... that was my target for this
evening. I'd found that people living in the Adirondacks
defined their lives and locations by the roads that cut
through the trees, around the lakes/ponds, and over the
mountains, and planned to use that to my advantage.
People tend to see their world by routes of travel, and to
ignore/discount the unknown. The people that I would be
visiting tonight very likely didn't see the miles of forest
behind their homes as more than backdrop, or a place to
get firewood or sap (*and those things from the edges of the woods,
not deep*). They wouldn't imagine people approaching them
from that side, when the road ran to within 50 feet of their
house. So I would be coming in from their blind side in my
visits to Tony Allen's Sugar Shack and Brent Martin's
Garage.

I'd parked my Honda Element off to one side of the
gate of the Lake Clear Transfer Station (*dump*) after they
closed at 3pm, walked in about a mile to a chunk of State

Forest Preserve along the Jackrabbit Trail, then hung my hammock in the woods and waited for dark. I made a simple, no-cook, supper of Cokes and jerky and orange slices (*the candy, not the fruit*), then climbed up into the bug proof hammock to read/sleep/wait (*each in turn, as my wait was nearly nine hours, and I haven't slept that long since being hospitalized for pneumonia when I was seven*). At a bit after one in the morning, I judged the timing right, grabbed my hydration pack, and headed out.

I was still getting used to the feeling of being in the woods at night, in the dark, having grown up in the eternal twilight and cocktail party noise of Manhattan for most of my life. I could hear insects chewing the wood in trees around me, frogs extolling the virtues of a pond that I would never see, and twice the sweep and brush of feathers overhead as a bird flew between/amongst the trees, doing whatever birds do at night in the woods. I could see nothing under the canopy of trees in which I had hung my hammock, save for the cone of light that my headlamp emitted. I found the path, checked my compass to make sure that I went in the correct direction (*a bit east of north*), rather than back towards my Element, and headed out at the fastest pace that I felt comfortable with … stopping every few minutes to stop/look/listen.

I had been walking along the trail that runs from Paul Smiths to Lake Placid for almost an hour, when I reached up and shut my headlamp off, letting the darkness rush back in all around me. After a few minutes, my night vision started coming into play, and I could make out a dozen shades of grey in the moonlight (*the moon was only a few nights away from full, and once I let it, gave me enough light to navigate by*). I had walked this path earlier in the spring, and remembered a series of side-trails shooting off to the east, and in the general direction I needed to travel … I skipped the first one, and turned down the second, hoping that it would pan out … it didn't.

I had a few simple landmarks memorized from my map-time before leaving the SmartPig offices, and as soon as I broke out and into a rutted field, I took a bearing on one of the airport beacons, and the signal light on top of Whiteface … I was still too far south. Instead of turning around and heading back down to the Jackrabbit Trail, I decided to walk along the edge of the field, taking bearings every five minutes to double-check that I was headed in the right direction (*as well as track my progress*). Somewhere between my fifth and sixth bearings, I had passed the sweet-spot, so I headed back along the edge of the field (*planted with … I guessed … corn*) until I found a jeep-trail, just opposite a farm house with a single light burning in it, and turned up the trail into the woods.

I walked up the jeep-trail back into darkness, but didn't dare turn my headlamp on so close to the peopled portion of the world, and my eventual target. It was slower going than I had planned on, but eventually (*probably no more than eight to ten minutes, although it felt longer*) I reached the sugar shack. I had no sooner walked around it, listened for people, creeped in through the unlocked (*and unlockable*) door, and scanned the room with my headlamp, when it occurred to me that my plan was dead in the water … I had failed to plan for everything, and couldn't imagine how to do what I needed to do and get clear cleanly, much less find and hit my second target (*Brent Martin's garage*).

I had brought a gallon of gasoline (*which was more than adequate to burn the wooden sugar shack*), but had no timing device, and couldn't be sure of getting all the way down the jeep-trail and back to the relative safety of the Jackrabbit Trail before someone from the waking farmhouse saw/came to the fire. I mentally went through the gear in my pack, and an inventory of the sugar shack (*based on my initial scan of the room via headlamp a few minutes ago*) frustrated with myself for not taking all factors into account before heading out so blithely … 41 seconds later, I had it.

I grabbed a box of long/thin/white emergency candles off of a shelf by the door, an armload of empty soda bottles from a container along the wall, and a spool of lightweight string (*it felt like cotton, but it was hard to tell*) from a junk-drawer/toolbox in the far corner of the building. I carefully filled all of the soda bottles three-quarters of the way with gas (*and screwed the lids back on*). I paced off the room, and cut/tied string to each bottle, connecting all of them to a single string with a loop at one end. There was a nail head sticking one quarter of an inch out of one of the floorboards at one end of the cabin, which would serve my needs perfectly.

I tied my Swiss Army knife to one end of the string for weight, and lofted it over an exposed ceiling beam at the opposite end of the cabin from my nail head (*on the seventh attempt*). Pulling on the string with a slow and even pressure, I reeled in the string until the bottles were suspended roughly seven feet off of the ground, and then walked over to my nail head, carefully paying out the thread as I went. I looped the thread around the nail head several times, and then tied it off. I went back and carefully unscrewed the lids of each soda bottle.

I lit one candle, and used drippings from it to place four more unlit ones around the room … three underneath the soda bottles, and a fourth laying on its side right next to the exposed nail head that bent the string slightly out of true in its path from nail head to ceiling beam. Finished, I stopped, looked around, made sure to gather all of my things back into pockets or pack, and lit the four candles I had placed.

I opened and closed the door very carefully, checking afterwards to make sure that my passage from the sugar shack hadn't blown the candles out (*it hadn't*), and traveled back down the jeep trail as fast as the darkness would allow.

Brent Martin's Garage, Gabriels, NY
Friday, 6/7/2002, 4:42 a.m.

I'd made it to the fields, and along the edge to the little trail
leading back to the Jackrabbit Trail when I could see a glow
and billows of smoke rising from the woods, slightly
indistinct in the general glow coming from the north and
east as morning light started to creep into the horizon line.

The candle must have burned sideways down to the
string's level, then through the string … even if the falling
bottles of gas had knocked over or extinguished one or
more of the candles underneath, there must have been at
least one candle left under the falling bottles of gas left to
ignite the fumes created by the spilling/splashing gasoline.

Relieved that half of my night's work was completed, I
moved along the Jackrabbit Trail more quickly as the
moonlight faded and was replaced by a more generalized
glow from the east. I turned off when the power line I had
been waiting for cut away towards the coming sunrise. I
followed the power line right-of-way for 10 minutes (*which,
given my usual pace over clean trail, should have been a half-mile*)
before cutting into the woods to the left of the power line,

heading north again and hopefully (*if the map in my head was functioning reasonably well*) bushwhacking through a few hundred yard of woods to the back of Brent Martin's property.

I came to the edge of the woods roughly midway between the Martin house and his neighbors' (*whose name I didn't know, as they weren't suspects in my bird-sniping investigation*). I couldn't see lights on in either house, nor could I detect any sounds or movements in the five minutes I invested in watching before crawling towards the Martin house ... stopping every 20 yards to look and listen before moving forward again. I got close to the house before it occurred to me to bypass it in favor of the big garage attached to the north end of the house that sheltered the deck from wind and noise and neighbors (*but not from me*).

I pulled out an elderly 3-liter hydration bag that I had loaded with paint and spent five quiet minutes defacing the Martin garage. Using the tube like a nozzle, and squeezing the hydration bag like a bagpiper might, I was able to spray the words, "guilty" and "murderer", as well as spooky eyes and fanged mouths and rifles shooting birds on two sides (*the deck side, and the side facing the woods*) before running out of paint.

I stuffed the old (*and now useless, to me*) hydration bag into a garbage bag, waited thirty seconds for lights or sirens or screaming or footfalls, and then quickly scuttled on all fours back into the woods, down to the power line, back to the Jackrabbit Trail, and eventually back to Element ... never seeing or hearing another human (*although I did surprise an extended family of deer, and a noisy tail-slapping beaver*).

SmartPig Offices, Saranac Lake, NY
Friday, 6/7/2002, 7:26 a.m.

I'd come home after dropping the containers I'd used to carry the gas and the paint into a dumpster behind the McDonald's in Tupper Lake, assuming that a long drive in the opposite direction couldn't do me any harm, and that nobody would be looking for a vandal's tools that far from the scene of the crimes. I also picked up a bag of sausage McMuffin sandwiches and a bunch of hash browns to replenish my protein and fat reserves after my moderately strenuous early morning ... all of it washed down with a huge serving of disappointingly syrupy Coke. I crept into SmartPig and waited to see what the day would bring ... I didn't have long to wait.

"Tyler! Most of the space in this ridiculous dorm-room fridge is taken up by Coke. There's no room for all of the bacon and the eggs that I brought," John said as he stood up and slammed a big wrapped package of bacon on the counter by the sink. "You either need to get a bigger fridge, or learn to drink your soda warm."

"Actually, I've been thinking of getting a bigger one just for my Coke, and keeping the small one for food ... you can see that I don't cook/keep/store much in the way of fresh food up here. That package of bacon looks

74

volumetrically similar to four cans of Coke laying on their side, so if you grab four Cokes off of the top shelf, it should just fit."

He did, it did, and I started working my way through the first can … wishing that it was a few degrees colder and tasted as good as the Cokes I'd enjoyed in Canada earlier this month.

"I took care of my end of things yesterday afternoon and last night. Sophia packed and was gone with tears and shouts before dinner, and once I walked her off the property and waited for her grandfather to come for her, I had a few hours before I could do the rest. The store windows were more difficult than I anticipated. Who knew that a one-horse town like Saranac Lake would make me wait so long for an empty street and a clean getaway. I managed to get both picture-windows and the stained glass one over the door before the sounds of the first breaking started echoing back at me. The Escalade was easy-peasy. I'm assuming that you got to your guys last night as well?"

"Mission accomplished," I said. "You could do a drive-by in that Helgafell Farm truck and be seen by each of the four guys before the end of the day to really drive the point home to the guilty party." I must have been tired, because I almost forgot, "although Sophia talking to them is probably enough … couldn't hurt to show the colors." I meant this both literally and figuratively, as the Helgafell Farm truck was painted in blue and white, and unmistakable to anyone who had seen it once.

"Good idea, Tyler," John agreed. "Whatever the guilty one had planned is out of the question now anyway … I've changed some of our security and procedures a bit, but I'm happy to broadcast the warning. It's a bit of a shame not to be able to neck-stomp this guy, just on general principles, but that's the old me talking, and the new me should be satisfied with a cessation of hostilities."

I nodded, and waited for the final, anticipated (*by me, at least*) shoe to drop ... it did.

"So ... it's good bacon and all, Tyler, but the last few days has me wondering. Why did you do all of this for me, for the farm, for Nick? We're nothing to you, really. So why help, why stick your neck out, why last night's shenanigans?"

He looked my way as I polished off the second Coke and cracked the third (*thinking about cozies or something to keep multiple cans cool while I drank my way through them*). I ordered my thoughts and reasons (*real and false, the ones I would share, and those I would keep to myself*) for 17 seconds before answering

"You first gained my attention with the threat of violent retribution on your part when you wrongly assumed that I shot the birds. I like a mystery. I dislike people hurting/killing animals. I had/have some interest in keeping Sophia safe and even good shots sometime miss, not to mention her or other people getting hurt during a break-in. And ... I like the bacon the farm makes."

John nodded and took out an envelope, thick and heavy with something, and chunked it down on the table between us and said, "I guess that I'm just old-fashioned, but I'd feel better if our relationship could be more traditional in terms of remuneration."

I pushed the envelope back toward him with my Coke can, "I didn't do it for money ... ten thousand dollars is far too much or too little for what I've done, if you follow."

"I think that I do, but how did you know the envelope has ten-k in it?"

"It's about a half-inch thick ... each bill is 0.0043 inches thick ... 100 of them is 0.43 inches, plus your nice heavyweight envelope makes it half an inch. You don't seem like the kind of guy to economize on the gesture with fifty dollar bills, so ten thousand dollars makes the most sense."

"Okay, that all parses, but why do you know it?" John asked.

"It's a fact, like thousands/millions of other facts that have passed in front of my eyes over the years … and like almost all of the rest, it stuck, and is a part of my brain now."

"You know that you're not like most twenty-somethings, right, Tyler?"

"I'm eighteen, John … and yes … I know."

"So where does that leave us … moneywise?" John asked.

"I have enough money to last me, in style, through an improbably long life, and as I said before, it's either too much or too little, depending on how each of us chooses to look at the last few days. I do like the bacon though, and also happen to know that Nick owns another place on the big island on Manicouagan Lake … I wouldn't mind checking that out sometime …with your blessing."

John looked mystified, which I've learned through the years is not a bad thing in this type of situation, so I didn't explain how Cynthia had followed the trail from Helgafell through lawyers and shell-companies to the property up in northern Canada.

"Consider it done. Get in touch with me a week or two before you want to head up, and I'll get the keys and other stuff to you. Enjoy the bacon, and don't be a stranger," he said and left the SmartPig offices, sounding as though he meant the penultimate, but not the ultimate, things he said, and closed the door … I could barely hear his bulk walking down the ancient stairs which ordinarily creak and groan under my 130 pounds.

SmartPig Offices, Saranac Lake, NY
Friday, 6/7/2002, 11:38 a.m.

I'd just begun entertaining thoughts of some sweat-inducing Chinese food when I could hear Maurice trudging and wheezing his way up the stairs to my door. I was still deciding which of my smiles to greet him at the door with, when he saved me the trouble by keying and dancing his way in, beaming and kissing me on both cheeks (*something I could go years ... decades ... without having it happen again*).

"Tyler, I don't know if it was you, don't care, but she came home last night ... in tears!" he exclaimed in a way that left me uncertain of whether or not he was happy or sad or angry (*his English is thick, and with a cigarette always in his mouth, his face doesn't move much ... which makes deciphering emotional cues, a difficult task for me in the best of times, even more difficult*).

"I'm glad to hear that she's home." Seemed like a safe/neutral/prudent answer, regardless of his mood.

"She got up this morning, and called the Registrar at NCCC about registering for her classes again. She pulled her stuff down from the attic. I've got my girl back, yes?"

He seemed happy, so I smiled at him (*my #1, 'just happy that you're happy', my oldest, always fully convincing*).

"I'm glad that it worked out, Maurice."

I didn't know how to segue from the resolution of his issue to the implied connection with my office space, but he managed it just fine on his own when he saw the pile of camping gear in my corner.

"So, Tyler, when you gonna get rid of that stuff and get a bed? I know Phil, at Gartner's, and his boy could get a nice bed up here this afternoon for you."

"That's a nice offer, Maurice, but I like camping ... even in the cold, and plan on doing that most nights. If you're okay with it, I'd like to spend a night (*or a part of one, since I seldom sleep more than three hours at a time*) on the couch from time to time ... but not every night by any means."

"Tyler, my friend, I don't know what you did, or said, to that man, to those people," (*Maurice was stringing together clauses in a way that was making me nervous, and think of Faulkner*), "for my Sophia, for me, for my family ... you can sleep here or anywhere, as long as you want. You keep paying the rent, and don't burn my building down, you can stay here forever." He grinned toothily at me, and gave me a hug and a series of pats and squeezes (*that, again, was miles outside of my comfort zone, a concept that he might have laughed at, or dismissed, if he understood it*).

"Thanks Maurice ... that's great," I answered, when, after a few seconds, it became clear that he needed some response.

"Lookin' at you, who could know you'd be so smart, so good at something like this? Not me, I'm not ashamed to tell you. I was desperate when I come to see you the other day, didn't think anyone could help, 'specially not some kid from downstate, sleeps outside most nights. But you did something right, something smart, brought my girl home to me, and she's glad to be home. You figured things out good, Tyler."

Maurice hugged me again, and was on his way a few minutes later, but I scarcely paid attention ... the idea/notion/plan/seed was turning around in the back of my head ... the lizard bit that work better/faster than processed cognition. I had 'figured things out good', and found an interesting way to pass the time, and was able to help some people out ... it was not an unworthy thing.

I called down to the Chinese place and asked the cook to make me something really spicy with chicken and broccoli and garlic, and turned it all (*what Maurice had said, the events of the last few days, and the shape of my life/world since the events of 9/11/2001*) around and around.

The food was hot and fatty and spicy enough to make me sweat. And as I ate, I realized that I was, maybe, a consulting detective with a place in the world (*where before I had had none*).

Life was/is/will be good!

Fair Play

JAMIE SHEFFIELD

Fair Play

SmartPig Office, Saranac Lake, NY
Friday, May 9, 2003, 11:47 a.m.

"TYLER! Are you awake? Get up! Get out! You gotta go ...
NOW!" Cynthia screamed in my ear as I picked up the
phone.

"Cynthia, of course I'm awake (*I hadn't been awake ten
seconds ago, but I certainly was now*). Calm down and tell me
what's the matter? Did we have a lunch? Am I late for it?"
I guessed.

I'm horrible at reading human emotions from tonal
variations, but she was obviously upset about something,
and one of our working lunches was the only thing I could
guess at (*although I seldom forget anything, especially tasty Chinese
food with a librarian who enjoyed servicing my wide-ranging research
needs*).

"Tyler, you've never been late to, much less forgotten,
one of our lunches, and we're not on until Monday. No, it's
that cop, Gibson, and a suit from downstate. They were
waiting when I came in this morning. I spent the last twenty
minutes answering all sorts of questions about you and all
of the crazy research and interlibrary loans and the

83

ridiculous amount of bandwidth you use with all of the library's online accounts and databases." She paused to suck in air for a few seconds before continuing.

"You haven't been using the library, using me, to do anything wrong have you Tyler? The suit with Gibson ..."

I made the connection now, Frank Gibson was a Saranac Lake Policeman, married to Meg, a woman I'd seen/spoken to numerous times at the Tri-Lakes Animal Shelter *(he'd picked her up once after a TLAS event, when her car wouldn't start ... it had been bothering me)*

"...flashed a shiny I.D. in my face and talked about Homeland Security and NSA and multi-agency task-forces and 'SIGINT' and terrorists and you," she said.

"Cynthia, I moved here to escape the shadow of 9/11, you know that ... you know me. I read/study/scan/upload information about all sorts of stuff. You've seen the kinds of things I, we, research," I said.

She didn't say anything for a few seconds, perhaps thinking about the sorts of things we'd explored over the past year and a half, and then spoke, urgently, but with her usual warmness, "You're right, of course, which is why I'm calling. I sent them to your old place, the apartment, but they'll find you and SmartPig before too long. You have to get out."

I'd rented both an apartment and this office for my first months living in Saranac Lake, before deciding that I only needed one space, and choosing this one ... despite the lack of a bed *(I chose wisely)*.

"Cynthia, I haven't done anything wrong. There's no reason to run/hide; it could only serve to make me look guilty of something," I said, but my mind was already turning things over and looking at them from various angles.

"I hear you, but we live in a different world now.

Suspicion may be enough, at least to hassle you, or hold you someplace unpleasant until they figure you out, which nobody around here, myself included, has been able to do. People, especially government people and suits, like easy answers, and for everyone to look and act and think the same as they do, and you, Tyler, do not. They may scoop you up on general principles, turn you upside down, and shake you until something falls out," she said.

Cynthia had something of a point about the state of the world, particularly the US (*and New York State*) in the post 9/11 world. I lived a life that I liked in Saranac Lake, but it, and I, were unusual, and the security apparatus of the US might decide to remove me for questioning. I was certain that regardless of the outcome (*even assuming they let me go reasonably quickly*), I would not like the interruption in the lifestyle to which I had become accustomed.

"Tell you what, Cyn," I said, "I'm going to drop out of touch for a few days, and see if I can figure out what's going on, why anyone would be interested in me. Can you email me your recollection of what the 'suit' was talking/asking about and our last six weeks of research aims? Bring any books or printouts you are currently holding for me down to the parking lot behind the Hotel Saranac (*a few minutes' walk from her cubicle at the Saranac Lake Public Library*). I'll meet you there in ten minutes."

"Tyler, if you access your email, and they're really looking, they'll know exactly where you are operating from," she said.

"I'm setting my Yahoo mail to re-direct through a couple of addresses that should make it prohibitively difficult for them to find me through regular, or even extraordinary means, but thanks for the thought ... and for the warning. I hope that I can make lunch on Monday and tell you all about it," I said, and hung up.

My first instinct had been to pack for a trip into the woods, but doing so would have made research/reading/communication impossible (*or at least highly impractical*), so I worked on 'Plan B' while grabbing a few changes of clothes, my laptop, a stack of articles/books/printouts relating to my research on dozens of subjects that had grabbed my fancy over the last month, and a few other items that I would need/miss/want in the next week (*if my absence lasted that long*). Everything fit in a backpack and a duffel-bag. I was barely able to resist the urge to make my call from the SmartPig phone before clomping down the stairs and out the back of my building to the parking lot, where my Honda Element was waiting.

I threw everything in the back, and drove away, deliberately quashing the impulse to look around for approaching police and FEDs. After picking up the materials I requested from Cynthia, I rolled out of town, towards Lake Placid and it occurred to me for the 233rd time (*I felt around the inside of my skull and pulled out 233 as the 14th number in the Fibonacci sequence … not a great grab, but I had other things on my mind*) that Saranac Lake needed a Dunkin' Donuts.

Olympic Training Center, Lake Placid, NY
Friday, May 9, 2003, 1:18 p.m.

I passed a forest ranger, two state troopers, a Saranac Lake
cruiser, and pulled into the Price Chopper parking lot just
as a Lake Placid P.D. vehicle was pulling out ... none of
them looked at me or stopped me or flashed lights or made
dramatic squeally turns before giving chase or shot out my
tires, so I parked near a few other big and boxy SUVs and
went inside the market to call Dave.

"Dave, do you still feel as though you owe me a favor?"
I said, when he picked up his extension.

"Wait, who is this?" he asked, although I am certain that
he could have figured it out from the context and the tenor
of my voice. Dave, like most humans, seems hampered
when not able to see the person they are speaking with
(*while I actually prefer it over face to face conversations ... I like
email even better ... I like nobody talking best of all*).

"Tyler, Dave, Tyler Cunningham," I said. "After that
thing with your father last fall, you mentioned that if I ever
needed a favor, that I should give you a call ... I need a
favor and am calling."

The phone hissed and crackled for a few seconds as Dave presumably thought about what I had done to help him and his father last November (*a minor bit of work that nonetheless kept Dave's father out of newspapers and jail ... never mind how I helped the person eventually convicted find themselves in the crosshairs of the judicial system ... justice, if not the law, was served*).

"Yup, I, me and my dad that is, we owe you. I don't have money, but I can prolly..." he said, before I interrupted him.

"Dave, I've got money, I need something else today. Do you still work at the O.T.C. (*the Olympic Training Center, where athletes are housed and fed and trained for Olympic winter sports*)?" I asked.

Dave was/is a mid-level mucky-muck in the O.T.C. facilities management hierarchy.

"Yes, although not much is going on here right now," Dave said.

"I need to stay in one of the rooms for a couple of days ... maybe as much as a week. Are there any empty rooms?" I asked, knowing that there would be at this time of year, based on a discussion of the facility that Dave and I had shared one afternoon last November (*they have 96 rooms, like hotel rooms, with keycards and maid-service, but no mini-bars, Dave had once said*).

"Well ... yeah, we've got a ton of rooms, but they're only for athletes and visiting U.S.O.C. folks and consultants and such. I don't know if I could ..." he started, before I cut him off.

"Dave, I need this if you can do it, but if you can't I have to think of the next thing, so skip ahead to the end, if you don't mind," I said, feeling exposed in the parking lot as the seconds ticked by.

Dave took a bit more than six seconds to reply after I

stopped talking. "Sure Tyler, I can set you up in one of the rooms; are you an athlete or a consultant?"

"A consultant, I think," knowing that I would not be able to convincingly talk about being an Olympic athlete. "Pick a name for me, not Tyler, not Cunningham. How soon can you be at the northeast end of the Price Chopper parking lot to pick me up?"

"Let me get you in the paperwork and the computer, so the guy at the front desk won't be surprised, and I'll be there in ten minutes," Dave said.

It was nearly 17 minutes when Dave pulled in next to my Element. We threw my bags in his Corolla and drove to the O.T.C..

We walked into the reception area together, medals/torches/skis from recent Olympics prominently on display everywhere, along with active countdown clocks to the upcoming games in Athens and Torino. The young man at the front desk watched Dave and I walk in and up to the desk.

"Hey Mitch, this is Bill Anderson (*an aggressively, almost too bland pseudonym, I thought*)," Dave said. "He's going to be here for a couple of days of meetings with various folks to talk about our computers and networks and things (*maybe a bit more than the front desk guy needs to know, I worried for a moment*). What do we have away from those gymnasts; I hear they're a bit noisy."

Mitch pulled out a laminated map on a clipboard, showing two floors of numbered rooms, less than a quarter with red dots on them; all of those on the first floor. "They're at the close end of the first floor," he said, pointing to a cluster of nine dots from rooms 103 to 111. "Housekeeping would rather keep it to the first floor if possible, so ..."

"Any of these rooms down at the far end should be

fine," Dave finished the thought. "Bill," he said to me, "do any of these look good to you?"

"137," I answered. "It's the best option down at that end (*which terminated with 147 and 148*)."

Both Dave and Mitch looked slightly perplexed, wondering (*I realized belatedly*) how I could know which room was better than the others.

"It's the handicapped accessible room in that pod, so the bathroom is bigger an' nicer, the bed's a queen, and it's mebbe twenty square feet larger than the other rooms nearby, but how'd you know?" asked Mitch.

"137 is an inherently more interesting and powerful number than any of the others at that end of the hall." They didn't look less bewildered, so I continued, "It's a Chen Prime, an Eisenstein Prime, a Stern Prime, and a strictly non-palindromic number ... oh, and a Strong Prime, which would be relevant for cryptographic purposes if it was a much larger ..." I stopped, because both Dave and Mitch had leaned slightly away from me during my explanation.

"Uh, I mentioned that Bill's a computer and network guy, right?" Dave stammered. "137 will be fine, Mitch, run a keycard for him, okay?"

Mitch swiped a plain keycard through a scanner after tapping some information into his computer, and handed it to me, holding the keycard in such a way as to minimize the chance of physical contact between us (*which seemed a bit odd, although fine with me*).

"Thanks," I said, and walked away and down the hall with Dave.

Room 137, Olympic Training Center, Lake Placid, NY
Saturday, May 10, 2003, 4:39 p.m.

The room was perfect. I spent most of the next 27.35
hours going through all of my research and reading over
the last six weeks of documents in detail, as well as looking
at my research notes for the last year. I stopped every few
hours to resupply on Coke and snacks from the dining
room. My keycard got me through a turnstile and into the
dining area where there was food left out all night, (*even after
the kitchen staff went home*). Twice I stopped to take a short
nap (*I don't sleep for more than two to three hours ever, and when
I'm 'working', it's often for much shorter periods*).

I arranged the information in piles by type/category/
location/subject, and kept re-shuffling the piles in an
attempt to find a pattern that would have brought me to
the attention of Homeland Security as an attractive
candidate for a possible terrorist threat. By my third
breakfast, at 11:19 a.m. (*the O.T.C. cafeteria opened early and
had an impressive omelet station*), I felt reasonably certain that
I knew the general shape of the concerns that had brought
the suit, an Agent Tyson Brimley (*according to the card that*

Cynthia had included along with all of the other materials she'd given me when we'd met the day before) and Officer Frank Gibson (*of the S.L.P.D.*) looking for me. I gave all of my piles/notes/books another, quicker, scan, and then took a nap to give the tiny gnomes I have always imagined live in the back of my head time to work/sort/straighten things out.

When I woke up, I called Agent Brimley on his mobile phone from the phone on the bedside table in my room. In the time it took him to answer, confirm that he wanted to meet as soon as was possible, and agree on a location, I undid all of the painstaking steps I'd taken to hide my whereabouts (*redirecting my email through multiple accounts/countries/servers more interested in anonymity than pleasing a post-9/11 USA, anonymizing my identity for online searches on cumbersome/sluggish web resources, and yanking the battery from my mobile phone to avoid tower triangulation*).

We agreed to meet at the O.T.C. cafeteria. The posted menu promised a hibachi station, and I hoped that either by logic or speaking slowly, I could convince the team of Brimley and Gibson to let me remain at the O.T.C. long enough to be one of the first to sample the food when service started at 5:30 p.m..

I assembled a short stack of papers and notes and books and went down the long hall of the dorm to wait for them in the cafeteria. I made sure to keep my hands empty and in plain sight when they arrived 17 minutes later (*I took this to be a good sign, as 17 is the third Fermat Prime, the minimum number of givens for a Sudoku with a unique solution, there are 17 possible symmetry patterns for hanging wallpaper, and it is the only positive Gennochi number*).

Olympic Training Center, Chadwick Cafeteria, Lake Placid
Saturday, May 10, 2003, 6:01 p.m.

Both men recognized me when they entered the cafeteria,
and adjusted their trajectories to spread out a bit, and
approach me from different angles; it was Officer Gibson
who spoke first.

"Hello Tyler, we've met before, at one of the shelter
things. My name is Officer Frank Gibson, I think that you
know my wife, Meg. I'd like to keep this friendly but I need
to inform you that you have the right to remain silent, and
that if you ..." Officer Gibson seemed primed to continue
Mirandizing me, but was cut off by a raised hand, almost a
shushing gesture (*but a bit more polite*) from Agent Brimley.

"Mr. Cunningham, I'm Agent Brimley, and I've got to
say that you've led us on a quite a chase. I have to admit to
being a little confused as to why you called us. In fifteen
minutes you'll either leave here in the handcuffs that
Officer Gibson has on the back of his belt, there, or you'll
leave with me, bound for someplace even less pleasant," he
said (*while I wrote a short note on a post-it, folded the piece of paper,
and slid it under the salt-shaker in the center of the table*).

"Well, Agent Brimley, Tyler called us because it's the right thing to do. Isn't that right, Tyler?" Officer Gibson said, with a confusing (*at least to me, being notably poor at pulling meaning from human tones and facial expressions*) mix of what I took to be irony and amusement at a joke that appeared to be funny only to him.

Brimley frowned a bit in the officer's direction, and gestured at the unoccupied seats around the table that I was sitting at, "May we join you?"

I nodded, and as they sat down, I began to answer their spoken and implied questions, "I called because I have no wish to hide. I've done nothing wrong, despite whatever impression you may have, and I assume that the quickest way to get back to my routine (*the one thing I value more than any other*) is to confront and show your suspicions to be erroneous."

"And what suspicions would we be harboring about you, Mr. Cunningham?" Agent Brimley asked, "And why?"

"You think that I'm going to make an attempt on the life of the President of the United States, sometime during the current election cycle, during a visit to New York, with a bomb." I felt odd saying this, recalling games of Clue with my parents as a child; I felt stranger still when I saw both men's faces register surprise/shock/disappointment briefly.

"You're partway right anyway, Tyler. May I call you Tyler?" Agent Brimley asked.

After a moment, I nodded.

"Screw this, he as good as admitted to both of us about making and detonating a bomb. Let me finish reading him his rights, and I can be home for supper," said Gibson.

"Relax, Frank. We have plenty of time to talk with Tyler, and still get you home for supper," Brimley said.

"No Tyler, we don't think you're planning on making a

run at the President, we think you've got your sights set on another target; one closer to your heart than George W. Bush. We have good reason to believe that you intend to assassinate Governor Pataki using an explosive device when he visits the Tri-Lakes in twenty-one days."

Agent Brimley leaned back in his chair and watched me to see what effect his pronouncement would have on me ... he was likely to be disappointed as I don't emote much, especially when people aren't acting/thinking rationally.

"That's stupid," I said. "Why would you think that?"

Officer Gibson cocked his head at an angle of about 20 degrees, looking at me for a full four seconds before speaking, "You expected that we would suspect you of planning an assassination, but seem almost disappointed that we think your target is the Governor and not the President. Care to elaborate on that a bit Mr. Cunningham?" he seemed to be vacillating back and forth between calling me by my first and last names, which I found interesting.

"I assume that you," I said, nodding in Agent Brimley's direction, "sift through searches and database accesses and library records for keywords and groups of associated terms."

Brimley nodded, and made a rolling gesture with his finger to keep me going.

"A number of my research interests in the last year would have grabbed your attention ... bombs and bomb-making technology, security-detail protocol, and President George W. Bush, among others of decreasing interest to you."

They both looked at me with similarly raised questioning eyebrows.

"You would have no interest in my studies of cicadas or

tontines or aquaculture or mines/mining in the Adirondacks or Wardian cases or any of the hundreds of books I've read in the last year, yet you pulled a select few of my areas of focus from millions, or billions, of records," I said.

"There was also some rather advanced mathematics and cryptographic research done, which helped draw our attention in addition to the other points of interest," said Brimley.

"But that doesn't seem enough ... can't be enough. Your being here is evidence of an interest in me, but what sparked that interest?"

"Why are we still talking with this guy, Brimley? Let's pop him in the back of my cruiser, and you can fly him down to Git-mo mañana," Frank (*since he was talking/joking about dropping me into a dark detention center, I felt that I could use his first name*) said.

Brimley waved Frank off, (*I wondered at their relationship, in terms of power/command/authority*) and turned his attention back to me, "Tyler, our records indicate that you're the smartest guy in the room most of the time, so let's work this together. Getting a peek at your library card was interesting; do you really read, or care about, all of that crap?"

I nodded.

"But that's not enough, as you said, to get our attention. What would be?" Brimley asked.

"C.T.R.s (*Currency Transaction Reports for those not in the know*) might have been another piece. I moved significant chunks of money up here in the first quarter of 2002, and a couple of times since then ... but I made a point of keeping them under the ten thousand dollar limit," I said.

Brimley smiled and shrugged, "We've broadened our charter and reach a bit since 9/11, and lots of banks are willing to share information with us, even if the amounts are below the Currency Transaction Report limit."

I was briefly resentful of my new banks' breaches of confidence, but then remembered the us/them climate that had taken hold since planes flew into the Towers on that Tuesday.

"Still, it's not enough, Tyler. What else?" Brimley asked, looking at me like a teacher trying to push a dim student to make simple connections.

He'd dropped the hint when talking with Cynthia, and now that I'd had a chance to think my way through it, it seemed the only sensible/logical/possible way for Brimley/Frank/Homeland to connect the dots in such a way as to draw a picture of me.

"Signals Intelligence ... 'chatter'. You/'them'/someone intercepted a message of some sort that pointed to an assassination up here, which got you started looking at a much smaller pool for interesting fish, which somehow led you to me ... it had to be the books/research/bank stuff, couldn't have been the message itself pointing to me," I said, drawing a small portion of satisfaction (*odd, since it might land me in a small and dirty cell near Cuba*) from having gotten there before Brimley could fill in the gaps.

"Why couldn't the message have implicated you, Tyler?" Frank asked.

"It couldn't have implicated me for a couple of reasons, Officer Gibson (*I could call him Frank in my head, but not out loud it seems*). First, I had/have/will have nothing to do with either the message or any plot/plan/cabal to hurt or kill anyone. Second, if I had been involved with any of this, I would have used an encryption scheme that Agent Brimley and all of the rest of the king's men couldn't have put together again, in any meaningful manner (*I occasionally try using metaphors in conversation, based on a childhood filled with speech/language teachers intent on improving the quality of my human to human interactions, and generally, as apparently in this case, fail pretty miserably*). Third, if I had been a part of this sort of activity, and for some reason decided to be lazy when encrypting my message, I can think of thirteen ways this instant to avoid sending a letter or email and still effectively communicate with anyone on the planet (*actually, I could think of considerably more, but 13 is a wonderful number ... the first emirp, the second happy prime, and one of only three Wilson Primes ... I like to twist and play with numbers when dealing with new and potentially unsettling situations, and this interview definitely qualified as one*)," I said.

Brimley parsed out what I had been saying, and his face reddened a shade, from the collar up, "Name two!"

Frank looked back and forth between the two of us, waiting, and smiling faintly.

"I could write an email and save it as a draft or in the trash or spam folder, never sending it; I'd give the recipient/target my login information and let them read and respond without ever hitting send. Alternately, I could establish a Yahoo group and post dozens of seemingly innocuous messages, each containing an agreed upon phrase or math problem that combined to make a message. These passive communication methods would likely elude the diligent efforts of the intelligence arms of our government," I said.

Brimley looked up at the ceiling and thought for a few seconds before he brought his eyes back down to mine. Although his flush had faded a bit, the collected shapes/positions/set of his mouth and eyes and hands and brows relayed what the speech/language consultants my parents had hired described as anger ... his was a textbook collection.

"You asked, Brimley," said Frank, then he turned to me

and asked, "Hey, Tyler, Meg tells me you're crazy about Coke?"

I nodded.

"Go and get yourself a Coke, and bring me mug of black coffee if you don't mind."

I got up and walked over to the beverage counter 20 paces away ... Meg had mentioned once within earshot that Frank liked a little coffee with his cream and sugar, so I didn't know what to make of his order (*simplicity, courtesy, distrust*) ... I went to get a Coke from the fountain and noticed the two men's heads close together during my absence. I tilted my head and opened my mouth slightly, to better hear what they were saying.

Frank's tone had grown skeptical as he said, "The more he talks, the less he fits with the profile document you forwarded me from the Shin Bet."

I had read articles about Israeli security consultants working with Homeland Security after 9/11, and filed Frank's comment away, with a note to try and find their profiling document

"That's crap!" Agent Brimley responded. "He's the guy, gotta be. There's too much stacked up against him, and too few other people in this wasteland for it to be a coincidence."

He ran down, like a grumpy clock that nobody had wound, and looked up at Frank, "Gibson, you said this guy was a whack-job the first time I called, and everything – the money, the lone-wolf thing, the research – it all points a big fuckin' arrow at him; but you're not talking about cuffing and supper anymore. How Come?" Brimley said the last bit with some heat/anger/challenge in his voice, but maybe a little doubt also; a little bit hoping that Frank Gibson would back him up.

"I said he was a bug, and I'll stand by that call, but I

never used the term whack-job," Frank said, nodding a bit in my direction.

I moved over to get the mug of black coffee for Frank and rearranged my face into my most functional smile (*the #3, friendly/sincere/helpful, which I had learned to imitate from people at an early age*) and continued to listen in to their conversation.

"He fits some of the criteria you gave, and all that shit he studies is weird, but after talking with my wife a bit last night at dinner, and sitting here listening to him now, I'm not so sure he's your bug. The 'Lone Wolf' paper presented most of these guys as low-average intelligence and jammed full of cardboard cut-out political crap. This guy doesn't present like that at all," Frank said waving a hand in my direction.

"As far as the money and research and reading shit goes, what can I say, sometimes coincidence happens," Frank shrugged.

"So what? We wasted two days, and got nothing? You're saying that there's a buggier bug than this guy up here? Are you fuckin' kidding me?" Brimley said, his voice edging up in volume and tone to the point that people arriving early for supper started looking their way a bit, until they noticed Frank's bulk and uniform (*although a S.L.P.D. uniform was a bit out of place in Lake Placid, nobody seemed ready to mention it … they might not notice the difference … I would have*).

Frank pulled Brimley's head in closer and appeared to be suggesting an idea. I could no longer make out what was being said so I came back to the table with the drinks.

"Thanks, kid," Frank said, taking a courtesy sip from his coffee after I handed it to him (*Mickey, a mentor and teacher of mine, also took/takes his coffee black when getting it from strangers, not trusting them to get it right … I felt 71 percent comfortable making the assumption that this was the case with Frank as well*).

"Officer Gibson has an interesting idea," Brimley said. "I'm not crazy about it, but it doesn't seem to have any significant risks or drawbacks. Since you're so good at research, we'd like you to work with Frank here. See if a different approach, different perspective, can move the investigation along. I'm still partway convinced that you're the guy, but I'm willing to give you a little rope."

I am horrible at metaphors, as I mentioned, and I paused for a few seconds wondering what he wanted me to do with a bit of rope, before answering.

"If you can get me the original communication you intercepted, and all of the raw data you've accumulated so far, I can help," I said.

I assumed (*based on a lifetime of reading mysteries and police procedurals*) that this offer was part of a long con that at least Brimley, and possibly Frank, was trying to run on me ... trying to get me to expose myself or my confederates in the assassination attempt by showing too much (*or not enough given the small amount of data they would likely allow me access to*). But, this possibility was outweighed by my belief that the quickest way out of a problem is by solving it.

"I have a box out in the car, but some of the information on it needs to be redacted before you can look at it," Brimley responded.

I shaped a frown for him.

He continued using a boss-tone, as if I worked for him, "The best I can do is to fax or email the stuff to you starting within the hour. Should I bring the paper to your office, once redacted?"

He seemed to like that word ... perhaps wanted me to ask what it meant, or why the papers had to be redacted ... I knew the answer to those and other related/unasked questions, so I just responded, "No thanks, I like the room here, and might stay for another night or two."

Brimley's face did some interesting things for a few seconds, before he smoothed things out and spoke again, this time to both Frank and me.

"Fine, we'll go now, but I expect you to present yourself here," he said, thumping the table, "at eight a.m. tomorrow morning for further questions and/or to work with Officer Gibson."

He stood and strode out through the turnstile, not looking back to see if Frank was following him (*which he wasn't ... yet*).

Frank reached across the table, slid the post-it from under the salt-shaker, and carefully unfolded it. His smile was magnificent (*I would spend half an hour later that night trying to copy it, in the mirror of my slightly larger than usual bathroom ... to no avail*).

"If he'd seen this, Brimley might have stroked out, Tyler. I'm glad he didn't see it, or forgot," Frank said (*the post-it said simply, 'you'll be accepting my help within 20 minutes'*).

"It's possible he knew, or suspected what it would say, and chose not to look for fear of losing face," I suggested.

Frank tilted his head again, looking like a dog listening to a far away and suspect woodland sound, and smiled a slightly less grand version of his earlier smile, "Might be. Meg said you were astonishingly smart, but not particularly clever; we'll see tomorrow."

"I'll be ready to start before eight, if you want," I said.

"I'll be here around 9:30. Don't care what he said," Frank responded, and walked out, turning partway. "Don't make me look like an asshole, Tyler. You be here. Don't make me have to find you and eat crow for that Brimley."

I nodded, but he'd already turned and hip-bumped his way through the turnstile the way some people do.

Olympic Training Center, Chadwick Cafeteria, Lake Placid
Sunday, May 11, 2003, 9:38 a.m.

I started receiving calls from the front desk about faxes
rolling in, as well as a number of emails, within minutes of
returning to my temporary living quarters (*they were serving
lasagna that evening, and I was powerless to resist three platefuls of
the hot and cheesy carb/protein festival ... which is probably what
gave Brimley time to redact and scan and send materials to me*).

There were entire pages clumsily blacked out save for a
sentence/line/word or two, here and there ... useless. In
this mode of research/operation, I'm like a whale
swimming through oceans or text, skimming out nuggets
of data with the baleen in the back of my brain. I read
dozens of reports having to do with some facet of my life:
credit, data-access, travel, family history, health history,
three psychological profiles, and a handful of interviews.

The interviews fell into two categories: people I'd
grown up with, and people I'd met/worked with since
moving up to the Adirondacks. I'd grown up in New York
City, but my social network was smaller than you might
think. I'd been collectively home-schooled by my parents
and a group of their friends, with their friends' children as

my school and playmates. The children didn't like or understand me, and their parents didn't understand me (*and were either circumspect or embarrassed about not liking me*).

Mickey, the one person from my previous existence that still occupied space in my brain/life/world had refused to respond to their questions (*whoever 'they' were*), other than to insist that they were insane to suspect me of any wrongdoing.

Adirondack locals in general didn't know me … I live a low-profile existence, and had worked to avoid social entanglements of all flavors. Most of their interviews were short and bereft of details beyond, 'likes Chinese food', 'goes camping a lot', 'seems a quiet and polite young man'.

The exception to this pattern was Frank Gibson. He was the first local law enforcement Brimley contacted, and Brimley's notes indicated that Frank suggested me as a 'possible unsub.' (*unknown subject … I googled it*) almost immediately … something I would have to ask him about.

Frank had started his investigation with his wife, Meg, and then quickly sifted through the tiny town of Saranac Lake for anyone with whom I might have had contact/relations with during my stay of almost 18 months. I was pleased to note that although he had interviewed a few of the people I had assisted in the course of my nascent interest in investigations, none of them had shared any details of our associations.

Later in the evening, I got a copy of the intercept that must have started all of this. Brimley had chosen to be difficult by including the ciphertext, without either key or decryption … my assumption being that he was angry/distrustful/petty, and foolishly wanted to punish and/or withhold information from me even though I was ostensibly someone helping him (*although I was actually engaged primarily in maintaining my status quo … it just happened to look the same to anyone observing from the outside of my brain).*

As I worked on the cryptogram, I ignored the periodic 'boop' noise from my laptop as emails rolled in during the next few hours, along with phone calls from the front desk when the pile of fax paper for me got thick enough to warrant a call. (*I noted a pattern of their calling after every fax at first, and then every third one as the night rolled on, and the tired guy at the desk got tired of me and my endless faxes).*

I stopped in my pursuit of the cryptogram only to lurch stiffly down the hall (*bent over the desk in the same position for hours at a stretch had an impact on me ... I'm used to a lot more physical activity camping and hiking and sleeping in the woods*) for to-go cups of Coke, (*too-sweet fountain garbage, not the good stuff I'd enjoyed in Mexico and Canada in the past*) and food left out for Olympians, (*and me*) by the thoughtful kitchen staff. On the way back, I picked up the faxes sent throughout the night and early morning.

This was the ciphertext:

FO	KA	KP	DO	NF	DN	FR	BN
AK	TF	DN	MU	RV	XA	XK	UT
MI	PB	KZ	CO	CO	MA	BL	EU
LY	DZ	AO	EH	AE	BZ	YB	NF
	PH	BO	QK	AE	SR	EP	KZ

By its structure, I took it to be a digraph rather than a simple substitution code scheme. Digraphs use pairs of letters instead of single letters, as the more basic substitution methods use, which makes the process of breaking the encryption substantially more difficult (*there are approximately 600 two-letter combinations, as opposed to only 26 letters in English*). Since this was a relatively short cryptogram (*under 100 letters*), it would be more difficult for computers to break it with certainty, absent a key ... so I assumed that one had been found/given/extracted at some point along the way by Brimley or his minions (*or betters*).

I had three things working in my favor when attacking the letter-pairs: the lack of double-letter digraphs (*like EE*) meant that it was likely a Playfair cipher (*erroneously/generally credited to Lord Playfair, when it was actually developed by Charles Wheatstone*). I had a good idea of a possible tell, and there was a repetition of two digraphs within the cryptogram. I took out a stack of graph-paper, laid out a line of my favored pens and pencils, balanced my caffeine level, and moved snacks to within reach ... all preparatory to digging in to play with the letters (*I could have waited until morning, and Frank would likely have the decrypted message for me, but I wanted to carve/establish/maintain an edge with team-suit, and this would likely help*).

Knowing that it was likely a Playfair cipher meant that I was working with a five by five grid, for the sake of substitutions ... this would inform all of my structural design when working out details. My plan of attack was a modified shotgun hill-climbing attack, making use of extant chinks in the armor of the encryption.

I started out designing a number of grids, and worked through the digraphs, looking for words or partial words in English, particularly 'Saranac' (*since my assumption was that the message had pointed Brimley to my town originally*). Similarly, the side by side occurrence of the 'CO' digraph implied a repetition of a pair of letters twice in the cleartext, most likely 'ED'. Working with 78 letters that I assumed would contain both the word 'Saranac' and the letters 'EDED' gave me a fair amount to work with, and it was simply a matter of guess and check and improve and check until I had tweaked the letter grid sufficiently to yield a message that had those components while the rest of the deciphered text made sense in English ... this took me a few hours, but eventually gave me:

```
ma ni ns ar an ac la ke
in pl ac em ay vi si ts
ho tn ex ed ed fo rb om
bt ow or km on ey tr an
   sf er sc on ti nu ex
```

```
man in saranac lake in place
 may visit shot needed for bomb
to work money transfers continueX
```

When the grid finally came into the correct arrangement, I studied/memorized/analyzed the words, and message it yielded, and lay down on the bed to think.

I took a nap for 157 minutes, which, as I struggled to sit up from the unaccustomed softness of the bed, it occurred to me was a delicious number … it's the center of a sexy prime triplet, and a balanced prime. The machinery in the back of my skull had been hard at work during that time, and I was reasonably sure that I knew the means and the method by which the 'evildoers' (*which my internal monologue said with all the irony I could muster, which wasn't/isn't much*) meant to try and blow up the Governor of New York … I spent the remaining hours until Frank Gibson had promised to return doing some online research that would have made all manner of three-letter agencies nervous and anxious to speak with me (*if they hadn't already been*).

I walked out to a series of computers that the O.T.C. kindly provides for athletes staying at their facilities, logged into my Yahoo mail account and printed out a number of emails I'd written to myself with some notes based on the findings and guesses generated by the gremlins living and working in the back of my skull (*my father first suggested this idea when I was solving complex chess and math and word problems at age four, and I'd never been able to entirely dismiss the concept*).

I was sitting at the table I'd met Brimley and Frank Gibson at the previous day when Frank walked in at 23 minutes after nine.

"I'm glad you didn't run. Whatsisname (*I couldn't imagine he had forgotten Brimley's name, so assumed it was some esoteric form of either 'good-cop', or simple disrespect*) called me at seven this morning to hustle me along, ninety percent sure you'd be gone," he said.

"Why would I run, Officer Gibson? I haven't done anything wrong and I find this all quite interesting," I said.

Frank looked at me, as if waiting for something, for nine seconds, and then spoke, "You are something out of the ordinary, Mr. Cunningham (*which my extensive history reading detective fiction would tend to indicate that he did not think me a suspect/criminal any longer … if he had, he likely would have used my first name only*), what'd ya make of all the stuff Brimley sent you last night?"

"A fair percentage of it, volumetrically, had to do with me, so I gave it only the most cursory of glances," I said.

Frank parsed out what I had said, and then nodded, largely inwardly it seemed.

"Most of the rest of the reports were highly redacted, or missing, but I was able to extrapolate and draw some conclusions from the way you, and Agent Brimley approached/dealt/spoke with me about my research/reading/studies."

Frank was bobbing his head in time with my word-groupings, so I stopped talking; he took that as me running out of things to say.

"I've got a decoded version of the chunk of code that Brimley and his people snagged. We'll have to take his word for it, it just looks like gibberish in the 'before' form," he said.

I shuffled to the third sheet down in my short stack, and

slid it over to him, "Yes, it took me a while last night."

He took my decryption, and compared it to a sheet that was waiting in a thin folder of papers, looking back and forth and back and forth and back and forth (*he did it a lot*).

"What the fuck? Brimley said that it was unlikely that anyone could figure it out without (*he looked at a scrawled note at the bottom of his sheet for an exact quote apparently*) 'massive computing resources', so he was positive that you wouldn't be able to do it."

Frank leaned back in the wooden chair, his big frame grinding the joints a bit, looking at me with renewed interest.

"Brimley's wrong, and possibly stupid, at least about cryptography ... the Playfair cipher is not too tough, especially with a couple of chinks in the armor like this cryptogram had. I was able to do it with a pen and paper and guess and check," I said.

"Good to know," Frank said.

"I'd like to know why you picked me when Agent Brimley got in touch with you initially, if you don't mind," I said.

"Nope, and as long as we're talkin', you should know that you're still at least partway my pick for the guy, especially after the trick with the code stuff," Frank said.

He looked as though waiting for me to respond, but when I didn't he held up a finger in the way that humans do when they want me to wait a minute, went over to the soda machine, and got Cokes for each of us.

"I'll tell you, Tyler (*I was aware, and a bit uncomfortable, that he switched back to using my first name, but perhaps it was a 'study-state' thing*), when the suits from Albany and points south got in touch with us, and then me, it took me about three minutes to draw up a list of guys they should look at first, and you were second on that list. I bounced it around the squad-room, and to a friend out in Raybrook (*at the State Troopers' barracks out there, I assumed*), and your name came up a few more times. Not in any big way, like you done anything seriously hinky, but just, you know, different. People notice different, and you stick out in a dozen little ways; a couple of not-so-little ways also, if you know what I mean."

I didn't/don't.

"The person, or persons, that you're looking for, that are planning this thing … they won't stick out … they'll blend in," I said.

"Maybe. One thing I like about police work, Tyler, is that most of the time, the obvious answer is the right one. Sometimes you gotta look deeper, harder, but playin' the percentages comes through most of the time, and doin' that, playin' the percentages, you're still the guy," Frank said.

"Besides knowing that I'm not 'the guy', I can tell you a couple of reasons I'm not your best bet. First, I made your list and the squad-room's list and your friend's list. Second, the living space the 'guy' or 'guys' is occupying is unattached to others for privacy and my office is in the heart of Saranac Lake. Third, they work at the hospital and I've never been inside the Adirondack Medical Center since moving to the Adirondacks," I said.

This last was a prod to move us along to the next phase of our conversation (*it worked too, I could see his head come up from the bored position it had occupied while I made my excuses.*

Adirondack Medical Center (AMC), Saranac Lake, NY
Sunday, May 11, 2003, 10:17 a.m.

"Why the AMC? I've looked at all that stuff of Brimley's,
same as you, and nothing in there points to the hospital,"
Frank said as we drove away from the O.T.C. in his squad
car.

He'd waved me out of the cafeteria, telling me to go and
get my 'computer and papers and shit' and waited
impatiently, with a freshly made breakfast burrito and a to-
go cup of coffee, for me to come back out of the dorm
257 seconds later (*the second largest known Fermat Prime*).

"I got some of it two nights ago, when I was trying to
see why you wanted to fit me for your conspiracy, and the
rest last night once I decrypted the message," I said.

Frank made some noises and gestures which I took to
mean/convey impatience or frustration … with me or the
situation, I had no way of knowing (*and I didn't know how to
ask without potentially making the situation worse*). So, I just sat
there, next to him in the cruiser, while he drove too fast
and tapped the wheel and huffed and snorted and kept
looking sideways at me.

"Still on why, Tyler. What do you think you know, and why do you think that you know it?" Frank asked.

"I don't know anything for certain, Officer Gibson ... if forced to gauge my level of certainty, I'd put it at ... fifty-three percent," I said.

"That's awfully precise, Tyler. How'd ya come up with fifty-three percent?" Frank asked.

"Well, I feel it's a bit more likely than even odds, and fifty-three is a great number ... it's a Sophie Germain Prime, and the sum of the first fifty-three primes is divisible by fifty-three," I said, and stopped talking, because he seemed to be slowing down, looking for a place to pull over.

We were on Old Military Road, at the crest of the hill above the L.P.F.D., before the private land gives way to a huge tract of state land (*I'd recently found a spectacular glacial erratic in the approximate center of that small island of woods bounded by Old Military Road and Carolyn Road and Route 86 while working to expand my personal map of my new world*).

"Mr. Cunningham, despite how things may have appeared yesterday, it was mostly Agent Brimley who wanted to scoop you up, with me willing to take a chance and give you some room to run, and see how things worked. I got picked to liaise with this guy because I'm pretty new and pretty green and my chief mostly wanted somebody to take care of this Brimley and drive him around. My wife, Meg, she says that she's got a good feeling about you, that you're a bit different, but generally a good guy. That's great, and she's mostly a good judge of characters (*I almost corrected him, but then it struck me that it might be exactly the word/phrasing he was reaching for ... consciously or not*), but she tends to think the best of people, and to give 'em the benefit of the doubt. That's a luxury I don't always have, an' right now, I'm wondering if I made a mistake keeping you on the field (*I'm useless with sports metaphors, although I can generally recognize them*)," he paused to breathe and pull over to the side of the road (*by the big open field that leads up to a house on the left-hand side of the road, there was nothing on the right-hand side*).

I could see him composing his thoughts into what he planned to say next. He slipped the shifter into 'P', apparently ready to wait.

"What I need from you, what's most important to me (*the structure/sound felt odd to me, I reached back into the files in the back of my skull, and wondered if Frank and Meg had watched 'The Godfather' recently*), is for you to help me figure this out, and stop someone from killin' the governor of New York State in my town, on my watch," he said. "If you can do that without continually pegging my weird-o-meter, and hopefully giving me a better than fifty-fifty chance of not ending up with egg on my face (*I started to point out that 53 percent was better than 50/50, but he waved me to silence before I opened my mouth*), that'd be great."

"One of the things in my research that rang a bell with Brimley and his brethren was a nested series of probes into Presidential security, the Secret Service, security detail work and procedures in general, " I said.

Frank nodded.

"Americans kill Presidents with guns. Security people know this and take measures," I paused.

Frank nodded.

"The guys running the security detail for the Governor are pretty good right? I bet they get training from the Secret Service or the FBI or similar (*I'd studied security matters having to do with POTUS, so I wasn't familiar with the details, but it didn't really matter*). Nobody's likely to get in close," I said.

Frank nodded and then he added, "Or even to know his route, unlike the President. The governor travels light, with a small detail, counts on an advance team to do most of the work. They'll have a few secure stops along his trip, ya know, for speeches and lunches and stuff, but the rest of the time, they vary the route and timetable enough to make it too hard for anyone to hit 'em," Frank said.

I nodded.

"That's about what I thought. I assume that even given all of that, most of their energy/worry/focus is spent on keeping the Governor safe from guns, long and short: safe from long guns by sight selection and security, and safe from handguns by screening and situational awareness (*much of this I had gleaned from my initial reading on the subject months ago, extrapolated to meet the current criteria*)," I said.

Frank nodded.

"Current air sampling technology can pick up infinitesimal amounts of explosives, which takes them off the board for the most part … except that we know they plan to use a bomb … after a shot, according to the cipher, which I'm assuming that I decrypted correctly?" I asked.

Frank nodded.

"That's it … what I just broke down for you gave me, and should give you everything that you need."

Frank started tapping and huffing and snorting and wiggling and turned towards me (*I assume angrily, I stink at reading faces, especially faces with facial hair as his did*). I rushed ahead without giving him the quiet time he might need to figure things out on his own.

"March 30, 1981. John Hinckley, Jr. fired shots at President Ronald Reagan on his sixty-ninth day in office (*it occurred to me, but I chose not to point out, that 69 is a Blum integer, and that 69 is the largest factorial number that can be computed on my scientific/graphing calculator … not a great number, but interesting nonetheless*). Upon getting clear of the scene, both the President and the agents with him in the car reported that he was fine, and that he would be heading back to the White House … he was, in fact, grievously injured, having been shot in the chest instead of merely having a broken rib as they all initially thought. If Secret Service Agent Jerry Parr had delayed redirecting the limousine to George Washington University Hospital by another minute or two, the President likely would have died," I paused.

Frank nodded, calmed.

"Thanks for the history lesson, Cunningham, I was twelve, and you couldna been born yet. What's this got to do with us, now?" Frank asked.

"Since then, starting March 31st, every security detail in the USA altered their manual such that if shots are fired at their principal, they get checked at the nearest approved hospital."

I could see a change going on in Frank Gibson's eyes.

"At some point in the Governor's visit, they'll have someone take a shot in his direction, knowing it's unlikely that they'll get him … not even really trying to get him, and then his detail will take him to the hospital. That's where they'll try for the Governor … an unscheduled stop, and therefore a somewhat soft target," I stopped.

Frank shifted the car back into 'D' and we pulled back onto the road and towards Saranac Lake.

"What then, Tyler?" Frank asked.

"A bomb of some sort. With a big enough detonation, they don't have to be precise, and in addition to being easier, it makes for good television … sends a more mediapathic message." I shut my eyes for a moment, remembering the endless flood of pictures and videos of the planes and towers and flames and rubble.

"Some sort? What the fuck do you mean, some sort? That's all you got?" Frank was spitting on the windscreen, and a red color was creeping up neck and ears.

"I can find out, with your help ... I mean I'd like to help you find out how (*I don't understand how human emotions/feelings work, and inevitably offend everyone I meet, which is why I live alone up in the middle of a six million acre park*). I would need a couple of hours with access to the hospital's H.R. files and purchase orders for the last ... twenty months (*probably only twelve would be necessary, but with today being the 11th, I naturally, for me at least, calculated back to that day*). I can find the who and how for you, Officer Gibson," I said.

Frank settled back in his seat and drove silently for a few minutes, waving to the statue of Smokey the Bear that we passed in Raybrook (*which indicated that the danger of forest fires was 'High' today*) in an unconscious gesture of the type that I most often associate with deep thought.

"Fifty-three percent, you said earlier. What's the other forty-seven percent?" he asked.

"Assuming the target is right (*I could reasonably assume that Brimley's peoples' signals intelligence which suggested that the Governor was the intended target was correct, but it was by no means a certainty*), then the other alternative could be a shooter with a backup mobile/car bomber to corner them on the way to the airport in Lake Clear or through the Cascades as they leave (*I didn't know what their protocol was for leaving the Adirondacks if an attempt was made on their principal*). It's certainly a possibility, but it seems chancier to me, and lacks ... artistry," I said.

Frank looked sideways at me, perhaps at my word choice (*although I did/do stand by the phrasing and sentiment*).

"If you were me, what would you do with this 'information'? Buncha guesswork and all sorts of privacy violations and long odds," Frank said.

"Give me time today looking at some of the paperwork generated by AMC, and you can talk with Brimley tomorrow. I'll know something one way or the other by dinnertime," I said.

Frank nodded, but seemed unconvinced.

"I'd like to help ... I don't care about clearing my name, you guys don't likely have enough to arrest/detain me, but I'd like to help if this is a legitimate terror strike, and not Brimley or someone at Homeland getting their wires crossed," I said.

Frank nodded, slowly, and looked down at his shirtfront.

"If I find something, you and/or Brimley can act on it. If I don't find anything, you've lost nothing except that I peeked at some files that nobody cares about except the A.C.L.U.. If I do or say anything that makes you and/or Brimley suspicious, you can put me in the lockup in Saranac Lake or let him take me to Guantanamo until things blow over or blow up. But none of that matters ... I want to help, and more importantly, I can help."

"I can live with that, Tyler. A friend of mine works for one of the head honchos, and if I explain it to him right, and you don't say a fuckin' word to him, especially about prime numbers and Reagan, I should be able to get you the paper you say you need," Frank said.

I nodded.

We pulled into a parking lot around the back of the Adirondack Medical Center (*at the northeast corner of the huge building*) and Frank had me wait in the car while he went in to find, and talk with, his friend. He came back 13 minutes later and waved me to join him inside.

Adirondack Medical Center, Saranac Lake, NY
Sunday, May 11, 2003, 2:39 p.m.

"Milt Lepak is my guy in AMC," Frank said quietly out the side of his mouth as we walked down an odd smelling hall at the back of AMC, leading eventually to his friend's office. "I gave him a snapshot-story of what we're dealing with, and he's going to help us take a look under the hospital's skirt (*a metaphor that managed to be effective, confusing, and make me mildly uncomfortable/ nauseous all at once*). Say nothing to him, less if possible; I'm assuming that you don't know him, as you say you've never been here before, and he moved to Malone after High School."

I nodded to let Frank know that I'd heard/understood him.

Entering the office, I saw a short and blocky man in his thirties, wearing a sweat stained shirt and thick/smudgy glasses. Frank said, "Milt, thanks for helping us. This is Tyler, he is a part of a multijurisdictional anti-terrorism taskforce being run out of Albany and Washington."

Before either Lepak or I had a chance to shake hands or say hello (*not that I would have, I avoid personal contact whenever possible, and generally don't speak to other people unless I have to)* Frank continued, "Tyler's gonna tell you what he needs, and we'll need a quiet room with a big-ass table and a data drop for his portable, okay?"

Milt grabbed a pen and a pad of paper, and looked over at me.

"I need information on anyone hired in the last twenty months, and every purchase order placed and filled during that same time period," I said.

Milt goggled at me, unbelieving and said, "The H.R. stuff is no big deal, I can get that for you from Phyllis inside of ten minutes. The P.O.s will be impossible. You have no idea what you're asking. It's gotta be tens of thousands of 'em, maybe more. Some in paper, some on the computer, from fifty different departments and a thousand vendors."

Frank looked at me with a look that was easy to interpret *(even for me)* as anger.

"Got it," I responded. "Let's try everything you can get on paper from your accounting department for the last month or so. My experience has been that almost everything starts on paper, even if it gets computerized later … so give me what you can lay hands on … sound better?"

Milt nodded.

"Most likely what we're looking for will be in an order from a custodial or lab supplies vendor, and should be filed with your OSHA coordinator as a hazardous material of some sort," I added as Milt prepared to leave.

"What can I do?" asked Frank.

"You've done it … getting me in the door and connected with Milt is all I need from you," I said.

"I could help you read through the stuff he brings back," Frank offered *(humans are surprisingly delicate creatures at times like this, experience has taught me … I reached around in all of my words for a gentle way to put him off).*

"Officer Gibson — Frank (*I've seen people do this to great effect, to establish a feeling of closeness … it didn't seem to work in this instance*), my methods are outside normal, but I can ingest/digest huge amounts of information with great rapidity, and at some point during the process, something in my consciousness makes connections. I don't understand it, but I know how to do it, and I have to read/see/touch everything. The best thing you could do, if you really want to help me, is drive to the nearby Mobil station, and pick up a cold twelve-pack of Coke, a bunch of their Amish beef jerky — the maple and cracked pepper flavor if they still have some — and a handful of Reese's Peanut Butter Cups," I finished.

I watched his face (*I'm always trying to learn/mimic how humans compose their faces to express emotions*) shift quickly through (*I think, based on my recollection of the pictures my therapists used to show me*) amused, surprised, and angry. I reached for my wallet, assuming that I'd angered Frank by letting him think that I expected him to pay for my food and drink.

"I got this, Tyler," Frank said. "I'll be back in a bit, and we can talk about Plan-B, as this is feeling more and more like a bust."

He turned and walked out of the room.

I plugged my laptop computer into the data drop with the blue cord I'd brought along, started the machine up, and opened a few browser windows in anticipation of a solid chunk of reading/research. I lined up my favorite pens and highlighters and sharpened five pencils, and arranged them next to a steno and a legal pad … for notes. By the time Milt Came back with a stack of thin folders, I had things the way that I like them.

"You didn't specify, but I included all people who were hired in the last twenty months, regardless of whether they're still here or left in the intervening time," Milt said.

"Great," I said in the flat tone that I tend to speak in, that makes people doubt me when I say things like 'Great'. "That should work fine ... it occurs to me that I'll likely find the guy and the 'device' from the orders of chemical or custodial supplies though, so that's really my top priority."

He turned, and without another word left the room.

"Hurry please, it's important," I called after him as the door closed.

I quickly flipped through the folder of new hires at AMC in the last 20 months ... there were 37 (*which coincidentally is the first irregular prime, the third Cuban prime, and the fifth lucky prime*). All of the files had some minor irregularities (*including one which had not a single irregularity, which in this chaotic and error-filled world is an irregularity in and of itself*), mostly attributable to unclear writing, fake references/job-histories, improperly filled out applications/forms, and poorly hidden criminal records.

None of them rang any of the tiny bells in the back of my skull, but I was able to divide them into three piles by likelihood ... possible, impossible, and unsure; these groupings were based on their potential access to volatile/explosive chemicals (*I try not to use the words flammable and inflammable, because it always causes confusion/debate, both of which are things that I prefer to avoid ... even though I just used both words in close proximity*), which I assumed would be the key to things once I could get access to records of what AMC had, who ordered it, and in what quantities.

Milt brought in a tall stack of messy folders and papers, grumbling about something. I'm not good at ferreting out the reasons for human upset, so instead I just continued working. I started skimming through the documents, flagging some with torn pieces of post-it notes, arranging others into piles for future perusal, and dropping the rest — a majority of the papers — onto a stack/pile/mess on the floor beside the long meeting table.

At some point, Frank came in with a small cooler and a couple of those opaque plastic shopping bags, filled with (*I assumed*) fuel for my brain and associated systems. He put the cooler on the floor, dropped the bags in one of the fancy-looking swivel chairs, and started to ~~pick~~ reach for one of my piles of purchase orders.

"Stop!" I said sternly (*I can do stern ... having practiced it for slightly longer than 15 years, thanks to my parents and teacher-parents, who were perfect study-subjects*). "I've got a system ... you'll screw up my piles. If you want to help, open me a pair of Cokes and a package of Reese's cups. I'll be done with this pile in (*a pause while I balanced what I've already done with what is left*) twenty-nine minutes. Can you find that guy and ask him if he can come here in thirty-one minutes?"

The room was silent for so long that I looked up at Frank, wondering. He was looking at me with his face shaped by odd and contrasting emotions that I had no business guessing at ... I didn't.

A few seconds later, I heard him crack the tops of two cans of Coke, and from the quality and tone of the hiss, I could tell that he had ice in the cooler (*which raised him up a notch in my estimation*). He ripped open a two-pack of the peanut butter and chocolate treats, and slid the items across the boardroom table to me before opening a Coke for himself (*which hinted that I might have to rush my research somewhat as the day wore on*). He sat down to wait in one of the swivel chairs. I could hear the chair sliding/squeaking/adjusting minutely as he rocked back and forth and from side to side. But he said nothing.

I reached the bottom of the stack in a bit more than 28 minutes, and out of the corner of my eye, I caught Frank hitting a button on his digital watch and just barely smiling (*I study smiles, and his was interesting … very little happened with his mouth, but the color and depth of his eyes changed and it altered his whole appearance*). He sat up fully and looked over at me.

"So, what's the what, Mr. Cunningham? Is it Dr. Goodhead in the surgical suite with the dynamite?" Frank asked.

"No. It's not going to be a doctor, they're significantly different than the profile of the person that Brimley and you (*and I*) are looking for … also, Dr. Goodhead was the worst Bond chick ever (*I used to watch those movies with my father, and he was adamant on that, and many other points*). Also, the sniffers that the Governor's security detail will be using would pick up on the tri-nitro-toluene in a second … we're looking for something both much more exotic and seemingly harmless," I said.

Frank focused on the least important detail in my statement, "I just watched 'Moonraker' with Meg the other night. I love that guy with the teeth, whatsisname?"

"Richard Kiel played Jaws, an assassin, in that and 'The Spy Who Loved Me'. My dad liked the redemption and sacrifice that Jaws showed at the end of 'Moonraker' … he said it was the only thing, besides the scenes shot in South America, that saved the movie from being total garbage," I said.

"Meg said you, um, lost your parents on 9/11?" It was a statement, but his tone went up at the end of the sentence, which implied a question … so I answered the ones I assumed he was asking.

"They both work at the Trade Center … worked … my father was in Tower 1, with Wexler Insurance, and my mum was in Tower 2, a director for Xerox. They were both well below the impact sites, and my research into the flame and fire and degradation/failure of the metal/building would suggest that they could have walked down with any of thousands of others who walked home that day … but they didn't."

I stopped.

"Were they ever … ?" Frank asked, as people always seem to, when they get the chance.

"Recovered? No, not even DNA. They weren't killed so much as destroyed or made to vanish, like Pickles the Clown did with Billy Madsen's silver dollar at that birthday party."

I ran down a bit, feeling a bit out of breath, and suddenly desperate to get back to work, "At any rate, where's Milt? I can be a bit more precise for the next batch of paper I think, which should help things along."

We both looked at the door, perhaps both hoping for a well-timed deliverance from awkward pauses … and even more awkward not-pauses … none came.

"Meg and I went down to Manhattan on the twelfth, for a week, no, ten days. She worked with the families of, um, victims, and I did some crowd and traffic work and shuttled food and water to the workers in and around the WTC," Frank said.

There was silence in the room.

"Thanks," I said, not knowing what else to say, and feeling that a person would say something in response.

Thankfully, Milt came in before we talked more about things I didn't want to talk about. He bumped into the door as he came through it (*no mean feat*), and then stood … looking … staring at the piles of once organized papers strewn around the table and floor, and feeling the residue of oddness left from the words that Frank and I had bounced off of each other and the walls of the AMC meeting room.

The good news was that the disruption of my mental processes, facilitated by talking with Frank about 9/11 and my parents and 'Moonraker', had given the wee gremlins in the back of my head time to shuffle things around and come up with an idea that made sense to me. I wasn't quite ready for the reveal as yet (*I'm a big fan of mystery novels, and have always appreciated a classic revelation/revelatory scene at the end of the book, with the cast assembled for accusations/denials/excuses and a final climactic chase or violent episode*). I wanted to be more certain before I shared my thoughts with Frank, and inevitably, Brimley.

"Milt, I can streamline your next trip into the paperwork warehouse (*I briefly pictured a cavernous room stretching to the horizon, like the one seen at the end of 'Raiders of the Lost Ark', but the reality was probably a temperature controlled room with floor to ceiling filing cabinets, overseen by a fuzzy-sweatered grandmother with pictures of cats on her desk*) substantially I think. For the next round, I need orders for bottled gases and chemical supplies … AMC seems to use three vendors for the various gases you use, and two vendors for the chemicals. I want a couple of months within the last twenty months for all three vendors, and also a couple of months five years back, and also a couple of months ten years back. Does that sound doable?" I asked.

"Yup, ya got the names of the vendors? That'd make it easier for Doree," he asked.

While he was speaking I reached for one of my post-it note piles, took out three sheets, did the same in another pile, taking out two sheets this time, and handed them to him after writing down the basics of the P.O.s on my legal pad. Milt waited for a second, looking at me.

"That's it, you can go," I said.

"Thanks Milt, this is great, and should be a big help," Frank added as the door closed behind Milt's receding form.

I've been listening to people stick addendums onto my (*presumably and predictably and preponderantly*) incomplete/improper/impolite interactions with other people all of my life, and could tell the tones that likely heralded a lecture. So, before Frank could begin, I went over to the cooler and grabbed a nicely chilled pair of Cokes from the melting ice and went to work on them and an envelope-sized sheet of beef jerky (*made by an Amish farm about an hour's drive north of our present location*).

"Would it hurt to be nicer, Tyler?" Frank asked.

"Of course not ... why, or how, would, or could, it?" I said.

Frank gaped at me, and then grabbed a Coke for himself.

"It's a figure of speech. You, um, well, you're not a moron. That stuff with the code and decoding and watching you reading and organizing this stuff faster than I could make piles. But, Jesus, the way you act. You're not messing with me or Milt or that fuckwit Brimley, are you? You're actually missing something that we, and most people, have, right?" he said.

"One of the parents that helped homeschool me and some other kids always said that I was assembled using different parts and directions, but that I'm not less (*or more, as I've sometimes thought, when I see humans struggling with the emotional components/complications that I lack*), just different," I said, thinking of my one remaining link to my old life, Mickey Schwarz.

"I see facts and logic and numbers like other people see puzzle pieces ... I don't always know how or why, but I can turn them this way and that, and make them fit more easily and quickly than other people do. When it comes to people, though, I've got no clue how they fit with each other ... or especially how they fit with me," I said.

Frank nodded to the ceiling (*as he was tipped way back in the chair, looking at the acoustic tiles*).

"I'm almost the opposite, Tyler," Frank said. "I'm good with people and feelings and expressions and nuance, but can't figure out the tough, school and book stuff, like on Jeopardy and Wheel (*I said nothing, assuming that it would only come out insulting/insensitive*). You can get along with, and get more out of people, if you work on your interpersonal skills a bit (*I wondered how he would react to some advice on him solving more cases if he worked on being smarter ' a bit'*)."

It occurred to me that in books and movies I'd read/seen, the differences/similarities between Frank and me would make for a great cop/buddy team-up, with the two polar opposite styles having a synergistic effect on the team's investigation ... resulting in a grudging respect fostered through adversity, and ending with an ongoing association built on the foundation of shared trials/tribulations and cemented in a final scene with the gnarled and wise police captain assigning the two as permanent partners. But, I wanted nothing more than to get away from Frank Gibson, and I could see him working out the same thing ... albeit from another angle. Luckily, we only had to wait 17 seconds before Milt came back in with a shorter (*but hopefully more relevant*) stack of papers and folders.

I worked through the purchase orders rapidly, categorizing them by date and materials ordered, taking notes as I went along. At one point I went over to my computer to check on a couple of things, using Google to refresh my memory.

I was reasonably sure (*79 percent, a fortunate prime and the atomic number of gold, which felt good to me*) that I had it mostly worked out when I compared recent orders with those from years ago, and went through the orders three times in sequence to get the progression and numbers straight in my head before switching back to the files from the human resources person. After filtering all of it through my brain once more, I drained another pair of Cokes (*a bit worried now about the lack of ice in the cooler and our dwindling supplies*) and then wandered through the antiseptic and oddly proportioned halls (*they seemed too wide, and with ceilings too low*) to try and find a bathroom to splash my face before telling Frank how they were going to kill the governor … and who he and Brimley should grab.

Adirondack Medical Center, Saranac Lake, NY
Sunday, May 11, 2003, 4:53 p.m.

"The guy you're looking for is named Altan Peebles, and
he's been working for AMC, for the Medical Infrastructure
department, for a week more than sixteen months," I said.

Frank wrote down the name, and nodded for me to go
on.

"Medical Infrastructure supports the medical staff with
supplies and equipment, and acts as liaison between the
medical staff and the administration and the custodial
department when it comes to the physical plant and space
allocation and layout."

I was parroting what I'd read on the AMC website.

"Yah, cause the docs and bug-hunters in their labs can't
be bothered to talk to the peons or order those wooden
things they stick in your mouth," Frank said, in a tone that
implied that he was agreeing with me (*although he seemed to
be overstating things*).

"At any rate, it was the perfect position for what Peebles
wanted to do, or was tasked with doing. He was able to take
advantage of a gap in their system of checks and balances

to essentially make the hospital pay for the bomb he's been making," I said. "He didn't order anything out of the ordinary, or anything that hadn't been ordered before ... he simply ordered the things that he needed for his project (*Frank glared at this word-choice, but I continued anyway*) in slightly larger quantities, and much more often than had been done in the past. In this way, he was able to accumulate what he needed, and set the stage for the big day."

"This seems awfully elaborate for a plot to kill a public figure, Tyler. Not to diminish the importance of the Governor of New York, but why go to this length?" Frank asked.

"Terror. They're not just planning on killing the Governor, they're going to kill a lot of people, and make a statement. Unless I'm mistaken, which I'm not, the plan isn't to detonate a bomb in the hospital ... the plan is to make the entire hospital into a bomb," I said.

"Explain that to me, this fucking second, using words that an eight year old would understand," Frank said loudly, spacing each word out with a tiny pause.

"A regular bomb, think a stick or bunch of sticks of dynamite like in a 'Roadrunner' cartoon, is a single point detonation/explosion which, while powerful, is limited by a number of factors ... most notably that it happens in just one physical space, it is mostly oxidizer and not fuel ... okay so far?" I paused.

Frank nodded a bit hesitantly.

I continued, "The explosive device that Altan Peebles has likely designed is called a thermobaric weapon. It will be much more far-reaching and energetic, pound for pound, than a traditional bomb for a couple of reasons, that are, you will notice, exactly the opposite of the shortcomings of a traditional bomb. First, the explosion takes place throughout a much larger volume of space, in this case the entire interior space of AMC. Second, the device is powered by nearly one hundred percent fuel, not oxidizer."

"A bit more detail now, but keep it simple," Frank said, taking some notes on a sheet he'd torn out of my steno notebook.

"Peebles stockpiled a sterilizing agent used in every hospital in America, ethylene oxide, along with a very fine powdered form of both magnesium and titanium ... which are also commonly used chemicals in hospitals."

I was prepared to continue, but Frank interrupted.

"How did he stockpile it without someone noticing? Is he working with someone else in the hospital?"

"Possibly, but I doubt it ... someone else's name would have been on one or more of the relevant P.O.s placed in the last sixteen months, or it would have started before he came to work here. I might have missed it if I wasn't looking for it. Peebles ordered the same amounts, or nearly the same amounts, as the hospital normally did, but monthly instead of on an annual or semi-annual basis. He also ordered it within separate departments' line item budgets instead of in a consolidated hospital order ... he might not have gotten away with it forever, but he didn't need to, just for a year and a bit," I said.

"Where is it? What does it look like? How will we find it?" Frank asked, looking around at the room (*and possibly beyond the walls of the meeting room we had taken over, sensing the hospital and people all around us*).

"It's everywhere ... and nowhere. When I walked around a little while ago, looking for a bathroom, I saw tanks of different gases everywhere. In patient rooms, in supply closets, in hallways ... who knows what the basement or roof or HVAC areas of this place look like.

My assumption is, and yours has to be, that he's got it set up all around the hospital."

Frank looked up from his note pad.

I continued, "There's a lockdown protocol for AMC which closes and locks all the main doors. If they put the hospital on lockdown when the Governor comes, it will become airtight-ish, and Peebles could (*for which I meant I would*) have tanks and piping set up to start dumping ethylene oxide and powdered titanium and magnesium into the air ducts all over the hospital as soon as it goes into lockdown. Once it reaches a certain density/saturation/ proportion in the atmosphere, it would be easy, nearly inevitable, to ignite and the whole hospital would go up … along with the Governor and between six hundred to one thousand (*depending on the day and hour*) people," I finished, proud of explaining it in relatively simple terms.

Frank looked like his stomach was bothering him … I popped the two remaining Cokes and generously slid one over to him.

"Why here?" he said, quietly, almost to himself.

"Why not? Angry people, filled with hate, taken advantage of by groups eager to hurt and scare. They did it in Manhattan and Washington in 2001, so why not go further afield? I would think that there may be similar projects happening all over the country … Brimley and his people with their ID cards probably stop most of them … others go off, and we hear about it or we don't, things blow up … mysterious explosions, tragic fires. An interesting fact about thermobaric weaponry is that one of the scientists who did some very interesting foundational work on the principle discovered it by accident when studying/investigating seemingly unrelated explosions across a diverse field of industries. He noted a pattern of aerosolized fuel igniting in highly energetic explosions when finely powdered materials as flour and coal and sugar and some metals ... even powdered milk, get in the air in sufficient quantities," I said.

Frank didn't look interested.

"Saranac Lake makes some sense, especially when the Governor of an important state like New York is visiting," I said. "It's going to be a softer target than a Manhattan or an Albany or Westchester, and would give a feeling of open-mindedness to Al Queda attacks, because of the area's rural nature ... most Americans don't live in New York or Washington ... nearly one in three live outside of cities, and almost one in five live in the country/woods."

"You think it's already in place, ready and waiting to go?" Frank asked.

"That's how I'd do it ... maybe with a cutout/failsafe to be taken out on the day of, so that a missing baby or psych patient doesn't bring on a lockdown and an early detonation ... although it would still carry roughly the same media-grabbing attention value," I said.

Frank cocked his head to one side again, like a dog, and looked at me with an odd mix of emotions, got up and left the room.

I went through the papers spread around the room, putting them back in their original order for Milt, stretching the last Coke, hoping that Frank would come back ... I needed a ride back to Lake Placid, either the Price Chopper parking lot or the O.T.C. (*although I'd been snacking all day, I felt confident that I could do some serious damage to an omelet from the omelet bar, or the baked ziti the menu posted this morning had promised for dinner tonight*). I was thinking about various incarnations of ziti I'd enjoyed over the years when Frank came back in, quietly, so that I barely noticed him until he spoke.

"So what do I, or we, do?" he said.

"Why ask me?" I said. "Brimley will certainly have a plan of action, probably something predetermined from some anti-terrorism playbook ... this is his now, or yours, but certainly not mine. I figured it out ... that's what I do ... the rest is people stuff, which is not what I do."

"I get that, I think. You're a bit of a bug, but I'm ninety-eight percent sure that you're not a dangerous bug, or at least not in this situation," Frank said and then took a deep breath before continuing.

"Brimley may have a playbook, but I went to school and grew up with these people. I don't entirely trust him, or the agencies he represents, not to screw it up," he stopped, looked at me, swallowed audibly, and continued. "If your parents were alive and worked in this building every day, what would you do?"

"I'd find where Altan Peebles lives, and kill him in his sleep, before he could set off the explosion," I said plainly.

"You get that I'm a cop, right?" Frank asked, his face doing that weird partial smiling thing again.

"If you don't want to know, don't ask ... there's nothing illegal about hypothetical murder," I said.

Frank looked hard at me, the trace of the smile leaving his face as I continued.

"If you're asking what I think you, a peace officer, should do in this situation ... given that you don't trust Brimley and his ilk not to screw things up or tip Peebles off, I do have some thoughts on that."

After a couple seconds of silence, Frank cleared his throat, looked at me pointedly, and then ... finally, said, "Oh, for Christ's sake, Tyler, tell me."

"Tell Brimley that I gave you some leads, but nothing too useful ... that you think I'm clean, but will keep an eye on me ... he wouldn't believe a totally positive assessment of me from you."

Frank raised his eyebrow (*a cue I'd studied a fair amount as a child, evidently Frank didn't give me a totally positive assessment anyway*).

I decided to move on and said, "I'd talk to whoever you know at the top of the AMC food chain, and have them find a genuine and relevant training for Peebles and one or two other people in his department to attend in Malone or Watertown ... something that will require two days and an overnight a couple of hours away from Saranac Lake. Get them out of town, and get a couple of guys you know and trust from AMC and the S.L.P.D. and the State Troopers in Raybrook to come in and go over the building with a fine-toothed comb."

I stopped, waiting for Frank to catch up with some hurried writing.

"First order of business," I continued when Frank looked up from his notes, "is to take the lockdown protocol/machinery, and his FAE-related modifications, offline. After that, find and photograph and then disable every tank of ethylene oxide ... it may be as simple as closing the valves. You'll be looking for forty-seven, or more, tanks of the stuff. Some of it will likely be in use for sterilizing sensitive equipment, which is its actual intended medical use, but AMC can live without it in the short term." I stopped.

Frank nodded and scratched at the steno-pad as quickly as he could. As soon as he had caught up I went on.

"The best way, the way I would do the powdered metals, is to have them almost blocking the outlets for the gas tanks, so that when the gas comes on, the microfine powder gets suspended and distributed along with the gas. Take pictures of everything before you disable it, for Brimley and/or the courts afterwards." I stopped and waited ... again, with diminishing patience for slow handwriting and imperfect recall/memory.

"At that point, you can probably loop in Brimley, and have him detain Peebles as a terrorist of foreign combatant or whatever, and squeeze him to see if you've decommissioned everything he set up at AMC. Can you take me back to the O.T.C. now? I'm starving and tired from not sleeping much the last two nights," I said.

Frank wrote for a few more seconds, checked back through his notes from the last few minutes, and then nodded ... to himself more than me.

"I want you to know that I heard everything that you said, but I'm not gonna do it your way ... entirely. I'm gonna loop in Brimley in three minutes, then you and I will head over to my office so that you can explain all of your thoughts to him for a coupla hours ... sorry. I'll get you some Chinese food, from the good place, while you're teaching him about oxy-acetylene or whatever (*Ethylene Oxide, I thought, but didn't bother to correct him*). If Brimley buys your thinking, then I bet that we'll scoop up Peebles tonight, as 'a person of interest in an ongoing investigation into a possible terrorist threat or event', and lean on him awful hard for details about his plans and associates and the possibility of other similar attacks at other hospitals," Frank said.

Frank's plan made sense. Why not launch a bunch of similar attacks, all at once, before Homeland gets up to speed. I agreed to meet with Agent Brimley.

Olympic Training Center, Lake Placid, NY
Sunday, May 11, 2003, 10:47 p.m.

Brimley was slow to give up on me as a suspect, but when I (*along with lots of persuasion/convincing/help from Frank*) connected the dots and information and guesswork in enough ways and enough times, he agreed to go and pick up Peebles as a person of interest, while Frank kept me (*eating pounds of Chinese food from the good place, and reading a paperback mystery that someone found in their desk, so I didn't really mind*) in a room that he called an office, but I noticed had no doorknob on the inside.

Peebles must have cracked quickly/easily/ convincingly, or had a bad poker face, because Frank came in to inform me that he was going to drive me back to the O.T.C. only 107 minutes after heading out with Brimley (*107 is a 'safe prime', which I took to be good luck for me, if not Peebles*).

"We're going to be working on this, but I need you to stay available for the next few days, in case I have questions about Peebles or you. Your analysis of this still feels a little hinky, too neat and easy, to me. I expect that I'll be able to find you at the O.T.C. or your office in Saranac Lake. Don't be a smart pig and try to hide if I need to find you, I'll be pissed," Frank said.

I nodded.

"I think that you did me a solid on this, Tyler, but some of it doesn't entirely work for me. Don't make the mistake of thinking that just because you may be book-smarter than me, that you can out fox me."

"So we're going back to the O.T.C. now?" I asked, not interested in threats or counter-threats or responding to threats.

"Yes," Frank said, and we did.

Things must have worked out roughly the way that I assumed that they would. Nothing/nobody went boom out at AMC, although I was perfectly all right staying at the O.T.C., (*on the far side of Lake Placid from the hospital*), for a few days, while they presumably took care of Peebles and whatever mischief he had wrought. Brimley and Frank each came out to ask me some additional questions about things that didn't matter. I'd already figured this problem out, so it no longer interested me (*and once I was certain they weren't going to arrest/detain/Guantanamize/harass me, neither did they*). I got to stay in the Adirondacks, largely unmolested, and Peebles didn't. Frank and I mostly avoid each other, speaking politely/minimally when forced to inhabit the same space by our common bond, Meg (*his wife, my acquaintance*). He doesn't trust me, and the feeling is mutual ... we serve different masters/interests/systems (*luckily, the Park is big enough to accommodate us both without too much friction*). We both play fair ... within reason, and allowing for different interpretations of the term.

Mickey Slips

Jamie Sheffield

Mickey
Slips

SmartPig Office, Saranac Lake, NY
Monday, 1/21/2013, 3:07 a.m.

When the phone vibrated in my pocket, I had just broken
into (*with some difficulty*) the locked den of a locked house as
a favor for my latest client (*who needed some pictures back quite
desperately*). I pulled the phone out of my pocket (*not many
people have my current number, so I assumed that it was important*),
saw that it was a "911" text from Mickey, turned around,
and let myself out in much the same way that I'd let myself
in. Sheila wouldn't be happy, but I was doing her a favor
for money, and Mickey was my answer to family (*since
everyone genetically related to me on the planet had died eleven and
three-quarters years ago*). I got back to SmartPig as fast as I
could, and called Mickey.

"Tyler, why are you awake at this hour?" asked a voice
that I eventually identified as belonging to Mickey Schwarz.
It took me a few seconds to be certain that it was Mickey
because his speech was both labored and clumsy (*and neither
was the norm for Mickey, regardless of the hour*).

"Mickey, if you thought I'd be asleep, why did you text
me?" I stood up quickly, displacing my rescue beagle Hope,

141

who had jumped onto my chest when I lay down on the couch in the world headquarters of SmartPig, my office, and lair, and home, and bat-cave. As I asked, it occurred to me that Mickey had never called me (*or anyone, as far as I knew*) at three in the morning. I broke back in to cut him off as he started to apologize for the lateness of the ....

"Mickey, what's the matter? Are you and Anne and the girls okay? Where are you? What can I do?" These were the four questions that I needed to have answered immediately. His ability to process the questions and answer them succinctly would give me more information about the state of affairs (*within one of the few people on Earth who can elicit something like an emotional response from me*) than the answers themselves would.

Mickey was in the circle of my parents' friends who chose to educate their children outside of traditional schooling, by taking advantage of all that they, and the city of New York, had to offer young and hungry minds. Twenty-some years into the experiment, I would argue that it has worked out well for me, as the communal approach was more responsive to my social/educational needs (*peculiarities?*) than either public or private schools would have been. When all the other doors in my old life slammed shut on 9/11/2001, Mickey was the one left partway open. It was important to me that he be all right.

"Tyler, I woke up in a hospital-bed fifteen minutes ago with a policeman outside the door. Anne and the girls are home, and fine. I'm in Syracuse, New York. I'm not sure that there's anything that you can do, but I was scared and lonely, and can't call Anne ... not yet." Mickey had answered all of my questions, in order and efficiently, so he was still essentially Mickey; but, none of his answers made sense given the kind of person that he was ... is.

"Okay, Mickey, everything will be fine. Start by telling

me about your injuries … were you in an accident?" I wanted to ask about the policeman, but needed to know about his physical condition first.

"I was apparently in a fight of some kind. I haven't spoken to the attending yet, but my nose is badly broken, I've got a split lip, my right eye is swollen nearly shut, it feels as though a number of ribs are cracked, and I'm sore all over. The policeman said that they responded to a call about a bar fight, found me alone outside of some bar, and took me to the ER to get checked out." Mickey mumbled this last part, not entirely because of bar fight soreness; he was both ashamed and lost at sea.

Mickey consults at hospitals all over the country (*and the world*) as an oncologist. I would bet (*if I was the kind of person who placed bets*) that he had never been in a bar fight in his life; to the best of my knowledge he has never gotten a speeding ticket or a been cited for jay-walking before, either. He was deep into the weeds in this instance, and far outside of his comfort-zone.

"The officer outside my room when I woke up said that they weren't going to arrest me for punching one of the cops that brought me in, because I was in an impaired mental state. They could tell that I didn't know what was going on; but I may have to appear in court for a bunch of other charges related to what happened."

"What did happen? Why are you in Syracuse? I'll be there in a few hours, but why haven't you called Anne?" I popped open the Coke-fridge, grabbed two cans, opened one, and chucked Hope a handful of homemade dog-cookies while I started making mental lists and checking them twice (*not too concerned, as is my way, with naughty or nice*). Syracuse is about three hours away from my base of operations in Saranac Lake, depending on logging trucks and winter-driving conditions.

"I'm ... was ... here for a cancer-conference, and I'm reasonably sure that I slept with another woman last night." He stopped talking to let his last words sink in ... to shock me as much as they shocked him.

They didn't, not that it wasn't shocking, (*Mickey worships Anne and their marriage, both the concept and the reality*), but I just don't shock much in the regular course of events. It was certainly noteworthy, as Mickey had often spoken with disdain about people with 'disposable' marriages and lifelong promises that meant nothing; but I was more surprised than shocked.

"It happens Mickey ... it happens all the time. You should call Anne. Call her and tell her everything, or you could call her and not tell her; you could make it work either way."

I prepared myself for his explanation about why he couldn't lie to Anne, and further, why he couldn't tell her everything just yet. In a way, I was looking forward to (*and had even set Mickey up to go into*) one of his complex logical discourses on why the right thing to do is the right thing to do, even (*especially!*) when you could get away with a falsehood. I had enjoyed and appreciated exploring these constructs of his over the years, even if I didn't always abide by them, and I hoped that his launching into one would give him some comfort on what sounded like a pretty rocky morning.

"Tyler, it gets worse ... there was a ... he might have been her pimp ... and there was video ... I think ... my brain still isn't functioning too well, but I keep getting disturbing memory-snippets and flashbacks to this woman and me in bed, and then this guy yelling at me and slapping me and showing me a little video camera and a movie of me and the woman," when Mickey choked out this last bit he sounded like he wanted to cry.

"Mickey, I know you are sore and tired and foggy, but this is important ... when she showed you the video and camera, what did it look like?"

"Jesus Christ, Tyler, my life is literally in the toilet and you're interested in ..."

Mickey, shut up and think ... I'm not shopping for a new camera, I need to know this ... what did it look like? Was the camera tiny, like a cellphone, or big like one that my mother and father used to have? Did it look heavy? Can you remember anything?"

"Okay ... sorry Ty, I just ache all over and feel so stupid and can't imagine what I'll say to Anne or my colleagues or the police. Let me think ... it was bigger than a cellphone and smaller than your parents' camcorder ... more like the size of a brick of Bustello (*Mickey drinks lots and lots of cheap/strong coffee that he buys in rectangular vacuum-sealed bags a bit smaller than a box of tissues*). Wait! I remember that she took out one of those little cassettes, and shook it in my face, and said something ... I can't recall what she said ... sorry, Tyler."

"Mickey, you did great ... that helps. Now don't talk to anyone about anything until I get there ... except your doctor. Tell me what hospital and room you're in, and I'll see you soon."

He told me, I hung up, made three quick calls to facilitate my next moves, grabbed gear for a week's car-camping in the cold, and was out the door ten minutes later.

Route 3, heading west, NY
Monday, 1/21/2013, 5:28 a.m.

Dorothy had been my first call, and was my first stop; to drop off Hope and pick up some supplies. Dorothy runs the Tri-Lakes Animal Shelter (TLAS), and introduced Hope and me the previous summer (*a perfect and lucky moment for both of us in what turned out to be the most exciting/dangerous/law-breaking two weeks of my life*). Dot wasn't happy to get my early morning call, but she had her lights on and a hug for both Hope and me as she handed over the waterproof container that had been waiting above the acoustic tiles in her bathroom for five years.

"What the hell are you into Tyler, and can I come along?" she asked as she handed over the OtterBox. She'd probably looked inside it within five minutes of my giving it to her (*Dorothy is able to resist anything except temptation*), and ten thousand dollars 'in case' money in a mix of bills will always raise both eyebrows and questions. I'd given it to her to hold for me 'in case' something happened and I needed a lot of money instantly … like tonight.

"Nope, your mission, should you choose to accept it,

and even if you don't, is to stay in town with Hope, since she hates every human on Earth besides the two of us, and I have to leave for a bit."

She looked disappointed, but understood, at least the bit about Hope.

"Tyler, what problem do you have that ten grand is gonna fix?" she persisted.

"It's better if you don't ask, and I don't tell, and it's entirely possible that I won't need the money (*or at least not all of it*), but nobody ever got to the far side of a jam and wished that they'd had less money to grease their way through the tricky parts." I answered her in a way designed (*hopefully*) to head off any further questions ... it did. I already had almost two thousand from the cache I kept at SmartPig, but I could always put any extra/leftover back in its hidey hole if I didn't spend it all.

Dorothy and Hope wished me well, walked me back down to my packed and gassed Honda Element. They faded into the dark quickly in my rearview mirror as I headed further west.

My next stop on the way to Syracuse was just outside the Adirondack Park, near Fine, NY. Dan was waiting for me outside of the cleverly named Dan's Pawn (*Loans and Payday Advances - Checks Cashed*), which did a booming business with the soldiers at Fort Drum, although his laissez-faire business practices occasionally landed him in trouble (*which was, in fact, how we had met nearly four years earlier*). While his problem had been interesting to me, I found Dan himself to be a repellent and immoral man, who improved his lot in life by preying on those in need ... that being said, sometimes a repellent and immoral person is useful to know and/or have around (*especially one who feels that he owes you a favor*).

Dan motioned me around the side of his building, and

had me back the Element into the attached garage. Before I had gotten out of the Element, he'd already opened the rear hatch and shoved in two obviously heavy and clanking duffels, and then met me with a handshake and an all-purpose grin/wink/head-bob that took in everything and meant nothing.

"Glad you called Tyler, I hate owing a man, and with this I figure we're about even ... I guess I thought you'd forgotten my number," Dan said to me as we walked back into his garage to lean against a dusty workbench for a minute.

"How could I forget your number Dan? It's the thirty-third number in Fibonacci's sequence ... if I could get a phone number like that, I'd stop using the burners, and settle down with one phone for the rest of my life." I smiled at the thought, Dan looked as though he wanted to hit me with the weed-whacker growing rust next to him, and quickly changed the subject.

"I got fifteen, like you wanted, mostly twelves, some twenties, a couple .410s, and a 10-gauge ... a few rounds for each ..." I cut him off.

"Dan, I told you, these will never be fired, I just need them clean and not easy to trace back," I reminded him.

"Yup, I heard you, but nobody ever kept or sold a shotgun without some ammo ... adds verisimilitude." He grinned a gappy smile at me and added, "My wife Doris gave me a 'word of the day' calendar for Christmas, and verisimilitude was January 10th ... been waiting to use it for almost two weeks now."

I smiled goggle-eyed at Dan, and left him to guess whether I was faking surprise at his vocabulary or the fact that there was a person who would spend time with him (*and even give him gifts*) by choice.

"So what do I owe you?" I asked, eager to be on my

way, thinking about Mickey in the hospital, hurt and scared and alone made me uncomfortable in a way that I was entirely unaccustomed to.

"Call it a hundred per ... none of them are in great shape, but they'll do for what you said," Dan responded.

He looked suspicious when I counted out twenty hundreds, until I explained, "Like we agreed, these don't go on a bill of sale, aren't in your books, don't get mentioned to Doris or anyone ... even through a lapsus linguae."

He nodded, and put the money in his pocket, moving his lips through 'lapsus linguae' a few times to remember it for later, and waved me off as I drove away.

I stopped off at the Kwik-E-Mart on the way out of Fine to top up on gas and Cokes and road-food (*donuts and pizza-flavored Combos*) in sufficient quantities to get me down to Syracuse; paying, as I would be for everything on this trip, in cash.

University Hospital, Syracuse, NY
Monday, 1/21/2013, 9:14 a.m.

I'd rolled into Syracuse at a few minutes before 7 a.m., coming south on Route 81, and queried my GPS for nearby Walmarts; there are four within 10 miles of the hospital. I stopped to buy a burner Trakfone, a set of cheap dark sheets, and a big microwave (*the same model luckily*) at each before heading to University Hospital, hoping that Mickey would have gotten some sleep in the hours since we had talked. I was able to get in to see Mickey without a hassle, being a friend of the family (*and arriving at a decent hour*), dressed neatly in slacks and a blazer (*as dressy as I own these days*). He was struggling with the foil lid of a tiny cup of orange juice when I entered his room, and gave up when he saw me.

I could see that it hurt him to smile; his face was misshapen by swelling and colored with bruises. This gentle man who had spent his life helping people had no business being here … like this. My mind was racing as we exchanged pleasantries and small-talk. I added a nasty refinement to the constellation of ideas that was trending towards a plan.

"So, what did your doctor say, Mickey?" I asked, once he had run out of the silly things that people say when they're embarrassed and don't want to talk about what you need to talk about.

"Pretty much what I told you last night," he replied (*this morning I thought, but didn't say ... it wouldn't help, and might slow things down*). "A guy that I know vaguely came in this morning and set my nose. Everything else is superficial ... my ribs are taped, but it doesn't seem to be helping much (*It never does, but they do it anyway*). Honestly though, the worst part was Bill, the guy who set my nose, seeing me like this, in a hospital johnny."

"Then you got off pretty easy," I said, at which point his face, which had been working on a smile, despite the swelling and tape and bruising, collapsed in defeat. Mickey had been trying (*somewhat pointlessly, or even counterproductively, although he couldn't know it yet*) to put up a brave face for me, and now gave up.

"If only Bill really was the worst thing ... he actually comes in third, maybe fourth. The officer that I struck last night came in to talk with me a while ago, and was quite nice about it, but they're charging me with drunk and disorderly, along with some form of failure to comply with an officer. What if I go to jail, Tyler?" Mickey hung his head in disgust.

"You won't. This is bad, but you're a somewhat important guy who's never been in this sort of trouble before, you can afford a team of flesh-eating lawyers to get you a deal with a fine and some community service at home ... and maybe some diet-form of probation or suspended sentence ... if they pursue it at all." I believed that this was true, but legal research has, strangely, never been an interest of mine.

"Worse ... after the policeman left, and just before you came, Lily came ... you might have passed her in the hall on your way in." Mickey's eyes filled with guilty tears, and although I felt that I knew, I had to ask.

"Who is Lily? Is she the woman you met at the conference?" Mickey grimaced when I used the word 'met', and just nodded. "What did she want?"

Mickey picked his wallet up off of the table that his tray of breakfast was sitting on, and chucked it at the wall with an angry gesture. This was the first such gesture that I'd seen from him in the 25 years that I'd known him (*it's possible that he had an angry outburst during the first three years of my life, but if he did, I can't recall the incident*).

"She wanted to return my wallet," he said, "which fell in the gutter during the bar fight last night, or so she said."

"And ..." I prompted. That couldn't be all that there was to the story.

"She mentioned what a good time she had last night in my hotel room, until I got too drunk afterward and wanted to head out to a bar," Mickey said this with a combination of anger and confusion in his voice.

"Seeing her this morning, I have no doubt about what happened last night between Lily and me ... but I can't understand it. I don't drink much, would never cheat on Anne, and don't go bar-hopping. Tyler ... just what the FUCK happened last night?"

In the ordinary course of events, Mickey would never talk like this, but he felt as though his life had come undone. I had to help him keep from falling apart, and also I had to see what I could do to fix whatever had actually happened. He had slipped, as people do, and I would help catch him.

"But wait, it gets worse! She said that I had encouraged her to make a video of ... what happened in my room, and that her 'friend' Shane had come by to pick her up later in the evening, and had seen the video at one of the bars we visited. He got mad and we started fighting, which was when the police were called to the scene." By the end of this, Mickey could scarcely talk ... he was red in the face and crying by this point and wouldn't look at me.

"Let me guess the rest Mickey. She managed to talk her friend out of pressing charges, but he (*not Lily, of course, but unreasonable Shane*) wants money or else he'll send a copy of the video to Anne and the girls, whose pictures they saw in your wallet," I paused for breath. "Is that about the size of it?"

Mickey just nodded, ashen.

"You got set up Mickey ... quite nicely. I'm pretty sure that she's not registered for your conference, but was trolling for a rich doctor. You enjoyed the attention of a beautiful woman, as men often do (*myself excepted*), and she gave you some drug to render you docile and impressionable. When she was done with you (*no need for too much in the way of details here, I don't like thinking about anyone having sex, much less a father-figure of mine being drugged and forced into the act*), she dragged you to a public place, and set you up for an embarrassment and injuries that would distract you long enough for her to get away and finish building the trap for you." He looked up at me with whipped puppy-dog eyes, and I jumped in before he had a chance to apologize ... again.

"That's all the bad news, and it's plenty bad. They built a nice trap and you were, unfortunately, the poor sap that wandered into it. The good news is that you've got me. I can never repay you for a million kindnesses and lessons and pieces of advice that you've given me, but I may be able to fix this; and that's what I am going to try, if you'll let me."

Mickey started to talk and I cut him off.

"You've been telling me and anyone who will listen about how smart and unique my brain and personality make me, and you helped (*more than anyone else alive*) to make me happy and proud about who, or what, I am (*not entirely true, as I don't really 'do' happy or proud, but Mickey would appreciate the sentiment anyway*), so it's fitting that you can benefit from who, or what, I am."

I paused for a breath before rushing into the closer, realizing that I could feel my flush and elevated heart rate, indicative of emotional involvement in what I was saying, beyond the show that I was putting on for Mickey. I do favors for clients, and sometimes acquaintances, but never get involved in their problems emotionally ... until now (*I wondered briefly how it would affect my process or the final product*).

"You've always known that I see the world differently than ordinary humans do. I use that difference sometimes to help people, and now I'm going to help you. I've already got eighty-seven percent of a plan, and the rest is coming together in the back bits of my brain as we speak."

"Do the police need you for anything?" I asked, and Mickey gave a tiny shake.

"Does your health, after the bar fight, preclude your leaving with me now?" Another tiny shake.

"Did Lily give you a deadline?"

Mickey spoke quietly, and to his lap, "No, Tyler, she said that she'd be in touch in the next day or two, on my cell phone."

"Okay, so we're going to get you checked out right now, and I'll drive you to your hotel and then to the airport, so you can head back towards Manhattan. You should check into an airport hotel until the regularly scheduled end-date of your conference here, and then go home and tell Anne that you were mugged, which is essentially true."

"Tyler, I can't lie to …" I interrupted Mickey, and started rounding up his things and herding him towards the bathroom to get dressed while I threw his stuff into a bag to carry out.

"You can tell her the whole truth if it makes you feel better, but you were the victim here, not Anne, and you should make sure that she sees it in that light," I advised him through the closed door.

I have never understood Mickey's preference for difficult truths over convenient lies, but I imagine that it's one of the things that makes him a good man, and makes me something just a bit less.

We made sure that he was checked out with the hospital and his conference and hotel, and I got him out to the airport in time for a 1 p.m. flight back down to JFK. He promised to stay in an airport hotel for a couple of days. I gave him one of my burner-phones (*generically activated this morning, along with the others that I had bought*) in exchange for his phone, and watched him enter my current phone number into the contacts list. If Mickey thought anything odd about the back of my Element being filled with microwaves and camping gear and duffels that clanked like firearms when jostled, he was tactful enough to keep his own counsel.

At the airport drop-off, I walked around to his side to take his picture with my phone, and endure a hug from him. Once he got past security, I breathed a sigh of relief, and then gave Kevin, at Dinosaur Bar-B-Que, a call in order to put the next bits of my plan together. I was comforted that the human element (*at least the one that I cared about*) was out of the equation now, and I could focus, once again, on the ends, and not the means.

Dinosaur Bar-B-Que, Syracuse, NY
Monday, 1/21/2013, 2:27 p.m.

"Try all of this!" Kevin crowed triumphantly, as he threw down the last of a seemingly endless parade of plates and bowls of barbeque and sides. I was working my way steadily through all of it, but he always tried to beat me with food whenever I came through town. The previous March, Kevin's ex-wife (*and her new boyfriend*) had grown sick of shared custody, and taken Kevin's six year old daughter, Tracy, with them (*absent permission or legal authority*) when they moved to Ohio. People we both knew through three degrees of separation had put Kevin and me together, and it had worked out well for everyone involved (*except the ex-wife and boyfriend, who might get out of jail in time to attend Tracy's graduation ... from grad-school*).

Kevin had a great relationship with his daughter, a wonderful job at the best barbeque joint in New York State, and no money at all to pay me (*to his ongoing chagrin*). It didn't bother me a bit, as the retrieval of Tracy was easy and quick (*and interesting*), and now I eat for free whenever I'm in Syracuse.

I finger-squeegeed the last morsel of brisket from the top plate on the stack twenty minutes later, and told Kevin once again that he put out a nice plate of food. "I won't be hungry again for hours!" I said, giving him a smile designed to show him that I was kidding and grateful and full.

"I wish that I could do something else to thank you Tyler," Kevin said, and dug out a picture of Tracy. "Here she is at the Christmas Choir Concert ... isn't she an angel?" he asked.

"She is, and that's all the thanks I'll ever need, but there actually is a favor that you could do me Kevin ... but certainly feel free to say no if it's a hassle."

"Whatever it is, it's done ... just say the word Tyler," he gushed, and for a microsecond, I thought about letting Kevin take a more direct (*and violent*) route towards settling Lily and Shane for me and Mickey (*just a microsecond, I promise*).

"You mentioned one time that one of the owners of Dinosaur owns a garage around here that he lets people borrow to work on their bikes and trucks from time to time." I remembered Kevin talking about it the last time I came through town.

"Yah, Mike's place ... not really a garage so much as an empty warehouse with a roll-up door and piles of crap in the corners. Why ... is your car busted?" Kevin asked guilelessly.

"No, the Element is fine, but I need a private spot to do some work for a couple of hours. Do you think you could set it up for me?"

"Sure, I can ask. When would you like it for?"

"Kevin, I need it for this evening if possible, or if not, as soon as he can manage. Also, since Mike doesn't know me, could you leave me out of it? Don't mention my name to him or anyone else, okay?"

"Sure, Tyler, I can do that, but why? What's the deal?" Kevin asked, clearly unable to imagine why I would need or want garage space on the sly.

"Kevin, I'm in town helping out a friend, like I helped you and Tracy out last year. I need to do some work in a quiet and private place for a couple of hours, and if you could set me up with it, I'd consider us more than even." I even tried to waggle my eyebrows meaningfully during this part, and I could see a low-watt idea flicker on in his head, and then he winked at me.

"I got it, Tyler, I'll go up and see him now. While I'm gone, try these fried green tomatoes … they're killer." He smiled broadly as a waitress brought a huge and heaping plate of battered and fried tomato slices based on some signal that I'd missed.

He was gone for seven minutes. The smile on his face when he came back was clear enough that even I could tell that he had good news for me. He dropped a greasy set of keys next to the now empty plate where the fried green tomatoes had been, wrote an address on the only unsullied napkin within twenty feet (*eating at Dinosaur usually ends with me finding splatter evidence of barbeque-sauce and bits of meat in my hair and clothes for days*), laughed when I asked for a bill (*although I did leave a twenty for the waitress who would have to clear and clean the table after I left*), and told me that the warehouse/garage was mine for as long as I wanted, as long as I promised to check in with him for another meal before leaving town. I agreed and headed out … thinking about a nap in the back of the Element to digest the 8000-calorie meal I'd just enjoyed, and let the lizard bits in the back of my brain work a few final details out.

While I was drifting off to sleep, Mickey's phone got the first of many calls and messages and texts from home/Anne. I replied just this first time, in text form, on

Mickey's behalf, telling Anne and the girls that 'I' was fine, keeping busy, enjoying the snow, and eager to see them in a couple of days. It didn't stop the calls/messages/texts over the next hours and days, but it would likely delay Anne from reaching out to the Syracuse P.D. for enough time to let me either fix or completely screw up Mickey's life.

I put the phone back in my pocket, cranked the seat back, and dropped into my usual dreamless sleep.

University Sheraton, Syracuse, NY
Monday, 1/21/2013, 7:12 p.m.

I called Mickey when I woke up, dialing the number for the burner-phone I'd given him when we'd said goodbye. He was fine, and had settled into one of the hotels by the airport after a short flight home. He said that he was sore all over, embarrassed, and wanted to call the whole thing off and just pay Lily.

"If you do that, she and Shane will own you, and they'll come back for more within a month. Give me two days to straighten this out, and if I can't fix it by then, we can talk." I tried to put some wheedling into my tone, but am pretty sure that all I managed was impatience.

We talked for another minute before I told him to order a room service dinner and a bottle of wine, and chase it with a handful of Advil and Tylenol before going to bed. He didn't fight me on the Tylenol/booze combination (*which had long been a hobgoblin of his*), and just before we hung up he admitted with a hang-dog tone that he hadn't yet called Anne and the girls. I couldn't decide how I felt about that (*it made sense to me, but not coming from Mickey*), and so left it alone. I headed back into the university area, and towards the hotel where Mickey had had one of the worst nights of his life.

I'd checked Mickey out of his hotel only a few hours earlier, but it felt like a different world now. Then, I had been sneaking him in and out as quickly and quietly as possible, both of us slinking and hiding to avoid both 'Team Lily' and all of Mickey's colleagues. This time, I was by myself, just the way that I like it. With nobody else on my side, I didn't have to worry about them screwing up in word or deed. I could move forward, adjusting on the fly, based on instinct and input, without having to pause (*or even slow down*) to explain any changes in the game plan. The facts and suppositions that I had about this situation had formed themselves unbidden into a possible solution (*or more accurately, a nested set of solutions*) since my initial contact with Mickey a bit over 16 hours ago, changing and reforming as new information was added to the mix; but I approached the front desk with a confidence born from the knowledge that I was smarter and more motivated to get Mickey out of trouble than Lily and Shane were to keep him on the hook.

"Can I help you Sir?" asked the solicitous, but slightly dubious, front man on the other side of the yard of cool marble at chest height. I was slightly rumpled-looking, and probably had some lingering chunks of barbeque on my earlobes and shirtfront, despite a quick visit to the bathroom at Dinosaur on my way out a few hours earlier.

"I sure hope so. I helped my Dad, Mickey Schwarz, check out a couple of hours ago. He got in an accident last night, and didn't get a chance to return some papers to a colleague of his before leaving, and I was hoping to take care of it now," I served up my opening volley.

"I heard something about some *unpleasantness* when I

came on this afternoon, but wasn't on last night, so I'm sure that I couldn't help you or your *father*. So sorry, Sir."

His eyes seemed to shut down a bit as he replied, and it occurred to me that he knew most of the story, and assumed that I was looking to pay off, or get revenge on, some hooker for a friend. I needed to redirect, and get away from this one without setting off any of his people-radar alarms; this is difficult for me in general, as I lack most of the empathic hardware/software that the rest of humanity is born with.

"I don't want to hassle you, or anyone … I just want to talk to someone who might be able to point me in the right direction to find this woman. Dad mentioned getting some drinks after the conference sessions yesterday … I assume that there's a bar in the hotel?"

The upside of a fundamental lack of emotions and emotional sensitivity is that I am pretty good at delivering a lie without the usual tells that people tend to exhibit. The guy behind the counter looked at me for a few seconds, and then just pointed back into the semi-darkened gloom of the hotel's extensive lobby.

The bartender was polishing and slicing and arranging and generally looking like a guy trying to keep busy during a slow shift. I've never had a good Coke from a fountain, so I try to avoid them whenever possible (*which is always*). I ordered a double measure of Lagavulin 12-year old Scotch with a splash of water.

I've never met a bartender that wasn't a snob about alcohol, and this one looked like a single-malt snob. My ordering a Coke or a Perrier or Clamato, as I might like to in this situation, would not enhance his calm, and could make my work here tonight more difficult. I had no intention of drinking the vile rope/iodine-tasting stuff he put down in front of me a minute later (*I'd seen the label and distinctive bottle as I sat down, so knew that I wouldn't have to reach for another name*), but it allowed him to put me in a series of categorical boxes that suited me for the moment.

"You know your single-malt," he said, as he set the chunky glass down with some ceremony. "Lotta guys, they'll order Glenfiddich or Macallan, and choke it down with their buddies, but they don't like it, you can tell. I haven't uncorked the Lagavulin in months."

"I like the taste of Islay … the salt and peat and smoke … go far enough back, and my family worked the sea off of Islay … maybe warmed themselves at the end of the day with Lagavulin." I'd done some research a few years back, and could talk for hours about single malts, although I hoped that I wouldn't have to. "Pour one for yourself, if you've got the time."

He looked up and down the bar, then smiled at me, and went back down the bar to grab the bottle. He poured himself a copy of my drink, and leaned in to clink my glass. "Happy days," he said, and I groaned inwardly, knowing that I was going to have to drink some.

We raised our glasses, and each took a minute amount into our mouths to vaporize. It burned my tongue and tasted like poison, but I made appreciative sounds, and rolled my eyes to heaven. His eyes shifted, saw someone over my shoulder, and he moved his glass quickly under his side of the bar. He shuffled down to the far end for a few minutes to talk with a tall, thin, gray man in a tall, thin, gray suit before coming back to my end of the bar with a wistful smile.

"Well, you're not in Syracuse for the peat and smoke, what brings you here?" he asked.

"Ewan's my name Phil, and I'm here to sort out some family trouble." Phil looked surprised and a bit nervous when I used his name (*which suited my needs at the moment*), but then remembered his nametag, and which side of the bar he was on. He looked hopefully up and down the bar for thirsty patrons to give him an excuse to flee, but was out of luck.

He looked into the bottom of his glass, swirled it once, took a sip, and brought his eyes back to mine with a neutrality that hadn't been there before; so I primed the pump a bit, "A friend was in here last night, got picked up and rolled by a pro pretending to be part of the conference, and ended up in the hospital minus some of his belongings. I'm trying to find out who and why and how to get back what they haven't already sold before they dump it."

Phil chewed over what I had said while he brought a basket of various bar-snacks up from under his side of the bar. He tilted his head this way and that, a bit like my dog Hope does when she's trying to figure something out. He pulled a single peanut out of the basket, and threw it in his mouth before he answered.

"I probably can't help you, but even if I could, I'd naturally want to make sure that it didn't get back to me."

Thankfully, I don't naturally smile or frown when other people do, or I would have had to repress a grin (*which is an expression I've been working on … smile #23*) when he tried to lawyer up his version of an admission of knowledge of the events that took place last night. I needed to be careful and/or bold, so as to avoid scaring him quiet.

"Here's a picture I took of him at the hospital this morning … imagine him without the broken nose and split lip and bruising. I don't want trouble for you or her or for the people that she works for … I don't care about the stuff they stole, except for some papers they took along with the rest. We just want the research findings, before they chuck them into a dumpster." As far as I knew, Lily hadn't taken anything from Mickey, and there were no research documents, but I assumed that it would make a better story for Phil, who had likely watched enough movies and TV to make up a scenario fitting his secret desires for adventure and intrigue.

"Yah, makes sense. So … you're not looking to put a hurt on anyone, or get anyone arrested, just recover your friend's papers or whatever?" Phil asked.

"That's exactly it Phil, can you get me another of these … and one for you as well? We just want the papers back, I pay out the reward money, and then I go back to the lab in Boston."

As expected, his eyes lit up at the word 'reward', and I needn't have lied about going home to Boston, for all he was listening to the end of the sentence. He hustled down the bar to grab the bottle, and after refilling both of our glasses, left it on the bar … perhaps hopefully. He hadn't noticed me spilling most of my drink from between my knees onto the carpeting on my side of the bar.

"There's a reward for anyone helping you get this stuff back?" Phil took a swallow of the sipping whisky as he obviously battled with a decision.

"That's right, so it's too bad you don't know anything. I may try the bar mentioned in the incident report next, although I'm sure they won't be pouring Lagavulin … pity." The mention of moving on decided Phil, and he blurted out what came next all in one long breath, the tenor of his voice rising and tightening as he ran out of air.

"The guy you want to talk to is Morty … I don't know his last name … he runs the 'Starlight' … this club, see, up near the Carousel Mall, and a string of girls that work the 'Starlight' and a few hotels … his girls are the only ones work the Sheraton … Christ, you can't tell him, or anyone, that I told you, or he'd fuckin' kill me, honest."

The final syllable came out with the last of his breath

(which smelled like mostly digested hot dogs and mustard) and some spit … I was ready to get going, so I moved on to close the deal … what I lack in street-smarts and grace, I make up for in directness and money.

"Phil, I don't have the time or the talent to fuck around or negotiate or threaten … so here's where the shit meets the shorts *(I could see that he liked that phrase, which I'd learned from Dan, and it seemed appropriate)* … if you can give me an address for Morty's Starlight Club and a glass of cranberry juice *(to wash the raunchy taste from my mouth)* in the next minute or so, I'll give you a thousand dollars and be on my way. If the information is good, nobody will ever know that it came from you, and you'll never even see me again. If the information is bad, you will see me again, and I'll be both unhappy and unpleasant. Does that sound fair and reasonable?"

He nodded, filled a tall glass with cranberry juice and a bit of ice, wrote down an address on a slip of paper *(after checking something in a phonebook under the bar)*, and then started to slide my bill across the bar.

"Here you go Phil," I said, as I slapped down a thin stack of $100 bills. "I think you can cover my drinks out of your end … right?"

"Uh, sure …" Phil's face was fun to watch … his fingers reached out to caress the money, and it made him happy, but he felt sad about spending some on pricey whisky. I was okay overpaying for information, but I was opposed to paying for the privilege of drinking that nasty slop in the fancy bottle. It was almost worth it to see the thoughts and moods slide back and forth across his face, until they settled on mostly grateful, with a side of slightly hoodwinked.

Mike's warehouse/garage, Syracuse, NY
Tuesday, 1/22/2013, 2:28 a.m.

Mickey's phone rang as I pulled up at Dinosaur Bar-B-Que for another snack (*hoping to avoid being seen and food-hazed by Kevin, if possible*). I dug the phone out of my bag and the screen identified the caller as 'Lily'. I had been expecting her call, and was glad to hear from her.

"Hello?" I asked.

"Mickey? Is that you?" Her tone was only a little guarded, probably in surprise at not having Mickey pick up ... she may have thought that she had misdialed.

"Hi Lily, my name is Tony, I'm a friend of Mickey's who's helping him with some stuff, since he's not feeling so well at the moment." My normal voice is somewhat lacking in expression, this is especially noticeable over the phone, but I didn't think that it would hurt in this instance, so I didn't try to push any feeling into the exchange.

"I need to talk with Mickey about a private matter, what number can I reach him at? Or should I call his home in Manhattan?" She was speaking loudly and I could hear her breathing, rapid and shallow ... I didn't want to lose her at the beginning, but it was a possibility.

"No need to go straight to the nuclear option, Lily. Mickey and I are old friends, and he told me everything about last night and this morning. I can help you get what you and Shane want, but we need to sit down, talk rationally, and not get excited."

She took a calming breath before her reply, "Why shouldn't I just hang up right now, post the video of Mickey and I fucking on YouTube, and send a copy to his wife?"

"Mickey and me, Lily ... but that's not important right now ... what is vitally important is that you understand that if you hang up and post or send or distribute that video, you have two big problems .... First, you lose your chance at seeing any money from Mickey ... ever. Second, you will hurt Mickey, a good man that I care deeply about ... if you do that, I will devote considerable effort to making your life less pleasant. I am a man not generally given to threats, mostly because I feel silly when I make them. Nonetheless, it would be much better for everyone involved if you agreed to meet with me, exchange your video camera for a large amount of cash, and then we each go our separate ways." I had worked out what to say and how to say it hours earlier, and was generally pleased with how it had come out.

"So you're Mickey's friend ... that's nice. He was a nice guy," she offered ... partway to a peace offering.

"But not so nice that you and Shane left him alone?" I replied, forcing a bit of edge into my voice.

"Shane and me, we've got plans ... the first step is getting out of Syracuse ... and part of getting out of Syracuse is getting some money. Doctors have money."

She built this logical sand-castle for me in such a straightforward and simple way that I could nearly see/hear her repeating it like catechism to/with her boyfriend and pimp, Shane.

"It's a shame your plans involve trying to hurt somebody that I care about."

"We … I just want money, not to hurt Mickey … not really."

"He did a good imitation of someone who had been hurt when I saw him this morning in the hospital." Again, I let some anger into my voice, just to keep her from getting too comfortable with me.

"That's nice you visited him, we must have just missed each other, cause when I checked in again a while later, you guys had already left. It must be nice having friends like you … like him. Someone who would come all the way from New York to see you laid up in the hospital."

"Shane isn't that kind of friend?" I asked, not really caring, but assuming that must be where Lily had been heading, and further assuming that if I got there first, I could hasten our way to the end of this conversation (*which could conceivably make me regret what I was going to do to Lily and Shane*).

"Shane's okay, but it wouldn't occur to him to visit me when I'm sick … I'm no use to him sick or hurt… just once I'd like a friend that cared about me, not what I could do for them." We had veered off track, and I needed to get back on message.

"Well, the good news is I am that kind of friend … the bad news is I'm Mickey's friend, not yours; and I'm here because of you and the injuries and threats you visited upon my friend. My only interest is in getting clear of this with no more hassle or injury to anyone. If money is going to make this problem go away, then I'm going to throw money at you … once. Are you ready to deal, or do I have to listen to you whine about life being unfair some more?"

"No ... Okay ... I'm still here, how are we going to do this? The money," she said, sounding just a bit defeated, (*which was okay with me*).

"We will meet tomorrow, at noon I think, at the Mykonos Coffee Shop in the western quadrant of the intersection of North Salina Street and Kirkpatrick Street. You will bring the video camera and video, and I will bring ten thousand dollars in used and non-sequential twenty and fifty dollar bills. We will share a snack and table in the coffee shop ... my treat, and you can count or inspect the money while I ascertain that the video has not, in fact, been copied and/or shared with the world."

"I didn't know you could do that? How can you tell?" she asked with a enough nervousness to make me think that she had thought about it, but hadn't, as yet, copied the movie of her and Mickey.

"The video has all sorts of information stamped on it by the camera ... I'm sure that you've seen pictures and movies that have the date visibly stamped on them, this is similar, but the data I'll be looking for keeps track of the number of times the file has been shared ... like a counter on YouTube." None of this was true, but I was hoping to keep her from making a backup copy before tomorrow, and she only had to believe me until our meeting.

I continued, "If I find that the data has been copied, the deal will be off, with unfortunate results for you and Shane ... and presumably Mickey. That would be a shame, and I sincerely hope that you are not greedy enough to spoil one payment in the hopes of coming back at Mickey again and again for the same material."

"No," she said, sounding a bit scared and relieved, "We wouldn't do anything like that ... I liked Mickey ... he's a nice guy."

"Remember that in the hours between now and our

meeting tomorrow, when you or someone else gets tempted to try something unsavory or simply stupid. This is the best possible deal for everyone involved ... if this falls apart for some reason, all of the other options are considerably worse ... for our mutual friend Mickey, to be sure, but also, and most especially for you." I went for a flat delivery, as I had concerns that I would be unable to pull off menacing with sufficient oomph.

"Yeah, okay ... I got it. Twelve at the coffee place at North Salina and Kirkpatrick. No copies of the movie and no funny business. I count the money while you check the movie. When we're both happy, we leave, and never see each other again." She had nut-shelled it quite nicely.

"Perfect Lily, I look forward to seeing you tomorrow. I'll be sitting alone with a red backpack in the chair across from me. Remember, stay smart and we all get what we want ... try and get tricky, and nobody does." I hung up, locked the Element, and went in for some food (*Kevin was thankfully off, so he didn't get the chance to stuff me again*).

I finished my meal in short order, paid, left, and went in search of Mike's warehouse. I found the warehouse with no problem, and it was perfect ... huge and well-lit, with lots of tables and power sockets, and even some tools (*both power and hand*). I spent five minutes covering all of the windows at ground level with scraps of house wrap that I found over in a corner; then I started tearing the microwave ovens apart, and modifying the guts for use at a later stage in my plan.

I had stopped on my way to the warehouse into one of the gazillion strip-malls that rings the downtown area of Syracuse to find some things that I needed at Radio Shack (*huge capacitors, lots of wiring, walkie-talkies, a soldering gun, and some parabolic dishes normally used for satellite TV*) and at Home Depot (*another microwave of the same brand that I'd found at*

Walmart, a trio of small fire extinguishers, nitrile gloves, some copper tubing, beefy power cables and plugs, a hundred foot heavy-duty extension cord, and some more giant capacitors for appliance repair, picture hanging wire, C-clamps, and a hacksaw and blades); paying, as always, cash for everything.

I used the fifth (*which I pegged as an extra*) microwave to experiment. I had to backtrack a couple of times in rigging the capacitors (*in parallel, not series*), rigging the dish and copper tubing for 'aiming', and wiring it all together before I was satisfied with the design. I needed to test the device. So I drove out to a deserted u-shaped strip-mall with some lights/electronics still active in one of the windows and an outdoor electrical outlet along one wall (*maybe for Christmas lights*). I pulled the device out of the Element and onto the tarmac, covered it with one of the dark sheets that I'd picked up at Walmart, plugged it into the outlet, and drove some distance away (*hoping that nobody, especially not a cop would pick that minute to come by*). I could see the device and the store window filled with flickering electronics. When I had waited long enough for it to reach a full charge, I activated it with the walkie in my hand.

I could see a brilliant flash and some smoke come out from beneath the sheet, and everything in the store window went dark. I was heartened to see that the lights in the store behind the device were still functioning, which lead me to believe that I could run the other devices from the back of my Element, assuming that I could repeat the construction process exactly. I waited five minutes to see if anyone would come to see what had happened, but nobody did; I went to pick up the device, found a dumpster behind a Circuit City to throw it in, and went back to Mike's warehouse to prepare the other devices.

The other four devices essentially assembled themselves. I let my mind wander through the map of

Syracuse that I had in my head, and explored the plans that I had for Lily and Shane and Morty's Starlight Club, while my hands moved across the landscape of gutted microwaves and capacitors and walkies like crabs; both mind and hands feeling for the easy or artful or elegant way to accomplish my goals. I was coming up on a nexus of high-risk elements in my nested plans, and the physical activity of disassembling and reassembling the microwaves and other components was perfect for occupying my forebrain, which allowed my backbrain (*what I generally refer to as the lizard bits*) to forage around my plans for pieces that could be altered or rearranged in such a way that would reduce risks for Mickey and me and other people (*even Shane and Lily and Morty*).

In this manner, I worked until long after midnight, first altering the microwaves, and then later, purpose-modifying some of the other equipment that I had loaded into the Element in the last 24 hours. Once I was done, and everything was prepped, I loaded it into the Element, covered it with dark linens, threw a few odd bits of lumber (*from one corner of the warehouse*) on top of the lumpiness in the back of the Element, locked the car and warehouse, hung a hammock from a pair of support beams, and got a few hours of sleep.

I dropped off thinking about some details of the next stage of the plan, and awoke with the answers I had sought.

Starlight Club, Syracuse, NY
Tuesday, 1/22/2013, 5:47 a.m.

People who frequent or run or work in clubs that involve drinking and drugs and prostitutes tend to run out of steam around the time that farmers are heading out for morning chores, so that is when I headed over to the Starlight Club. I'm sure that it looked nicer with the lights on, and people lined up outside, and music thumping from inside ... but with dawn whispering in the eastern sky, vomit drying in the gutter, and garbage ripening in the alley it didn't look like anybody's idea of fun (*or so I would imagine ... I don't drink, don't like crowds, and don't understand sex or sexuality beyond the biological basics, so I'm probably not the best person to review a nightclub and whorehouse*).

I had changed into dark pants and a fleece back at Mike's warehouse, and only stopped for a few seconds to offload a couple of duffels of gear behind one of the dumpsters in the alley behind the club before parking the Element a safe distance away. I kept my eyes and ears open as I walked back to the club, but didn't see or hear a soul. When I ducked into the alley to grab the duffels, I slipped into a pair of thin gloves that I could work in (*while hopefully avoiding leaving any fingerprints or DNA*). I found an emergency exit right where I had hoped one would be, pounded a foot-long spike through the door at just the right height (*noisy, even with the wooden mallet, but it has been my experience that you tend to get one big noise for 'free' in these situations*), and stuck a bent coat hanger through to hook the push-bar and let myself in.

Once inside, I threw my gear into a pile in the middle of the room, stood still, and listened for a few minutes. I could hear water dripping, and air being heated/pushed around, and the soda system behind the bar pressurizing (*twice, it must have a leak somewhere*), and a window rattling upstairs, and a big refrigerator compressor cycling in the kitchen through some double doors ... but no human sounds, waking or sleeping. I had thought that it was possible that some prostitutes (*maybe even Lily*) might live upstairs, which would have changed, but not aborted, my mission parameters for this morning. The room smelled like old beer and locker-room and hot-wings and deodorant and various cleaning fluids ... again, not as glamorous as I had anticipated for a 'nightclub with girls upstairs', but I was in Syracuse, not Paris or Berlin.

I was glad, but wondered momentarily, about the emergency door not being wired or alarmed, and looked around for other evidence of security alarms ... none. It made sense in a way ... they wouldn't want police response in most cases, and would likely prefer to handle most break-ins/emergencies on their own; this worked in my favor. They were too big for local criminals to mess with, and too small for bigger criminals to bother with ... this left them perfectly exposed to my form of hijinks. I listened for a further minute, and then searched the entire club.

Being a student of the writings of Lawrence Block, and

especially (*in this instance*) Bernie Rhodenbarr, I believed my ears, but wanted to verify that I was alone in the Starlight Club. I made my way slowly through the whole place, from basement to an attic crawlspace, making certain that nobody else was in the building. Going at a reasonable pace, it took me 17 minutes to check every last human-sized space. I could feel the seconds weighing heavily on me, but had to make sure; the time spent also served to find the best places to leave my surprises.

With C-clamps and hanging wires, I rigged a number of the shotguns that I'd picked up at a few of the entrances to look like booby-traps; I did the same with some of the basement windows and an attic hatch that lead to the roof. Last night, in Mike's warehouse, I had sawn all of the shotguns off to below legal length (*"sauce for the goose, Mr. Saavik" my inner trekkie reflected as I rigged up one after the other*), and now rigged them with C-clamps and hanging wire to doors and windows at critical access points around the club. I rigged all of them to miss their supposed target-spaces, but not by much ... I wanted to scare (*and possibly piss off*) but certainly not injure anyone who got in the way of one of my traps.

When I had rigged the most likely places with poorly executed booby-traps, I salted the rest of the club with the leftover sawed-off shotguns ... behind the bar, in the kitchen, in the offices, at the top of the stairs where it appeared that there was a 'reception desk' presumably manned by a guard or pimp or some such. When my duffel bags were empty of guns, I took a final look around, and left the same way that I had come in, plugging the holes in the emergency door with matching disks of some dull metal that I crazy-glued in place over the holes I had punched to gain entrance to the club ... not a perfect match, but if you didn't know, they would look a part of the door.

Nobody screamed and pointed as I walked out of the alley and away towards my Element; the street and neighborhood seemed as dead as it had when I'd entered the club some 68 minutes ago. I drove slowly back towards the club and parked for a minute from a few blocks away. I watched for any signs of life and/or alarm, but saw none.

I dialed 911 and described, for the operator who answered, two men that I had just seen drag a screaming young girl down an alley and into a building at the address that Phil had written down for me for the Starlight Club.

Two squad cars rolled up from opposite directions, with flashers, but no sirens, 193 seconds after I ended my call (*despite the ongoing questions from the 911 operator*). I heard a shotgun blast, and shortly thercafter, sirens from multiple sources as I rolled away from the scene, programming my GPS to find the nearest Dunkin' Donuts for me.

Dunkin' Donuts, Syracuse, NY
Tuesday, 1/22/2013, 7:19 a.m.

As usually happens, my request for a dozen donuts (*in what I consider the perfect grouping: four each of regular glazed, sugared jellies, and chocolate glazed*) without coffee resulted in their checking (*twice*) to make sure that I didn't want coffee (*as if I might have forgotten*). I took the box back out to the Element, and enjoyed one of each type with a pair of frosty Cokes from my cooler as I dialed home. Dorothy answered on the third ring, which was quick for the Tri-Lakes Animal Shelter (*TLAS*), where she works.

"Hey Dot, how's Hope behaving?"

"Tyler, are you okay?" she asked because on my last adventure I called to ask her for a rescue when my brilliant plan didn't work brilliantly (*because people seldom act in the ways that I expect them to*); it hadn't occurred to me that she would be worried about me.

"Dorothy, I'm fine … just calling to check on my dog, and because I miss home." I was surprised to find that this comfortable lie (*as I don't generally miss things or people or places*) was to a surprising degree true. I would have liked to share some donuts with Hope, my rescue beagle, this morning. I also found that the cityscape of Syracuse was wearing on me ... I wanted the woods and waters of the Adirondacks to fill my field of vision instead of strip malls and tall buildings and crowds of people. I needed to be here for Mickey, but I found that I wanted to get home, which gave me a pleasant feeling (*a glow?*) of humanity that I was unaccustomed to; Dorothy shook me out of my reverie in her usual straightforward way.

"Tyler, are you sure that you're okay? You sound as though you've got an extra tongue in your mouth."

"Nope, really fine." I took a swig of Coke to clear my mouth a bit, "I was administering a bit of donut therapy, and it made me think of you." Nothing makes Dorothy happier than being surprised with a box of America's favorite source of carbs and fat (*although she prefers those carnival ride donuts labeled 'manager's special', or the holiday-themed ones*).

"Nice ... anyway, Hope's fine, although I think that she misses you. She refused to come into work with me, so I had to drive her back home ... pain in the ass dog! I think that Frank must have some kind of radar that tells him when you're up to something. He was in yesterday to ask if I'd seen you. On general principle, since I knew you were heading South and West, I told him that you were heading to the Northeast Kingdom in Vermont for some camping with friends."

Frank Gibson is a cop that I know, who is somewhat aware of what I do, and how I get things done (*"sideways and seldom legal" is how he describes it*). I helped him with a delicate problem a while ago, and ever since he's been grateful and a bit nervous about my living and working in his town (*not to mention being 'friends' with his wife, Meg, which makes him queasy*).

"Thanks, but unless I've seriously miscalculated, Frank will never hear about anything I'm involved with … here in Vermont." I tried for a joke, but it must not have worked, because Dorothy didn't even slow down to snort or snigger.

"How's your shoulder?" This was a cheap shot, referring to my last major miscalculation, which resulted in my getting shot.

"The shoulder's fine Dot, there's no heavy lifting involved in this job," I answered, double-entendre-ing like the warden at a pun-itentiary.

"I hope you get back soon … this year's Ice Castle is looking fantastic, and you promised to take me winter camping in February."

I'd called to get a piece of home, and it had worked … I was missing the Adirondacks, which helped prepare me for the last part of my plan.

"I'll be back before the fireworks, and we'll go camping after the parade." I would be helping her, and TLAS, transport and walk dogs in the parade at the end of Saranac Lake's Winter Carnival, an event that Dorothy both loved and hated, looked forward to and feared.

"Okay, take care, and hurry home … you're dumb dog growled at me in my own bed last night," she said, but ruined the effect with a tiny giggle at the end. I said my goodbye, hung up, and reached for a sixth donut.

After the eighth donut, I called Mickey's burner-phone, and he answered on the first ring, as though he'd been waiting … which he probably had been.

"Tyler … What?!?" It made sense … I was the only one who had this number, so he knew it would be me calling.

"Hi, Mickey. I'm just calling to check in, and make sure that you're okay. Things are going well up here, and if the creek don't rise, I should be tying things up in the next six hours or so."

"I'm glad to hear from you. What sort of text did you send Anne, she's been email bombing me since last night. I replied that my phone's not holding a charge, and that I've been in executive committee meetings and incommunicado to try and deal with some potentially embarrassing issues." That seemed a little close to the bone, I thought, but gave Mickey props for trying.

"Sorry about that Mickey ... I sent a generic text, based on others you had saved in your phone, but it must have sounded off to her. I've never been able to fool Anne into believing that I was human." It was a joke, but only just ... Anne had always thought that I was damaged goods, and might hurt her husband or kids, despite Mickey's instant and ongoing interest (*and eventually love*) for me.

"Never mind ... so can I go home now, Tyler, or do I have to go on pretending? Every second is a lie, and a burden that I have to carry."

I don't understand Mickey, but I certainly do enjoy studying him. I was tempted to push him, see how he would react to a proposal of even greater deceit, but I had no wish to be more cruel to him than was necessary.

"I'd feel better if you would wait until later in the day before I answer that question if you don't mind," I responded. "But you should do what you think is best. How's the hotel? How are you feeling and healing? Do you have enough to read?" Mickey, like me, was a reader ... he could likely survive the end of the world, so long as he had adequate reading material.

"I moved to a Radisson near the first place ... this one has a pool, which feels good on all my sore joints. I'm almost past the need for the pain meds and my swelling is all coming down, although the bruising is spectacular. I'll have to explain it to the girls for certain ... it'll be weeks before I'm back to anything like normal. I have a couple of hundred books on my iPad, so I'm fine for reading material unless I end up having to flee the country ... which I won't have to do, right, Tyler? You're not doing anything illegal are you?"

(*Now he asks!*)

"Mickey, if you want, when this is all over, I'll answer any questions that you care to ask, but for now, I have to go, and you'll have to be satisfied with my promise that things are going well, and nobody is going to get hurt."

"I guess that'll have to do then. I'll expect your call this afternoon or evening. Love you, boy!" It made me feel good (*as though things could/would return to normal*) that he ended the call with his traditional closing.

"Love you too, Mickey," I always said this, although we both knew that it wasn't exactly true.

I finished the box of donuts, and instead of the expected sugar rush, I was overcome by a nap attack, and decided that I could afford to close my eyes for a few hours.

Mykonos Coffee Shop, Syracuse, NY
Tuesday, 1/22/2013, 12:03 p.m.

It was, as it always seems to be doing in Syracuse, snowing when I arrived at the intersection of North Salina and Kirkpatrick Streets at sixteen minutes after eleven. I saw nothing that made me want to keep driving, so I pulled into the big parking lot that the cafe shared with a Kinney's drugstore, and parked in such a way that pointed my rear window at the front door and window of the Mykonos Coffee Shop (*not, I noticed, a coffee shoppee, the spelling of which drives me to distraction every time I see it ... and apparently sometimes even when I don't see it*). The geography of my parking also avoided the external video cameras placed to record drive-up pharmacy traffic. I went into Kinney's, and saw a manager-type a few isles over stocking shelves with drugstore things.

"Excuse me," I spoke loud enough to get his attention, but I didn't want to distract him too much from his task. "My car battery died, can I plug my charger into the outlet I saw on the side of your building by the parking lot to run the battery up a bit?" I asked, using a slightly modified #3 smile (*friendly/ sincere/ helpful, with a touch of honest added for effect*). Lacking the usual range of human expression, I've always been surprised at how much of human communication is non-verbal; and as such, have had to learn how to fake smiles and frowns and shrugs and such ... I have twenty-four smiles in my repertoire, not counting slight variations, like the one I was using now.

"Sure, no problem," looking up briefly but barely noticing my effort at personality. "But could you throw something over the cord, so nobody trips over it?"

"Great! I've got to pick up some stuff anyway, and I'll just add a towel to my basket," I said jiggling my partly full hand basket ... I have a towel in the element (*I've read 'The Hitchhiker's Guide to the Galaxy' seven times after all*), but I decided to use the one from Kinney's for a couple of reasons: it makes me a customer, it shows him that I'm interested in complying with his wishes, and I don't get my own towel all covered with Syracuse.

With my new towel (*and some other assorted stuff that I didn't really need, but could always use*) in hand, I headed back out to my car, popped the hood for verisimilitude (*thinking of Dan for a second, and wondering what he'd think of the role his shotguns were playing in today's fun*). I ran a heavy duty extension cord from the back of the Element out to the all-weather wall socket, plugged it in (*cringing slightly when I did so, hoping that it wouldn't short circuit the plug/ building/ neighborhood, or cause the gizmo in the back of my car to explode ... it didn't*), and laid my new towel down on the cable and snow and dirt of the narrow walkway. I added a traffic cone that I'd picked up off the side of the road on my way down here (*people respect a traffic cone and always assume that it must be there for some important reason*). I'm sure that I only imagined that I could hear a hum from the back of the Element as the massive capacitors built up their charges.

I opened the backdoors and pulled some lumber partway out to explain the open backdoor to the casual (*yet curious*) passerby, chucked my watch up to the front seat (*so I wouldn't lose it if everything worked as it should*), grabbed the red backpack that Lily would be looking for, and went over to grab a Coke and a snack before she arrived.

She arrived a few minutes late by the clock on my burner-phone (*which placed her well within the acceptable range of 'promptness' for the majority of humanity*), alone (*I assumed that Shane was busy and/or arrested this morning*) and looked past me twice before her eyes came back to the red backpack that 'Tony' had mentioned yesterday in their/our phone call.

I needed things to happen in a specific order in a pretty short time span, so I waved her over and initiated the conversation to try and insure that things went in the correct manner. While she was walking my way, I turned on the walkie I had in my lap, and made certain that it was on the correct channel to initiate a link with the device in the back of my Element.

"Lily, you're late. Show me the camera and video and tell me that you haven't been dumb enough to make a copy for 'insurance', please." She recognized my voice and manner, and stopped just short of sitting to pull a coffee-brick-sized camera from a shoulder bag and put it down on the table.

She pushed a button on the top of the camera, and a noise preceded a small door on the side opening and partly ejecting a little videocassette. "I didn't make a copy … this thing's not as easy as the new digital ones, but …"

I didn't care much about where she was headed with that sentence … I pushed the 'SEND' button on the walkie, imagined that I could feel a surge of something racing through the air at the speed of light to damage my central nervous system, and the lights and radio and TV in the coffee shop went out with a couple of expensive sounding pops and puffs.

I stood up, probably before anyone else had really noticed, grabbed the backpack, and turned to head back out into the snow; only pausing to check the coffee shop to make sure that I hadn't killed anyone with a pacemaker (*I had failed to think of that until after I pushed the button ... oops*). I hadn't.

"Wait, what, wait ... what the fuck is going on? Where the fuck are you going?" Lily asked, scooping up the camera as she followed me outside.

"We're done here 'Lily', take a look and think about it for a second," I said as I held up my burner phone for her to see ... not that there was much to see. I had bricked it with what amounted to an electro-magnetic pulse (*EMP*) using the high energy radio frequency energy from the modified microwaves in the back of my Element. I had made use of the stuff I'd picked up at Home Depot to aim the wave generally into the coffee shop, where it fried everything with circuitry (*especially stuff with magnetic data storage like Lily's video*).

"But I've still got the camera... the tape ... I can ..." she seemed to run down as she looked at her watch, which had stopped at a few minutes after noon.

"Can what?" I dug into my pocket for a folded packet of hundred dollar bills (*ten of them*). "Here's the new deal, I give you one thousand dollars for the time you spent in bed with Mickey, so it wasn't a total loss, and you walk away from me, from here, from Mickey."

"But Shane ..." she started, but I had neither the time nor the desire to hear idle threats or more whining.

"If Shane was going to do anything about today, he would have had to be here, which he isn't. I'm betting that his life got more complicated this morning ... the good news is that yours just got much, much, more simple. If you want my advice, which you probably don't, you should also walk away from Shane ... go pack a bag, get on a bus, and pick a new home with this and any other money that you might have."

She spent four seconds with her mouth open and gaping, seven seconds getting angry, and eleven seconds thinking her way out of anger ... I appreciated both her silent thoughtfulness and the Fibonacci-ness of the timing of her thought progression. She started to say something, thought better of it, plucked the hundreds out of my hand, turned her back on me and walked away, pausing at the corner only to peel off her watch and throw it, along with the camera, into the garbage can.

I will gladly admit that a small part of me had wanted to explain my actions, and was disappointed when Lily walked away from me in the parking lot. Mostly, however, I was enormously relieved that this thing was over for Mickey.

I like to think that she will leave well enough alone, that my tricks and treats at the Starlight should serve to hobble whatever backup or muscle or help she might hope to access. She may even take this opportunity to change her life, although I doubt it.

I checked afterwards, and found that one of the responding officers had been treated for minor injuries from a ricocheting shotgun pellet or fragment. The owners and various staff at the Starlight face multiple weapons charges, assault/battery/attempted murder of peace officers, and a hearty stew of drug and prostitution charges ... all of which added up to significant and multitudinous felonies for Morty and company (*presumably including Shane*).

After Lily had turned a corner and walked out of our lives forever, I quickly walked over to the Element, unplugged the extension cord, picked up the dirty towel, wrapped the cord around it, threw it into the back along with the traffic cone, pushed the lumber back into place, slammed the rear door and hatch, closed the hood, and was ready to drive away 28 seconds after I had turned away from Lily.

Just then there was a tap on the passenger-side window. A Mister-Rogers-looking man, just closing the door on his 1970s era Monte Carlo made a rolling-down motion (*old school*), so I did, feeling my heart and respiration rate pick up a bit.

"Everything work out?" he asked.

It took me a second to parse out his meaning.

"With your car … you looked to be having some car troubles, everything work out?"

I smiled, nodded, turned the key, and when it (*thankfully*) started, said, "Yup, everything worked out pretty well … thanks!"

We nodded at each other and I drove off.

Gas 'n' Go, Star Lake, NY
Tuesday, 1/22/2013, 2:47 p.m.

I drove just under the speed limit all the way to Watertown, got off of Route 81 long enough to find a Walmart dumpster that I loaded with all of the leftovers of the stuff that I'd bought in the last few days. That done, I went inside to use their bathroom and load up on a bit of road food in the form of protein and caffeine (*beef jerky and Coke, not feeling the need for fats or carbs after my donut-tastic breakfast*), and then got back on the road heading north and eventually west, back into the park … back into the woods … back home.

I stopped at the Gas 'n' Go in Star Lake, certain from past experience that I would be able to get cell service when parked at the pump, to gas up. I dialed the number of Mickey's burner phone.

"Tyler! I've been going nuts all day! Tell me you're okay!" he shouted into the phone, not even noticing that I was calling from a different number.

"Easy, Mickey, you'll run out of exclamation points," I said. "Everything's fine. I just wanted to get home before calling you (*a slight exaggeration that he wouldn't understand, but that I felt I could be excused for*). You're off the hook with Lily and Shane, it's as if the video never existed. Nobody got hurt (*not 100% true, but he didn't need to know*). You can head home whenever you want. What you tell Anne and the girls is entirely up to you … if you asked me, I'd advise you to say that you were mugged, which you essentially were." I stopped talking to let him in, knowing that by now he'd be waiting.

"I've been doing a lot of thinking during my imprisonment at the Airport Radisson, and I have decided to go with what I call the 'Mugging-Plus' explanation. The girls will hear that I was mugged, and beaten, and woke up in the hospital. Anne will get the full story."

I cringed as he finished, "Mickey … the full story could involve some significant trouble for me, and maybe even for you if absolutely everything came out. Don't get me wrong, you do whatever you think/feel is right, but it may bring some substantial headaches for you and Anne … and me." I was surprised to find that I wasn't lying when I told Mickey to do what he thought was best.

"That's sweet of you, Ty, but by the full story, I meant that Anne gets to hear about my screw-up and Lily, not what you may, or may not, have done to get me out of trouble. My plan in that department is to tell her nothing about the proposed extortion, just leave it at drugged infidelity and a mugging."

"I still think it's a lousy idea, but you're a much better person than I am, so it must be the right thing to do," I replied, to which he chuckled … as he always did when we talked about my not being exactly the same species as him.

"I assume that you will have some loose ends to tie up in Syracuse with the police and hospital and maybe some of your colleagues? If you tell me ahead of time, I can meet you there and buy you the best lunch you've had in years," I offered. Mickey gets up so early every day for work that lunch is his big family, and talking, meal.

"That's nice, Tyler, I will be coming up in a few weeks to deal with some of the aftermath of the last few days, but I'll also be coming up to Saranac Lake for a visit after I finish up, and I expect you to do the right thing and talk with me about how you were able to rescue me." I heaved a deep internal sigh, and tried to imagine how I could dodge his questions.

"And don't waste time trying to aim that great melon of yours at the problem of dodging my questions. I've known you all of your life, and you're a horrible liar. You had something to do with fixing that creep up in Malone a couple of years ago. You were into something last summer which has had an impact on you physically, the range of motion in your left arm and shoulder is diminished, and you're too thin. You were able to come up with some solution to my problem in seconds after hearing about it."

Mickey, what you're saying is ..." He cut me off.

"Stop. I've always known that your mind works differently ... if you've found a way to make that work for you, and also help people, I'm all for it. I just need to know what it is, and that you approach what you do with some form of moral compass, or a reasonable facsimile."

I don't think that I necessarily do have a moral compass, but my actions always make sense to me, and are based on my understanding of the situation and the preservation/restoration of order, as I see it ... I hoped that would be enough for Mickey.

"Okay, Mickey, just tell me when and I'll make sure that I'm in town and presentable. You can meet my dog, Hope, then, too."

"Sounds good Tyler, I'll call you next week when I

know more."

We ended the call in our usual way, "Love you, boy!" Mickey said, with a slightly thick voice.

"Love you too, Mickey," I answered.

I filled up the Element, picked up some road and camping food, and headed for a chunk of State Forest Preserve I'd been wanting to explore. I set up camp, made a big campfire (*mostly for Frank's sake, so that when I ran into him tomorrow morning, I'd smell like camping*), enjoyed a few hours of quiet and cold and dark (*unlike anything that could be found in Syracuse*), and then climbed into my hammock, happy to be back in the woods, back in the Adirondack Park, back in my world.

Promises
To Keep

Jamie Sheffield

Promises to Keep

Forest Home Road, Saranac Lake, NY
Monday, 1/20/2014, 7:23 a.m.

I listened to the sound of the horn for a few minutes in the quiet morning before it occurred to me that it was coming from my Honda Element, and beyond that, that somebody must have opened my car in order to then draw attention to themselves ... Frank.

Frank was the only person in my life who made sense. Dorothy has a spare key to my car. Meg couldn't break into a loaf of bread with a firmly attached twisty-tie. John would have tracked me from the Element to my campsite. Maurice stays inside drinking coffee and brandy all winter. Cynthia's still gone ... dead. Barry is incapable of honking the horn of my Element (*and I hadn't seen or heard from him in months anyway*). There was nobody else that I could think of who would make noise after breaking into my car.

The woods were cold and filled with that special quiet that only comes with half a foot of new snow over everything. I was snugly cocooned in my hammock and hammock-sock (*essentially a sleeve that fits around the hammock and my sleeping bag and me to create a warmer microclimate ... much like a tent does*), swaying gently in the slight breeze and thinking about getting up to make some breakfast when I figured out the message implicit in the horn blasts. I jounced the hammock/sock a few times to shake off most of the snow that had fallen during the night, rotated into a sitting position, pulled my boots off the ridgeline that I had hung them (*and the 'roof' of the hammock-sock*) from overnight, and slid them on my feet before stepping down to Earth.

Frank is not a morning person, and not likely to visit on a lark in any case, so I had to assume that he was here on official — that is, police — business. Frank works for the Saranac Lake P.D., and has some familiarity with what it is that I do as an investigator … and how I do it; this has also earned him the dubious honor of being the one that tracks me down for local and state police when anything happens that is weird enough to be one of the tricky cases that I've stuck my nose into. Normally at this time of day, he would still be ungluing his eyes and drinking a second or third cup of coffee and working his way through notes and phone calls; being out in the boonies at this hour meant that he needed to talk to me, so I skipped breaking camp and just walked out to meet him, shrugging into my coat and gloves on the way.

He was sitting in his patrol car, warming up and talking to someone on his cell phone when I came out of the woods; when he saw me, he closed the primitive clamshell phone and got out to greet me.

"Tyler, I been up and down every road leading into or out of Saranac Lake for hours looking for you."

"And you found me. What do you need?" I asked … beating around the bush is not in my nature, nor is it usually in Frank's, but this morning I could see him thinking about what to say next … avoiding both the point of his visit, and my question.

"It got down to ten degrees last night, Tyler, were you really warm in that hammock thing, and why camp here?" he asked.

"Yup, the hammock sock has kept me warm down to thirty below. I was planning on climbing Spruce Ridge Mountain, and depending on how I felt, maybe continuing with Spruce Ridge and then onto Boot Bay Mountain. Why are you here, Frank?"

"Lotta snow. Can Hope manage it okay?" he asked. Hope is my aging rescue beagle from the Tri-Lake Animal Shelter (*TLAS*).

"I have snowshoes back at my camp. I brought them along in anticipation of this snow," I said, gesturing around at the winter wonderland-osity and general snow-globiness of the woods around us. "Hope is staying with Dorothy for a couple of days, because she doesn't like deep snow, and her joints hurt in the … what?" I stopped the health update on my grumpy dog because Frank had winced minutely during my last sentence.

"Tyler," he paused to take a deep breath before continuing. "We gotta talk."

"Fine, tell me what's up with Dorothy?"

He hadn't known that I didn't have Hope with me (*maybe he had thought she was back at camp*) and given his facial gymnastics, during my previous and current statements, I could tell that I was correct in my assumption that he was here with news about Dorothy. I often wonder if someday he'll connect Dorothy and me to some of the extra-legal things we've done over the years, but today was obviously not that day (*the day he figures out the truth about what happened to George and/or Barry and Justin, he'll come with backup … maybe SWAT*).

"She's in the hospital in Saranac Lake, Tyler. Mike

Lawrence, the doctor I spoke with, thinks she'll live, but she was pretty busted up and hypothermic when they brought her in. It seems a bit odd, but you, not Lisa, are listed as her emergency contact. Lisa was the one who brought her in, so it doesn't ..." He looked as though he was going to continue in this manner for a while, so I cut him off.

"Frank, stop talking. You drive in front with flashers and the siren, and I'll stay on your bumper. You can give me the rest after I've seen her," I said.

Frank looked as though he was about to say, maybe finish, something, but reconsidered when he looked at my face (*I was puzzled about what he might have seen, as I don't emote much, or tend to express facial expressions unless I'm trying to*).

He started up his car and lights, waited for me to get the Element going, and then took off with sirens clearing the roads of both cars we passed between my campsite and the Adirondack Medical Center in Saranac Lake.

Adirondack Medical Center (AMC), Saranac Lake, NY
Monday, 1/20/2014, 7:48 a.m.

I followed Frank into the parking lot at AMC, and found
an empty parking space 243 steps from the door to the
hospital; 243 being a notable number in that it is: the largest
three digit number that is a fifth power, the sum of five
consecutive prime numbers (*although clearly not a prime itself*),
and the number of Earth days in one Venusian day (*I play
these number games when tense or scared and have since I was very
young … I searched for, and found these facts somewhere in the back
of my head before we had cleared the lobby*).

Frank's badge and uniform and knowing (*and having
grown up with*) everyone in town eased our passage
through/past various gates and gatekeepers, until we came
to a door with an RFID reader, which slowed him down
long enough to fumble a card out of his wallet and slap it
on the scanner. When the door greenlighted (*greenlit?*) us, a
lock clicked in the heavy door, and we passed into a much
more quiet suite of rooms seemingly inhabited by an old
woman lying in a vast sea of white hospital bed, and
surrounded by machines that beeped and binged and

pushed and pulled various fluids into (*and out of*) the wretched wreck on the bed; pale as death on most of her exposed skin (*most of her face was covered in bandage*), and a macabre rainbow of bruising and scabbing on what remained.

When Frank did not move past her and into another room, I did a double-take and was forced to conclude that it was Dorothy. A miserable Lisa came back into the room from what appeared to be a bathroom a few seconds later, her washed face not masking her tears and lack of sleep a bit, but definitely confirming the identity of the ruined thing in the hospital bed. She saw us, scowled at Frank, and rushed over to hug me (*and apparently wipe her freely running nose on the shoulder of my shirt*).

I'm not a hugger, never have been … I dislike even casual physical contact like handshakes … this was way outside of my comfort zone. Beyond that, I was confused because Lisa not only doesn't like me … she barely tolerates my presence in Dorothy's life. We've developed a routine (*a bit like shared custody*) such that only one of us is with Dorothy for any length of time (*mostly, her*).

I was starting to pull away when she said quietly on my non-Frank side, "Don't say anything, Tyler. Dot begged me not to tell, and said that you can't either."

I nodded and then whispered my assent in her ear; we broke off the, by-then, lengthy hug to a look of astonishment from Frank (*who knows, even if he doesn't understand, my dislike of human contact*).

"Tell me about her condition … Frank or Lisa," I said. "Better still, get a doctor in here."

They both looked angry at my demand, probably for different reasons that I failed (*and would likely continue to fail*) to understand.

Frank pulled out his notebook, found the correct page,

and began, "Ms. Baker," he said gesturing to Lisa, "indicated that she received a call from Ms. Bouchard," he nodded at the bed, "at approximately 1:30 a.m., in which she stated that she had been mugged outside of The LumberJack's Tavern and Grill, in Tupper Lake. Ms. Baker drove to pick Ms. Bouchard up, rather than call an ambulance, due to a misunderstanding about the nature and severity of Ms. Bouchard's injuries. Once she saw the shape that Ms. Bouchard was in, Ms. Baker drove her straight here to AMC, where Doctor Stevens in the E.R. examined her."

I looked over at Lisa, but she refused to make eye contact with me or Frank.

"Stevens reports an orbital fracture," Frank looked up from his notes to me ... I nodded understanding, and pointed to my eye socket to prove it, "on the far right side of the right orbit. In addition, the doctor reported a catastrophic nose break involving bone and cartilage in and around the septum."

I nodded, relieved that it wasn't worse.

"Before you get relieved that it wasn't worse, let's take a look behind door number two," Frank said, unnerving me slightly in his seeming prescience.

He pulled back the sheet covering Dorothy's torso, with a flourish that reminded me of the magician at David Silverman's eighth birthday party, revealing pinkening bandages, with inflow and output tubes, doing their thing.

"She suffered massive blunt-force trauma, with accompanying broken ribs and some associated organ damage." He looked momentarily at Lisa, colored (*perhaps regretting his colorful reveal of moments ago*) and continued, "Fractured ribs penetrated her left lung in at least two places, and her liver appears to have been nicked by a rib fragment, as well. There has been significant internal bleeding, and the left lung collapsed just after her arrival in the hospital."

Lisa let out a moist and whistling sob, and fled the room as Frank finished.

"Frank ..." I didn't know how to continue, what to say, but luckily Frank did, and steamrolled through my ellipses.

"I know, I was tough, maybe heartless with that girl. Thing is though, Tyler, she's lying to me. There was no mugging in Tupper. Dorothy had no alcohol in her blood. Her wallet is among her effects, with eighty-seven dollars and some change. Lisa is lying to me. Dorothy was lying to me before she passed out, or went to sleep, or fell into a coma, or whatever the fuck happened while I spent the last six hours driving up and down every goddam road in twenty miles, looking for you." He stopped to breathe ... pant really ... for a few seconds before continuing.

"The doctors are watching her vitals and those tubes, trying to decide whether to open her up and try to fix what someone did to this woman who's eaten dinner with me, at my table. She cried with me, literally over my dog, the day we had to put him down, and I can't do a thing to help her with that bullshit story they served up. If you can talk Lisa into giving me something, anything, to work with, I can maybe try and make this right."

He gave me a hard stare for a few seconds, waiting for me I guess. "If you know about what happened last night, Tyler, the best thing you could do for your friend here is to tell me everything."

"If I knew anything, Frank I'd tell you in a second. I'll try and talk with Lisa when she comes back, and see if I can get you any information." I said this with a straight face and a slightly obsequious smile (*a modified #2, with a dash of my #8 mixed in*). It must have worked, at least partly, because he snorted disgustedly, and stormed out, saying something about finding one of her doctors.

I closed my eyes and breathed in the nasty soup of hospital smells: disinfectant, blood, urine, feces, for a minute while I tried to sort through the messy piles of thoughts in my head. I was, of course, lying to Frank. I very likely knew where and why she'd been beaten. I needed more information about why Dorothy (*and to a lesser degree, Lisa*) felt it important to keep the truth from Frank before I could proceed. I wasn't looking forward to cross-examining Lisa (*the only thing on Earth that we had in common was Dorothy ... I hoped that would be enough*) about the previous night, but needed to get more data to feed the hungry beasts living in the back of my brain ... they would digest it and (*following my unfortunate metaphor to its inevitable conclusion*) poop out some form of answer or plan for me to act on.

I was saved having to track Lisa down to grill her, by a dry whisper from the Dorothy-wreckage on the bed at my waist, "Tyler, I'm awake. Been awake, playing dead. C'mere. We don't have long."

I didn't know whether we didn't have long because Frank would be back soon, or Lisa would be back soon, or because she was going to pass out or die, but after 1.3 seconds of deep thought, I decided that it didn't much matter at the moment. I slid a chair in front of the door that Frank and Lisa had left by (*a primitive alarm system, but the best I could do with what I had to work with*), and bent down to talk with Dorothy.

Adirondack Medical Center, Saranac Lake, NY
Monday, 1/20/2014, 7:52 a.m.

"You can't tell Frank about the dog fighting. You can't tell
Frank about Bronsen. I need you to not do anything."
Dorothy's short declarative sentences were dumping vast
amounts of information into my fore and back brain, but
I was missing essential chunks.

"Dot, what are you talking about?" I asked. "You got
these injuries in, or at a dog fight? Who's Bronsen? Why
would you think that I would do anything, what do you
think I would do, and why is it important for me not to?"

I could see her eyes glaze and then refocus as she battled
fatigue and pain and drugs to parse out my questions, and
try to formulate answers to them ... she lost the fight
momentarily, went still and closed her eyes for 23 seconds.
It was long enough that I reached out and took her hand
(*I'm not big with human contact, but it seemed the right thing to do*);
she still had a pulse ... I waited.

Eventually, she opened her eyes a bit, and tilted her head
like a confused dog, goggling at me to make sure of who I
was.

"All of this is the result of two punches from that ass-wipe Bronsen," she whispered. "He flattened my nose for sticking it where it didn't belong, and hit me in the gut to show his guys that he didn't have a problem hitting a girl." She said all of this without animus or rage ... like she might report a tree branch falling on her car or a storm breaking a window.

Something clicked in place for me (*slowly, which slowness I attributed to being off-balance because of the injuries to Dorothy*). I said, "Bronsen is the guy who arranges/hosts dog fights out in the hinterlands. You found out enough about his operation to go and confront him, and this happened ... and you brought Lisa along as your minion."

She nodded. Dot had enjoyed her role as self-titled minion in a number of my trickier investigations, and had joked in the past about including Lisa.

"So why the secret? Tell Frank. Frank will scoop him/them up and put him/them inside." This seemed a logical progression to me, but now she was shaking her head, and the way that she winced I was a little worried that it might fall off.

"I told you, Tyler, he did this to me with two punches. He said if I talked with anyone about it, that he would beat on Lisa until he got tired, then take a nap, and then burn down the shelter." A tear rolled partway down her purpled cheek, catching in some partly dried and scabbed up blood, bringing it somewhat back into a liquid solution.

I was concerned that Frank and/or Lisa would be back any second, and needed to know more before she clammed up in their presence. I had no plan to act on the information as yet, but I needed to know ... it's the primary condition of my personage on this planet.

"Okay, I won't tell Frank a thing, but you need to tell me," I said.

She nodded minutely, either because she only partly agreed, or because it hurt to nod ... or, more likely, both, and said, "We talked last week about the dog fighting."

I nodded, to move her along. We had talked about it numerous times, and not just last week. A number of dogs' bodies had been found over the course of the last year ... badly decayed, but showing some evidence of trauma suggestive of fighting, as well as of primitive medical repair (*nylon stitches, crazy-glue wound closure, inexpert bone splinting, and so on*). They had been found in various parts of Franklin and Essex and St. Lawrence counties. Dorothy suspected that someone was hosting dog fights, and asked me to help figure out the who and where ... she had a good idea about the why and what and how already.

Maps marking the locations in which the corpses had been found yielded no useful results: they were in the middle of nowhere, roughly equidistant from what passes for population centers up here in the Adirondacks, and when taken as a whole seemed to lack a center point. My assumption was that the people running the dog fights lived within the irregular circle described by the outer marks on my map, but were happy to find a new spot for each fight (*there being no shortage of out of the way places in the six million acre park that I call home*). I hadn't given it much more thought, as it was a dead end without a radical evolution/improvement in the quality of our information. Dot had published a couple of letters in the local papers, asking for help, but got nowhere/nothing for her troubles (*until very recently apparently*).

"I got a call at the shelter (*Tri-Lakes Animal Shelter, TLAS, which Dorothy runs, here in Saranac Lake*) yesterday afternoon. A guy I went to school with said that he knew where a dog fight was gonna be held tonight ... last night. You were off camping somewhere, and I just wanted to see. I didn't want to send Frank on a wild goose-chase, so Lisa and I went after dinner." She finished this last bit, and ran down a little, chin drooping/dropping towards her chest.

"And you got there, and ..." I prompted, aware that other humans might/would feel bad about, or simply stop, pushing at this point.

Her head came up again, and started talking again, but more quietly and slowly than before, "There were maybe thirty cars and trucks parked outside an old barn. I could hear sounds from inside the barn ... men and dogs and laughing and screaming. I started to go inside, but Lisa stopped me. She told me to take pictures of license plates, and give it all to Frank."

'Clever Girl' I thought to myself, flashing as I always do, on 'Jurassic Park'.

"She stayed in the car, I got most of the way through the cars and trucks before she honked to warn me about the guys that were about to grab me."

Dorothy shuddered at this point, maybe remembering the fear and pain and helplessness ... I still remember them perfectly from being in a similar situation a year and a quarter ago. When you go off the edge of the civilized map of the world, you sometimes find monsters living there who make their living instilling those feelings. I was sorry that Dot had learned that particular lesson ... it would change her (*had changed me*) forever.

"He had a pair of guys hold me, and he did this," she flopped a hand at her face and torso, "not caring that Lisa saw. After, he leaned in close and whispered about Lisa and the shelter, then he and his guys let me fall in the snow and they walked back inside the barn. His guys asked if it was cool to just let me go, and he laughed, knowing that I wasn't going to say anything. Lisa dragged me into the car, we got our stories straight, and she brought me here." As she finished, I could hear heavy steps slowing as they approached the door.

The knob started to turn, she grabbed at my hand, which had still been by hers on the bed, and whispered fiercely in my face (*the smell of injury and swallowed blood on her breath*), "Don't do anything, Tyler; promise me."

"Okay," I said, as the chair skidded out of the way and the door opened. I was thinking about promises, and the two-way nature of promises made and kept.

As Lisa and Frank came back into the room, Frank looked down at the chair blocking the door, grew instantly suspicious, and said, "Okay, what?"

Thanks to long practice on her part, and the lack of emotional software on my part, Dorothy and I didn't look at each other, and I offhandedly replied, "Dorothy suggested that I should pick up Hope, since my dog regrettably hates Lisa ... I said okay."

Frank nodded, not entirely believing me, but well aware of my rescue-dog Hope's virulent and unreasoning hatred of most every person on Earth (*myself and Dorothy being the only real exceptions ... she tolerates Maurice, my landlord, and will now let one of the vet techs at the animal hospital approach her ... but just the one, and Hope still growls at her*).

Lisa nodded meaningfully, and perhaps revealingly, at Dot and me ... I hoped both that Frank didn't notice, and that he hadn't/wouldn't spend much time questioning/talking with her (*if keeping secrets was a long term concern of theirs*).

I straightened up and moved towards the door, "I'll check in with you later, Dot ... for now I'll head over, get Hope, and feed your cats." The cats living with Dorothy and Lisa feel the same about me as other cats I've experienced ... they seem to sense that I'm missing something that other humans have, and are unnerved by it. That being said, they don't mind my feeding and watering them, which was all I had in mind for today.

I was ten feet down the hall when I heard the door to Dorothy's room open again, and Lisa said in a slightly too loud stage voice, "I'll just catch up and give these to Tyler, since you and I won't want them."

I waited for her to catch up with the Cokes I'd seen in her hand a minute earlier.

Adirondack Medical Center parking lot, Saranac Lake, NY
Monday, 1/20/2014, 7:56 a.m.

"So, you talked with her?" Lisa asked me, after handing me
a pair of Cokes. I was interested in why she had come
bearing these particular gifts … she knew that I was partial
to Coke, but had never before given me one, in the years
that we'd known each other. It was possible that she had
simply wanted an excuse to talk with me, but there was
something about the way she passed them over that felt
like … an offering.

"Yup," I replied. I didn't know what or how much she
knew, so figured that less was, in this case, more, or at least
better.

"That thing broke her into pieces with a single punch
from each fist."

"Bronsen?" I asked.

"Yes, who'd ya think I meant? He's ten years older than
Frank if he's a day, and he doesn't weigh much more than
you, Tyler, but it was like he dropped a piano on her … on
my Dorothy." Bright spots of red spread outward from her
cheeks, her neck was flushed, and her breathing and pulse

were rapid; I was both interested and disturbed about where I felt/suspected that this was going to go in the next minute.

"Why didn't you tell all of this to Frank?" I asked. "It sounds like he'd be inside a cell by this afternoon, and good riddance."

I wasn't trying to poke at her ... her sadness shone out of her like a beacon ... I genuinely wanted to understand. If, as I assumed, she didn't know about the threats that this Bronsen had made to Dorothy, then it seemed ridiculous not to tell the police, Frank.

"Dot made me swear not to last night while I was white-knuckle driving back here from Union Falls Pond, sure she was bleeding inside and going to die. I begged her, Tyler, begged her and screamed at her while she moaned and threw up and shat herself and sounded like she was drowning in blood from her flattened nose."

She was up close and huffing, tiny droplets of spit hitting my face while she nearly yelled at me. I tried to smile comfortingly at her, but it must have fallen flat (*as my fake expressions often do*).

"She said that she had to not say anything to anyone. You didn't tell did you? What you know, or think you know, about the dead dogs and the fights?"

"She made me promise too, Lisa," I said, and cracked one of the Cokes ... feeling the caffeine and sugar start to make me whole (*or as whole as I get, in any case*).

"Fine, now promise me. Promise you'll do whatever it is that you do, and fix this for Dot."

Her eyes were full of tears, and some started to spill in the coming seconds. I got sidetracked watching her face ... I'm a student of human emotions, having none of my own for the most part ... and her face was a swiftly changing kaleidoscope of partial emotions that I wasn't used to seeing in the same context: anger, greed, shame, savage glee, excitement, hope, and fear.

"I'm confused," I said, when I came back and reached for an appropriate response. "You've both asked me not to say anything to Frank, and Dorothy made both of us promise to leave the truth behind her injuries alone ... how do you see me fixing this, Lisa?"

"She talks, you know. When she's drunk or sleepy or sleeping or distracted. She talks about the things you do, who, or what, you are. I've never believed the things she says. I've never gotten it, gotten you, understood her fascination with you. I never cared before today. I've always thought you were like the brother she never had, or that you just fill some gap in her life that I can't." She gasped for air, feeling ahead for the next steps she was going to take.

"Now, today, I want her to be right; want you to be more than you seem. I want you to fix this person who hurt her so that he can't touch her, can't hurt her, again."

Her eyes were still leaking tears, but she wasn't exactly crying. Her skin was blotchy, and her breathing ragged. I saw the thing that Dot talks about sometimes, when she's trying to fix/help/educate me about the human condition. I saw Lisa's fierce love, bigger than she was, washing over me like waves of heat from the woodstove. If I was a touch more human, I would have been jealous ... of Dorothy for having someone love her so much, or of Lisa for being capable of loving; instead, I felt cold and empty inside, and made a nested set of decisions, designed to: make nobody happy, actively anger/ disappoint nearly everyone I knew, but keep a more important promise.

"I'm sorry. I can't do anything. I wish that I could, but I made the same promise that you did. Dorothy must have her reasons, and we need to trust her. I'm sure she'll be fine."

Her swift/strong slap caught me by surprise, and the noise first startled, and then embarrassed everyone within 50 yards of us in the hospital lobby, where we had been talking. Anyone who hadn't heard the slap certainly heard what she yelled/sprayed into my face next.

"Fuck you! Just leave! We don't need you or your help. I don't want to see you again, here, or at my home. Go get your crazy dog and leave the fucking key my wife gave you on OUR kitchen table when you go. I don't want to see a trace of you in our house when I get home later."

She was a mess by the time she finished this final bit of yelling, nose running, eyes red and squinting. She flailed her arms out madly, and both Cokes that had been in my hands (*the nearly empty one and the unopened one*) clattered to the ground.

I turned and walked away, from her, the hospital, the growing crowd, Dorothy, Frank, and out into the parking lot and towards my Honda Element. I noted the huge shape of Barry, a ghost I had picked up last year, but not seen in a while, leaning against my Element, waiting for me.

"Duck!" he said, smiling, miming throwing something, and I heard a low whistling of something lobbed through the air at me; the full Coke can flew by my ear; it clonked off of a Hyundai next to me, popping open and fizzing/spurting all over me as I kept going.

Lisa had followed me out into the parking lot, and screamed at me for a few more seconds, unintelligible rage-fed noise. I walked towards my car without turning, feeling on the back of my head the spot where the next Coke (*or brick*) would hit, but there was only silence from behind me ... and then I heard the wheeze of the sliding doors opening and closing in the distance; she must have gone back inside ... hopefully to Dorothy (*where they would each comfort the other in the righteous glow of protective love that I neither understood nor respected).*

I hadn't believed that Lisa's poker-face would be good enough to fool Frank and/or Dorothy, but her genuine anger might serve for both people. I had 79 percent of a plan in place by the time I had started the car, and was polishing off some rough edges by the time I'd swung by Dunkin' Donuts for a box of cogitating donuts to split with Hope back in the SmartPig office, my Batcave ... once I'd picked her up and left my key on the table in Dot and Lisa's place.

Barry rode with me in silence, smirking a bit, and looking as though he wanted to say something, but each time he drew a *(fake)* breath to begin, I waved him off ... not ready, as yet, to debate/explain my motives/actions with my P.T.S.D.-induced hallucination.

SmartPig Office, Saranac Lake, NY
Monday, 1/20/2014, 9:23 a.m.

Hope had been glad to see me, not least because she could smell the donuts on me when I picked her up from Lisa and Dorothy's home. Although the cats fled (*as they always do*) back to the bathroom to hiss and hide when they saw who it was, I nevertheless filled their food and water bowls, and poured fresh litter over the box in the bathroom (*I have an entirely rational fear of toxoplasmosis rendering all of mankind, including most importantly me, into zombies ... or at least something no longer entirely me ... which is one of eleven valid reasons why I don't mess around with cat feces*).

Before I left the bathroom, I stood up on the toilet, moved the correct ceiling tile aside, and removed the waterproof container that held the "in-case" money I had stored with Dorothy (*and Lisa, albeit without her knowledge*) for nearly eight years. The heavy cast-iron pan that I gave Dorothy and Lisa for Christmas two years ago was hanging over the stove in their kitchen, and I pulled it down and took it with me when I left a few minutes later, hoping that I would re-open that door at some point in the (*hopefully*) near future.

Barry was not waiting in, or next to, the Element when I got back down, but I had the feeling that I would be seeing more of him in the coming hours and days. I drove around to the parking lot behind the building that houses SmartPig in downtown Saranac Lake, and parked at the far end of the lot, by the river, and river-walk.

I often see dogs walking at heel off leashes with their people along this walk, but that's not how either Hope or I are wired ... she would chase/attack squirrels or people she hates (*everyone*) or get scared by a car backfiring and run away, I would worry the whole time that she would chase/attack squirrels or people she hates (*everyone*) or get scared by a car backfiring and run away ... neither of us would have a good time. The leash allowed her to ignore the squirrels and unwashed mass of humanity, and me not to worry about her killing or being killed.

She found a used Starbucks cup, popped the lid off, got her nose stuck inside, and walked back to SmartPig that way, daring me/anyone to call her on it (*or even point it out*). We swung by the Element on the way up, grabbed the box of donuts and what I think of as my 'carry-on' (*the small backpack that I always bring/have with me, containing the bare essentials for camping and everyday life*).

My office was cold and smelled empty. The oddly blue light from the saltwater tank drew my attention, and I ran the tap warm enough to top it off before doling out the first donut to Hope ... a chocolate glazed (*don't start ... she enjoys them, and is old enough that it won't be donuts that kill her*).

I grabbed a trio of Cokes from the Coke-fridge, and fell back into the squishy embrace of my sitting/thinking/sleeping couch, the box of donuts in easy reach. The first Coke drained quickly enough to give me a barely manageable case of brain freeze (*I know that applying my tongue to the roof of my mouth will hasten recovery from the condition, but Mickey taught me twenty years ago that, like getting hit by a wild pitch, you just have to endure the pain ... I can't imagine why I/ anyone would get in the way of an errant baseball, so I have always just taken his word for it*). I had to think my way to a solution to the situation that everyone (*which in this case included me and Dot and Frank*) could live with, and also be off and running before Frank either got the truth (*or enough of it, anyway*) from Lisa/Dorothy, or decided/assumed (*rightly*) that I knew enough to point him in the right direction.

It was a nine donut, and four Coke, problem (*as Holmes would have said ... if he lived in 21st century America*). Hope enjoyed her share of the donuts, as well as the added bonus of tearing the box into tinier and tinier pieces, while I wasted my time (*from her perspective*) preparing my next moves. I looked over the maps Dorothy and I had generated, thought about dead dogs, made a few phone calls, checked a few things on the web, gathered stuff and bits from the closet and various big Tupperware containers and put it all into piles and then eventually bags.

Hope could probably tell from the outset that I was going to foist her off while I did my thing, but she hadn't figured out yet that she wouldn't be staying (*couldn't stay*) with Dorothy ... Hope and I were both on the edge of the known map of our world, about to sail into the unknown (*and unknowable*); the next day or so would be ... interesting. I went downstairs, locking up on my way out, carrying Hope and various bags of clanking and bulky gear over my shoulders.

Barry had been waiting for me down by my car, and spoke before I could pack my gear and dog into the Element, "Tyler, we need to talk about this before you rush into battle to protect the girls and dogs (*and cats, I mentally added, but since he's a figment of my imagination, Barry didn't need to hear it from me ... he left cats out because we both prefer dogs)."*

"I've got this Barry," I said, freaking Hope out a bit ... she couldn't/can't see Barry, but could see the space that I was addressing, and growled a bit, deep in her chest, and hair stood up in a thin ridge along her back. I didn't explain further, both to spare Hope the stress, and because Barry could obviously root around in my head to see what I had planned, since he lived there anyway *(thinking, 'I'm crazy, but not stupid' ... a distinction that the person at my first stop would ... might appreciate).*

I coaxed Hope into the back seat *(imaginary Barry won't tolerate, much less fit, sitting in the back of the Element),* and put my gear into the way back, drove out of town, stopping at the Mobil-Mart to fill the car with gas and the bag hanging off the shifter with junk food, and then made my first stop on my roundabout journey to safeguard Dorothy and the various and multitudinous beasties living at the TLAS.

Some would argue, especially given the clear vision of hindsight, that a healthy dose of revenge or retribution was built into my actions, but that was not my intention ... it would simply be an added benefit enhancing the efficacy/outcome of the plan I was assembling to re-establish order.

Helgafel Farm, Gabriels, NY
Monday, 1/20/2014, 10:13 a.m.

As we passed Donnelly's on our way to the farm, Barry broke the silence, "I sorta get it Tyler. You've got a pretty good idea, but you, and more importantly Bronsen is gonna need more if you wanna close the deal without any more dykes or doggies getting hurt."

I cringed at his word choice, not least because, although I believed that Barry probably wasn't the most open-minded and/or forward thinking guy when alive, his side of the conversation undeniably came from some nook/cranny/attic of my brain, and I wasn't fully comfortable with the way he talked sometimes (*and beyond that, wasn't fully comfortable with not being fully comfortable with it*).

Hope hadn't heard his side, obviously, but she started whining and trying to come up front when I responded, "I disagree … logically, he'll be left with nowhere to go, and have to pick up his toys and go."

"If this jamoke, Bronsen, was a 'logical' person, he would have put Dorothy and not-Dorothy (*it annoyed me that he couldn't/wouldn't remember Lisa's name, but I refused to debate*

219

things like that with Barry … you have to draw lines with your imaginary friends, or they'll take over your life) in the ground last night, a shallow grave topped with logs somewhere in the woods. Leaving them alive was stupid, show-off-y," he said. (*I cringed at his word, but had to agree that trusting Dorothy to keep quiet didn't make much sense, it wasn't one of her strengths … our secrets, I hope, aside*).

"Doubting my brain … my abilities … whatever it is that I am … that I do … it doesn't leave me anywhere useful to go." I addressed this over my shoulder to Hope (*wanting to convince her that I was actually talking to her*); she actually settled down a bit, listening, and smiling at me from between her paws, wrapped in a tight ball of dog.

Barry was right however, the weakness in my process … my plans … was never in the analysis of data, and always in my predictions of what people would do with the situations/alternatives/ultimatums that I created for them. I had been entirely wrong about George and Barry and Justin nearly a year and a half ago, and it had come very close to costing both Hope and me our lives.

I signaled for the turn into the farm stand at Helgafel, and Barry surprised me by saying, "Maybe John will have some advice about how to deal with this mess; maybe you'll listen to him."

John Heimdall (*almost certainly not the name his mother gave him*) was one of the few people who knew about my seeing, and talking with, Barry. We had talked a number of times last summer during (*and immediately after*) a bit of complicated missing persons work I'd done, about P.T.S.D. (*which all three of us agreed that Barry most likely was*) and imaginary friends. Our talks had given me the confidence (*or comfort rationalizing, which may be the same thing*) to accept Barry for what he was, and ignore him when I needed to. Barry had largely disappeared following these discussions … until today. John would have said (*and I would have to agree*) that Barry was manifesting himself in the world outside of my skull (*as opposed to the world inside my skull, where he is constantly muttering and bemoaning his fate from a perspective that sounds as though it is ten feet behind me, and slightly to my right*) as a result of the stress and confusion the attack and injury to Dorothy had introduced into my otherwise orderly (*boring by most peoples' standards*) life.

The snow in the turnaround for the Helgafel farm stand was deep and rutted and messy, evidently they didn't bother plowing it in the winter. John appeared from around the corner of the farm stand (*not the little cabin by the gate where he lived, as I had expected*), surprising both Barry and I (*which is, I think, why John does it*).

"Christ, for a not-tiny, sorta-old guy, he moves pretty good," Barry said.

Barry judges everyone by his size/scale … so we're all either tiny or not-tiny, nobody (*yet*) has been described as 'big' in our conversations (*Barry stooped his way through doorways in life, and probably squashed the scales at 400 pounds*).

"Yes, he does … try not to let Hope out," I said as I slid out of the Element, only catching myself at the last minute (*remembering that since he wasn't here, Barry didn't need to open, much less re-close the car door to join me in the driveway*).

I looked over in time to see John scanning the passenger side of my car before turning to speak to me … it bothered me that I was obviously rattled enough by events to slip up like that in front of (*real … human*) people.

"Tyler, nice to see you," he said, with a smile that looked real (*although I've practiced a lifetime, and can produce relatively convincing fakes myself*). "Do we have company as well today? Barry?" he asked, looking in Barry's general direction.

"Nice to meet you," Barry said, aiming a wiseass smirk in my direction, waiting to see how I would handle it.

"Barry ... shut up. Yes, John, Barry's here, insofar as he is anywhere (*except at the bottom of a mineshaft near Tahawus, I thought to myself*). It would be easier for me if both of you would address yourselves to me, even if you need/want/wish to speak to the other," I said.

They both gave me similarly amused and skeptical looks, so I added, "John obviously can't hear you Barry ... and you aren't looking in the right place, John," I said.

"Let's all go inside then, shall we?" John offered, with a sweeping gesture of his arms that took in me and Barry ... and Whiteface Mountain in the distance behind us, and any imaginary friends that Barry might have (*a mirror-in-mirror thought that I cut off before it could get any footing in my already addled brain*).

We trudged through the calf-deep snow, and went into his little cabin ... to the comfortable smell of books and wood smoke and expensive tobacco and espresso (*the sharp smell of which I enjoy, although I find the taste and temperature of it repellent*). Barry had either been absent, or stayed outside, during my recent visits, and now spun around taking it in and grunting with approval.

"Nice place," he said.

John spoke at the same instant, "What can I do for you, both?"

I walked over to the dorm-fridge that John kept in one corner or his somewhat Spartan cabin, and took out a Coke, "A Coke to start, and then I think that I need to bounce some thoughts around, if you have the time/patience/inclination to listen."

Barry seemed put off that I hadn't passed his compliment along to John, and moved over to the window to stare out, and up the hill, at the big farmhouse behind us, pointedly ignoring me.

"I'm guessing that something has happened. It must be

something major to have brought Barry," John gestured around the room. "Sorry Tyler, where is he?"

I pointed to the window, while Barry raised a hand (*pointlessly*), "... to have brought Barry out of 'retirement', and brought you here on this snowy morning, when I'm sure that you'd rather be hanging from a tree in the woods somewhere (*John is convinced that both hammock-camping and winter-camping are foolish life-choices ... and that the two taken together, and at the same time, are lunacy*)."

I quickly filled him in on the basics of what had happened last night and this morning, while he fiddled with his tricky coffee maker, which hissed and burbled and produced cup after tiny cup of tarlike espresso for him. When I was finished telling him what I knew and what I suspected about the events leading up to and surrounding Dorothy's assault by Bronsen, he nodded slowly, tipping the last of his coffee shot into his mouth and looking at me first, before turning to address Barry.

"So now he's planning to head off to fight the dragons to save the honor of the fair maiden, but that unusual brain of his doesn't really understand human beings, and he's likely to forget, or more likely overlook, some behavioral quirk or pattern among the black hats that will result in our boy Tyler ending up chopped into high-protein food for fight-trained pit bulls and shepherds," John said.

"Too fucking right," Barry agreed, looking at John and nodding.

"Barry thinks you might be right, which is why I came to talk with you, John," I avoided looking over when Barry gave a choked laugh.

"And glad I am that you did. I find you a bright young lad, with an interesting way about you, and feel the world's a richer place with you in it. I'm sure our friend Barry feels the same, since without you (*and because of me, I think, but don't bother to say, since they both are well aware of the events surrounding Barry's death*), he would have less of a place in this miserable world than he does now."

"Which is saying something, since living inside your melon is the pits, Tyler. No offense," Barry said, cutting in before I could reply to John.

I ignored both of them and attempted to charge forward, in hopes of regaining the point of this conversation.

"So in the hope of regaining the point of this conversation, and visit, let me tell you what I'm thinking, and the two of you may be able to help me tighten things up here and there ... hopefully resulting in a plan ... or series of connected plans that leaves me alive and Dorothy and Lisa and the shelter all safe," I said.

They both wore human facial expressions indicative of attentive listening as I went through my nested plans, smiled and nodded and chuckled at various points, but were both frowning and shaking their heads when I finished. I found this dismaying, as it felt (*to me*) like a logical plan that took in all of the variables/factors, and was likely to yield the desired effect(*s*).

For John's sake, I gestured at him and Barry, "The two of you are giving me the same skeptical look. What I've laid out should end his dog fighting business up here in the Adirondacks, and with that off the table, Bronsen and his minions (*a term I associate with Dorothy these days, which made me wince slightly in this context*) should shut down operations."

John gestured in the direction of imaginary-Barry, and then spoke, "I'm sure that Barry'd say much the same thing, but since I wouldn't hear it, let me break it down, yah?"

Barry nodded at me and I passed it along to John, curious to hear about my mistake/underestimation of the human element … this is something I am continually guilty of, although normally in ways that don't have much impact (*whereas errors in these proceeding could have dire consequences for myself and other people/things that I care about*).

"To be sure, he'll have to close up shop for sure after your tricks, but it'll just make a man like Bronsen, or me, or Barry, want to come after you all the more, lad," John said.

"You can beat him this way, but what you need is to knock his dick in the dirt. That or kill him," said Barry.

I must have made a face, because John asked; I related Barry's answer, including the imagery (*which surprised both him and me, as it's not something in my wheelhouse to even think of, ordinarily*).

"He's not wrong. Jaysus, I'm taking sides with your P.T.S.D. in an argument against you, boy; that's us deep in the weeds, sure enough. Remember the lesson of Bonzo Madrid in Ender's Game, you need to beat him so badly that he never wants to try you again."

"Bonzo died, John, Stilson too, and I have no interest in killing anyone … ever again." We'd had this discussion numerous times, from numerous angles.

"Then he may have already won, Tyler. If he's willing to go further, fight dirtier or get bloodier than you, and he knows it, and he's as bad as you surmise, then you either need to find a soft spot, or chink in his armor, or rent a U-Haul and start gathering boxes for your move."

John finished this with a smile, but some sadness in his eyes as well. He had 'retired' from (*what I have always assumed was*) a criminal life downstate, and presumably knew what he was talking about in this instance.

"Jeez, Tyler, I wish you had this respect for life before you dumped me and Justin in that shitty hole in the woods," Barry grumped. "Prolly coulda worked something out to stop things short of killin' us all."

"You tried to kill me first, Barry ... twice if memory serves (*which it always does*)," I said.

John stared from me to the space that Barry seemed to occupy. I continued, "What soft spot might you have had that I could take advantage of, Barry?"

"Family," both Barry and John said at once.

"Friends and associates are in the game, and understand, or at least live with, the rules; family is different," John said.

Barry nodded over by the window.

I felt a series of little ideas coming to me, and covered/stalled by walking over to the tiny fridge John kept Cokes in, and grabbed two more. I popped the first and drained it in a few seconds under a minute.

"Ha! Fifty-seven seconds is a prime, right?" Barry said, having obviously started counting when I popped the top. His recent contributions/vocalizations had been limited to fishing around in my brain for math facts related to occurrences in my everyday life (*a longtime hobby of mine that he seemed to be adopting the longer he lived in the back of my head*).

"Sadly, no, Barry ... it is a semi-prime though, having two primes, nineteen and three, as factors. Additionally, you'll be happy to know that you're not alone among the great minds of our time in mistaking fifty-seven for a prime ... mathematician Alexander Grothendieck once made the same mistake, and he essentially fathered the modern theory of algebraic geometry," I said.

"He lives inside you, and makes math mistakes. How's that work?" John asked.

"I don't know how Barry works ... neither does he," I answered.

"What I do know is that you two gave me an idea for a strategy ... let me talk it through to see how dumb the more functional humans in the room, real or otherwise, think it is," I said.

I had 72 percent of my idea formed when I started talking, and when we stopped 15 minutes later to take Hope for a walk, it was up to 81 percent. Barry and John poked holes and highlighted flaws in my plans and reasoning, and by the time I had finished all of the Cokes that John had in his fridge, 97 minutes had passed, which I pointed out to Barry was not only a prime number ... it was a happy prime ... he grumbled and went out to wait by the car, mumbling about haunting supermodels in Hawaii, instead of a math-geek in the frozen north.

"It can work, but you'll need a poker-face, or a change of heart," John said.

"I can do my part, if you're sure that you don't mind the role we jointly assigned you. Can you leave the farm once/if you find out the stuff we'll need?" I asked.

"No problem, I sneak away a few times each year for various reasons, and mid-winter is a great time not to be in the Adirondacks. I'll have one of the kids from the farm stay down here in my cabin with your nasty beagle," John said.

I hadn't asked, hadn't really thought about Hope yet, but he'd skipped ahead, and I had to agree that it made sense.

"She's no picnic, even for the people that she likes, both of whom will be unavailable for the next few days at least," I said.

"There's a new kid, Terrence, who's like a turkey whisperer, and those things are at least as horrible as your wee dog, Hope. They'll get on fine, and he'll be happy for a few days light work," John said.

I counted three thousand dollars from the money I'd been keeping up in Dorothy and Lisa's bathroom ceiling out of my pocket and into John's hand; he tried to refuse, but I countered, "This project will cost you time and money. You have to at least let me help with the money end of things."

He agreed, called up to the big house for Terrence to come down, and walked out with me to the Element. I grabbed Hope's food and toys and blanket, and we waited ... all of us. Terrence came down and was perfect when meeting Hope ... she bit him.

"We'll get on fine, Mr. Cunningham, don't you worry," he said once John had filled him in on the favor Terrence was being asked to do for me/Hope/John/us.

I was surprised to find that I was (*in fact*) worried, and gave Hope's greying chin an extra-long rub before climbing into the Element to head south and east, towards the next of my many stops on what would turn out to be a busy day.

Hinckley State Forest, north of Utica, NY
Monday, 1/20/2014, 6:27 p.m.

Barry made a good passenger, by which I mean that he sat there without speaking for the next three hours while I drove down to Albany, stopping at Scotty's Truck Stop (*Exit 16 on the Northway*) for gas and junk food and a shower.

Scotty's is my favorite place to stop when driving from up to down in my part of New York State, because they have everything I could need for the rest of my life under a single roof. The best part is that nothing I do, or want, or buy 18 of, hasn't been done or bought by scarier/smellier people than me a million times in the last week.

I got clean and dressed in what I think of as my functional artisan costume (*worn canvas pants and shirt, lightly spattered with paint and such, along with ancient steel-toed work boots with burn marks on them*) ... some of the time, my SmartPig office/home/batcave serves as an art studio, and I play the part of artisan, painting and building and stitching any of dozens of different things I've tried my hand at while living in the Adirondacks.

At the check-out, while paying cash for most of a cubic yard of junk food (*and a few choice other items*), I noted that the young woman behind the register wore a moderately ugly broach crafted from a mélange of metal and clay and semi-precious gems, obviously made by someone with technical competence in various fields that would be of use to me in the near future.

"Great," I said, as she handed me my change. "Say, that's a nice piece of jewelry. Where did you get it?" I asked, hoping it wasn't from a recently dead grandmother, or fiancé serving in the Gulf … her minute frown when she looked down to remind herself what I was talking about told me most of what I needed to know (*which is saying something, since I am not very good at reading facial expressions and gestures in other humans … strangely, I'm not bad with dogs … go figure*).

"Some girlfriends and me found it at a street fair down in the city one time when we went down to see 'Lion King', why?" she asked.

"My sister's birthday is tomorrow, and I haven't been able to find the right thing to get for her … she loves that kind of steampunk-y, handcrafted stuff."

I was taking a risk, but remembered a discussion with Dorothy about how to talk with girls/women about other women, and that sisters are a safe and non-threatening topic. I almost continued with an offer, but she broke in first.

"Hang on a second, okay?" she said, and turned to speak briefly to the other woman behind the counter before walking back towards the Red Bull fridge at the end of a long rack of candy.

"It's a pretty piece; that's for sure, and I love that you're looking for your sister. My brother don't remember my number, 'cept when he needs somethin'. You want it?" she asked.

"Yes, very much," I replied, eager to save myself another stop along the way to try and find something like this piece.

"How does fifty bucks sound?" she asked.

"Sounds good," I said, reaching for my wallet, and peeling off two twenties and a ten (*and thinking that she might have paid twenty for it*) before she changed her mind or upped her price.

"Hey, my friend Carol is working in the restaurant end today, and has a pair of earrings from the same guy, the same trip. Wouldja like me to see if she'd sell hers also?" she asked.

"That would be great, if you wouldn't mind," I said.

I peeled off another fifty in mixed bills and gave it to her, and she dashed away and back again in a 84 seconds; handing me a pair of earrings still warm from her friend Carol's lobes (*I tried not to shudder, with only marginal success, but already had the loot in hand, so it probably didn't matter*).

"Thanks mister!" she said, and turned to walk, and then duck back behind, the counter. "I hope your sister has a happy birthday."

It didn't appear that more interaction was required, so without answering I grabbed my bags of road food and headed back out to fill up the Element and was on my way.

I made it the rest of the way down to my first stop in the Albany area in 43 minutes (*as I made my turn off of the Northway, it entered my head that 43 is the third Wagstaff Prime ... something that is only important to a few cryptographers associated with the New Marsenne Conjecture, and notable to me because Wagstaff himself is working at Purdue on something titled "The Cunningham Project"*).

I had called ahead to my destination to be sure that someone would be around, that they would have what I needed, and because fore-knowledge would dull any suspicions that they might have.

"Robert Noble?" the man in the Dynasty Chemicals office asked when I walked in.

"Call me Bob, but yes, that's me. I called a while ago to inquire about some supplies for my jewelry business," I said.

"Yup. I'm Phil, and I took the message. Two hundred pounds of iron oxide? Is that right?" he said.

"Yessir," I said, thankful once again for the lack of affect my personality makeup includes, which prevents nervous tics and tells.

"That's quite a pile of the stuff, whatcha need it all for, if you don't mind my asking?" he asked (*heedless/regardless/ clueless of the fact that I did, in fact, mind his asking ... quite a bit*).

"Not at all. I've been lucky the last year selling my jewelry, and other things I make," I said, pulling out the newly acquired broach and earrings, "I use iron oxide in paints and glazes and alloys ... throughout my process, really ... you'd be amazed (*something that I have found is always a sure sign of something I will find non-amazing*)," I added.

As a cop, Frank has become somewhat of an expert in the ways people lie so he has been tutoring me ... he assures me that details and props and being just a bit boring are the keys to the kingdom of confidence-scams.

"Just look at the colors I'm able to bring out in these pieces."

Phil's eyes glazed a bit, and he almost visibly backed away from my artist shtick. He pulled out a clipboard and pen, and started going through the details of payment and loading.

I was so pleased that when he asked if there was anything else, I almost added the aluminum oxide. I wanted to insure a low profile though, and was certain that I could get it at the next place with as little trouble, and less chance of raising flags or eyebrows when (*if*) my endgame made the papers (*it seemed unlikely, but why take chances*).

I paid him with cash, backed the Element up to their loading bay, and let a guy load the surprisingly small paper sacks into the space in back that I'd cleared. Once loaded and thanked, I drove off to repeat the process (*only this time for 75 pounds of aluminum oxide*) at SureChem, with the help of Diana and a near-twin of the guy who had loaded the iron oxide for me.

I spent the rest of the afternoon circling Albany, eating donuts, finding a Walmart, drinking Cokes, shopping at EMS, stopping for dumplings at a Chinese place Dorothy had one mentioned, cleaning out whole shelves at Dick's and at Sports Authority, before heading out again. This time I aimed west along Route 90.

I pulled into the parking lot at the Utica Zoo 73 minutes later (*straining for meaning for a few seconds before it came to me that 73 is the fourth star number ... the third being 37, which is a permutable prime — an emirp — with 73*), to visit with Tony, a man I'd helped the previous April (*and who had forced a promise from me to stop in for a minute every time I drove through town*). Promise kept, I headed north and east and (*more importantly*) back towards the Adirondack Park on Route 28.

I felt tired and buzzed from road food and lots of Cokes, and turned off 28 and onto Route 365, which took me to the Hinckely State Forest, where I searched for, and quickly found, a nice enough spot to park for some fraction of the night, to hang my hammock, to cook myself a dinner, and to get some rest before getting back to the business at hand.

An hour later, fed and watered and stretched and peed, I climbed into my hammock for the night (*safe from the cold night air thanks to the hammock sock enclosing me and my sleeping bag)* and prepared to go to sleep (*a process which ordinarily takes from 15 to 90 seconds*); I was surprised when sleep wouldn't come ... when instead, I was visited by visions of the Dorothy I met in the Spring of 2002, nearly twelve years earlier.

Tri-Lakes Animal Shelter, Saranac Lake, NY
Wednesday, 3/20/2002, 10:05 a.m.

The hall was noisy/smelly/busy/crowded, all things I
dislike and try to avoid whenever possible in my life. I
almost turned around, seeing the short walk back to my
Honda Element, and similarly short drive back to my office
(*which would be quiet/smell-free/idle/empty*), with only a small
detour for a minimally interactive exchange with the people
behind the counter at the Chinese restaurant that could fuel
an afternoon of reading/research ... but before I could
leave, I was pulled/yanked into human contact by a tall,
thin woman who grabbed my arm and spoke into my ear
from only inches away.

"Don't leave. The dogs need to get out, and we don't
have time this morning," she said.

She must have felt the muscles and tendons in my arm
tense and jerk at her touch, and instinctively backed away
from me ... either out of fear or respect or courtesy or
some mix of those things, and maybe others (*none of which
were included in my factory installed software*).

"Who hasn't been out for a walk in the longest?" I

asked.

"Miles," she said, without having to stop to think, "nobody takes him out but me."

"Why?" I asked.

"He's big and he jumps and barks and pulls," she said.

"Will he bite me?" I asked.

"Not unless you're another dog and you try to take his food or toys," she answered, smiling a bit at the end (*this sometimes is indicative of humor, which is lost/wasted on me, but sometimes means other, equally alien things, so I generally make a policy of ignoring the subtleties of human emotions/expressions*).

"I'm not, and I won't ... may I please take Miles for a walk?" I said.

She looked at me for a few seconds, perhaps hoping for me to return her smile of moments before, or laugh, as people sometimes do, but I don't smile naturally or easily (*although I do have a collection of eleven smiles, I've practiced at length over the years*) and I'm even worse at modifying my speaking voice to impart meaning, or responding to signals from people (*beyond shouting if they are on fire, or whispering if someone holds a single erect finger in front of their mouth*).

Three seconds later, she turned and walked down the hall to a door with a 'TLAS Staff Only' sign on it, opened the door, and disappeared. She reappeared 47 seconds later (*one of my lucky numbers, so I took this to be a good sign*) preceded by a variety of scratching and thumping and metallic clanging sounds from behind the closed door.

She was pulled through the door by a very tall, but very thin black dog with sores/scabs/blood on and around his ears. The cats (*23, I had counted and classified them by size and colors upon my arrival*) scattered like the townsfolk in the westerns I used to watch with my father on Sundays (*Spaghetti Westerns, he used to call them*). The dog started towing the woman back down the hall towards me, barking with each lunging yank of the leash. They arrived, and the woman wrapped the leash around my wrist a number of times, being careful however, not to touch my hand or arm while doing so.

"Whatever you do, don't let go, and don't sit down, or he'll be all over you. He sometimes calms down in ten minutes or so; if he doesn't, or if he freaks you out too much, come back, and we'll find another dog that needs a walk," she said.

"How long can I keep him out?" I asked.

"Nobody has ever asked that … ever."

She tilted her head, staring into my eyes until I looked down at the dog and said hello to him, "Hello Miles."

I looked back up and she was still looking for something in my eyes or face … I worried that she might not see what she wanted to (*or worse might see that there was nothing to see*), and took Miles outside and into the melting snow of an Adirondack spring day before she could stop me.

The fresh/cold/still air was soothing after the smell and warm humidity and noise of the shelter, and I might have paused to enjoy it if Miles hadn't taken off at top speed for the horizon. I assumed that he knew what he was doing, and since I had no destination in mind, I ran (*was dragged*) after him at the end of the leash. We ended up in the woods behind the shelter, cutting across a series of short trails winding through the woods; stopping every 30 seconds or so when the nylon rope between us would get hung up around a tree or Miles would shimmy under a fallen log, and I would have to dive and squiggle to keep up. It was during one of these high-speed limbo maneuvers that he jumped on my back, firmly planting my face in the cornmeal snow and crusty ice.

I tried a push-up to dislodge him, but he maintained his balance on my back despite my rocking from side to side as I tried to rise. Eventually, some 17 seconds later, he saw something off to our right, and leapt that way, pull my arm out from under me, but also freeing me to stand again ... I did so as quickly as I was able, and just as quickly sat down on a rock that was mostly free from snow. Miles had lost interest in whatever had drawn his eye a moment ago, and took my sitting as an invitation to sit in my lap ... he barked some insults/warnings in the general direction of whatever it had been, and bounded up and onto my legs and chest (*all 70-ish pounds of him*).

A few seconds later, Miles had tasted my entire head, and was looking at me, waiting for me to do something ... I felt in my jacket pocket for a granola bar, and his eyes followed my hand, delighted by the crinkly plastic sound my fingers found in the hardest to reach pocket. I was trying to figure out how to unwrap the bar with one hand when Miles solved my troubles by gently/nimbly/instantly taking it from my fingers with bared teeth ... he threw his head back, presumably catching the bar at a better angle, chewed and rolled his jaws around for 32 seconds, and then spit out the emptied wrapper on the ground for me to pick up.

I entered the shelter 67 minutes after leaving with Miles. I was met by the woman who had given me Miles to walk. Her face was interesting to study as she relieved me of the dog (*I got a book for Christmas once from a well-meaning friend of my parents with exaggerated pictures showing human emotions, and they looked much like hers in the first few seconds that I was in the shelter after my walk with Miles*). I saw worry at my wet and lightly ripped clothing, surprise at the not-jumping/barking dog at my side, and happiness at my (*or perhaps the dog*) having returned to the relative safety of the shelter. There was a cat sitting on the counter, watching everything (*as cats do*), and when I leaned on the counter and began to talk with the cat (*and move my hand in to rub its ears*), it gave me a skeptical look, jumped lightly to the floor and ran away from me (*as cats also, inevitably, do*).

"Funny. Miles is impossible, and Lila," she said, pointing down the hallway at the tail behind the retreating cat, "is easy; friendly with everyone."

"I like dogs, and dogs like me. I feel the same way about cats, but for some reason they don't like me ... ever," I said.

This is the sort of thing that more standard humans feel embarrassed about, but I'm missing embarrassment in much the same way that I'm missing a natural capacity for, or understanding of, smiles.

"I can see why they like you. Miles hasn't had that kind of attention for a long time, maybe ever. The real question I have to ask is why do you like him, and dogs in general, so much?" she asked it lightly, but I could see from the way that she was looking at me that she was interested in my answer.

"I've never disappointed a dog. I disappoint every human I've ever met at some point, because I don't understand what they think/want/need ... they get sad or angry, I think, and leave ... or make me leave," I said.

"I'm Dorothy," she said, moving minutely to stick out her hand and then covering/continuing the motion to scratch her left arm instead.

"My name is Tyler Cunningham, Dorothy. I am pleased to meet you," I said, falling into human-greeting patterns I'd learned ten years earlier.

"We're open tomorrow at 9 a.m., and there are plenty of dogs who would love a long walk in the woods, Tyler," she said.

"Okay," I said and left.

Tyler Note:

I came the next day, and a few days each week for the next twelve years to help with dogs (*and sometimes the cats, although they continued/continue to dislike/fear me for some reason that they keep to themselves, as they do with most things*). I am certain that I have disappointed Dorothy a number of times, but she has neither left, nor asked me to leave because of who/what I am ... this, in the end, will be the simple reason for Bronsen's undoing

Hinckley State Forest, north of Utica, NY
Tuesday, 1/21/2014, 4:39 a.m.

The waning moon was bright enough to shine through the
bare tree limbs above me and my hammock as I floated,
suspended between earth and sky, seeing the light through
the sheer nylon of the hammock-sock. I reached up to grab
my headlamp off of the ridgeline and got a shower of
shocking/refreshing condensed snow in my face for my
efforts, as my hand brushed the roof of the hammock
sock. I swung up and out of the sock and hammock, found
my shoes rolled up in a tarp on the ground, oriented myself
in the dark and quiet woods, and headed out to find a tree.

Once I took care of elimination and hydration (*the former
at the base of an ancient birch tree three feet in diameter, the latter
after opening the hatch and digging out the cooler in the back of my
Element ... although in winter, it often serves as a warmer*), I
switched off the headlamp and waited for my senses to
come back into night-function. Because my light was never
in my eyes, my vision came back quickly, followed soon by
my hearing (*mouth slightly open seems to let me hear the night
sounds better*), and then my sense of smell ... smoke, distant

but definite … campfire with leftovers and food packaging tossed in.

I can't think before I pee when I wake up (*if that's more than you need to know about me, then pretend you didn't read that*). This is why I didn't note the smell immediately upon waking; in fact, it occurs to me only now, that the faint/distant smoke/campfire was probably the reason that I woke from my sleep. A winter camper up and around at this hour is unusual. In the ordinary course of events, I would indulge my natural curiosity and ninja my way through the woods to the other camp to see what, if anything, was up … not for any reason beyond wanting to (*which is generally how I live, and have lived in recent years, my life*).

On this day, I would not … could not … investigate. I had miles to go and people to see and important wrongs to right, and refused to let myself get sidetracked before dawn. I tried to project myself through the woods as I broke down, and packed up, camp … tried to get a vision of the people at the other end of a dark and woodsy walk. It's a mystery, but it's someone else's mystery … on this day I belonged to Dorothy, which meant heading north and west toward Lowville and Billy … Wild Bill Dunham … a man who owed me a favor.

13 Ridgeview Terrace, Lowville, NY
Tuesday, 1/21/2014, 7:14 a.m.

The drive from Hinckley to Lowville was unremarkable, except for a Quik-E-Mart in the middle of the woods, shining like a lost Las Vegas, jam-packed with relatively fresh Dunkin' Donuts and genuine Canadian Cokes. I got two dozen of each, and had made an impressive dent in my supply of both by the time I pulled (*significantly too early*) into Billy's driveway. I listened to the car cooling and clicking, powered down another donut and Coke, and was about to give him a call (*inefficient given our proximity, but I've been told that it's more polite than knocking on peoples' doors before six in the morning*) when he rapped on the window by my head. (*He later admitted that he had seen me pull in without recognizing the car, snuck out his back door, cut through a neighbor's yard, and approached my Element from the rear*).

"Tyler, you're a bit more than three hours early. C'mon inside and I can start a pot of coffee to go with all of those donuts."

Billy, like a number of people spread throughout northern New York, likes me, feels grateful to me, feels as though he owes me, but doesn't really know me at all. I cannot tolerate beverages that are any hotter than cold, and coffee tops my list of disliked food/drink (*it's tied with hundreds of others, including every alcoholic drink I've tried, papaya, watercress, gluten-free bread, and honey ... although that's 92 percent because bees creep me out*).

I helped Billy (*who was introduced to me as "Billy" by his uncle Tommy, which is why I think of him by that name although the rest of the known universe refers to this man as "Wild Bill Dunham"*) through an interesting (*for me, troubling and likely terrifying for him*) time 73 months ago. One of his numerous firearms was involved in a homicide and he was incorrectly implicated. I had discovered the truth, found that revealing it (*and the actual murderer*) would be impossible, and so created the appropriate (*to my way of thinking*) evidence to place in such a way as to identify the murderer and insure Billy's release and complete exoneration. This was effected through the relatively simple use of a rifle and bullet similar to those used in the murder, and the enthusiastic use/wounding of the victim's more than willing twin (*interestingly enough, the science contained within a study published only months after I was able to help Billy would have made my workaround fail utterly*).

In appreciation for my efforts, Billy and his uncle "loaned" me a family house near Moab, Utah at the end of one particularly cold and dark winter. While I considered us more than even, they continued through the years to contact me at fairly regular intervals with offers for other homes in other places, or begging me to ask for something — anything — that I needed ... ever.

It had likely been something of a relief when I had called Billy yesterday to arrange our meeting ... it has been my experience over the years that people don't like the feeling of gratitude hanging over them for years and years.

"I'm alright, Billy," I said, grabbing the full box of donuts to bring along for both of us, "but we can talk inside, and I need to use your bathroom."

He showed me where the bathroom was, and when I came out (*having splashed my face and brushed my teeth with a travel toothbrush I grabbed on my way out of the Element*) there was a breakfast spread with my donuts as the centerpiece. I poured myself a tall glass of milk from a glass bottled labeled from a Lowville organic dairy farm, and filled a bowl with a variety of fruit that would make a locovore cry.

I heard a slow scuffing/scraping sound, and turned to see Billy's ancient German Shepherd, Dutch, limping in, and then over to sniff hello to me.

"Hey Dutch, old boy," I said, thumping his side. "How's it going?" (*This is a cultural construct I'm told most people understand, whereby I appear to be talking to the dog, but am actually making the inquiry to his owner*).

"Fucking Lyme Disease!" Billy sighed, with enough despair to grab even my attention, "He's having a rough winter."

The truth is that Dutch has ehrlichiosis, which is in many ways similar to Lyme, but often, and somewhat unfairly to Dutch and Billy, worse, especially for German Shepherds.

"Were those papers of any use to his vets?" I asked. I'd done some research on the subject after talking with Billy 17 months ago, and sent him some materials that offered promise, or at least hope.

"Yah, his doc got some of the meds and pain-stuff for Dutch, but there's just so much any dog can do with that monster raging around inside of him. His kidneys are done, platelets too, he bruises and bleeds when the wind blows, and the cold hurts his joints something awful. I started sleeping downstairs because he can't climb up to my bedroom anymore."

Billy looked as though he was angry and sad and tears were running down his face, as from an open tap. I spent a minute looking very closely at the fruit to give him time to hide that part of him that I find interesting (*real people do that, all the time*). He coughed and started in, brushing the other talk aside.

"You were a little vague on the phone, Tyler. What can I do for you? What do you need?" he asked.

"You're still a 'gun fancier' and hunter, correct?" I asked.

Billy nodded, gesturing around the room/house at the mounts and stuffed beasties everywhere, as well as the guns on display on the walls and in glass-fronted cabinets.

"I need to borrow some of your camping and hunting gear, a few rifles with some ammo, your wallet and its contents, and the truck that I saw parked in the driveway," I said.

"Oh, is that all?" he asked, in a tone that should have (*but didn't*) tell me something beyond his spoken words.

"Yes ... no," I said.

He looked at me, smiling a little ... another expression that in this instance I was unable to wring meaning from.

"I'll have to damage the truck in order to meet my goals, but the rest of the gear will likely be fine ... possibly untouched."

"How the fuck will crashing my truck help you, and why my truck? Why not your weird boxy-thing?" he asked (*77 percent of the population fails to see the Honda Element for the spectacular vehicle that it is*).

"I need to be you for a couple of days, Billy," I replied. "A person that I care about is in trouble on par with the trouble you had six years ago (*I knew from prior experience with people that my ordinary level of precision would confuse and distract*

Billy from the matter at hand, so I didn't use months/weeks/days).
As with your problem, traditional solutions will not work
(*or at least I couldn't see how they would*), so I need to take a
more roundabout approach to get to the other side of her
current issues."

He nodded, possibly encouragingly.

"I promise that I will repair your truck before returning
it to you. In fact, getting it repaired is a much more
important component of my plan than damaging it in the
first place."

At this point, Billy tilted his head, in much the same way
that dogs do when they are confused.

"You're not going to shoot anyone with my guns this
time are you?" he asked.

"No, and remember, she was willing, even eager that
time. The rifles ... and maybe that ridiculously ginormous
handgun you showed me last time I stopped in (*on my way
to the Utica Zoo, 17 months ago*) ... they likely won't even come
out of their cases," I said.

He started to say something, but I had to cut him off.

"Except I also need a shotgun, and some of those
special rounds you showed me that time ... and I probably
will be shooting someone with that, although they won't
die unless something goes dramatically wrong."

Billy shook his head, and slid over a pad and pen for my
list.

"Whatever. If I've got it, you can have it. If you kill
someone with it, drop it in a river. If you don't and can
bring it back, great. I owe you; always will."

He looked at my hand scribbling furiously, read the list
upside down, and continued, "I'd love to hear about it
afterwards if you can, but I guess that, like with me that
time, there might be whole chunks not for sharing."

"I can only agree to tell you what I can when it's over,

assuming it all works out okay … if it doesn't, I may call and tell you to report everything stolen … probably won't happen that way though," I said.

We spent another 23 minutes going over the list, schlepping the gear and guns from his well-organized garage (*which was sized for two cars and held none*) out to the showroom-clean pickup truck in the driveway, moving some of the stuff from my Element into his truck, and then saying awkward goodbyes. (*My goodbyes are always awkward, and Billy seemed grateful for a chance to show his thanks, but kept patting his truck, while looking doubtfully at my mud-spattered Element*). The last thing I did, before climbing up into the big Ford truck, was to trade wallets with Billy (*he looks somewhat similar to me, but if I was stopped or checked out, his ID wouldn't fool anyone looking at it closely*), and hand him a stack of cash for incidentals for the next few days (*although I kept the majority of the cash with me for my expenses, which doubtlessly would be heavier*).

I drove out of his driveway and headed back towards home with him waving at his receding truck (*and probably me too … but mostly the truck, I think*).

The Quik-E-Mart on the way out of town had a rack of burner phones. I picked up a semi-smart phone, found the town's library (*to steal Wi-Fi and setup one of the burners with a 315 area code phone number*); I texted the new number to John and headed back into the woods of the Adirondack Park, my home on most days.

I swung back by Billy's house, thinking to grab one more thing from the Element, but kept going when I saw Billy, red-faced and struggling, carrying Dutch back up the three stairs and into the house, presumably from a walk … a Dorothy-memory, from years ago, popped up and consumed the present-day real world.

Tri-Lakes Animal Shelter, Saranac Lake, NY
Saturday, 9/17/2006, 1:49 p.m.

Dorothy's call woke me from a short nap that I'd been taking on the couch in the world headquarters of SmartPig, my offices in Saranac Lake (*I have no 'home', per se, since I can nap on the couch at SmartPig, and sleep most nights outside in the Adirondack wilderness*).

I'd been up reading through the night about diagnosis rates for autism in the US, the continued spread/rise of invasive mega fauna in the Florida Keys and Everglades, an interesting survey of cryptographic methodologies in World War Two, and collections of camping recipes. I'd reclined on the couch when my brain was full, to let the warehouse workers in the back (*I pictured an even mix of glasses-on-chains shushing librarians and sweaty/stinking/cursing stevedores organizing the newly deposited information into piles and files, and then moving them around the dusty shelves in the back of my skull to best effect*) organize things. At any rate, the process was only partly finished when the phone shrieked from across the room, and I lurched upright to answer it.

"What?" I said.

"Tyler, it's Dorothy," she said.

"Yes, I gathered."

I can identify most of the people that I am familiar with after only a few syllables, so it always seems a waste to me to use additional syllables with pointless identification.

"You need to come over, as soon as you can; Miles is crashing," she said simply, nothing else was necessary.

Miles and I had met four years and six months previously, and while I had found a home in Saranac Lake, he had not been so lucky. I walked him a couple of times each week, and had started making cookies and collars for him (*and the other dogs as well*) in the hope that exercise and play and treats would help him socialize sufficiently to attract/keep the attention of a forever home ... to date it hadn't worked. His behavior over the years of our acquaintance had mellowed, but some (*probably much, or even most*) of that had been due to his declining health. He had not been a puppy, or healthy, when we first met, and the stress and isolation of the behavioral room in the back of the shelter had not helped ameliorate his condition. A combination of kidney and liver and heart failure had been robbing him of his strength and vitality increasingly in the last year.

"By crashing, do you mean ...?" I started to ask.

"I mean that he's suffering, dying, and that we need to do the right thing by him (*I could tell by her tone — I had studied Dorothy's speech patterns extensively — that she was using the royal we, referring to the shelter that she ran/runs*). He likes you more than anyone else at the shelter, and I think that you might want to do the right thing by him as well."

She left that hanging in the air, nearly, but not quite, a question. I was flummoxed as to what she meant.

"Is it expensive?" I asked.

"Shut up, and get over here Tyler," she said and hung

up … I had obviously guessed wrong.

I splashed my face and brushed my teeth, and did the other things that people do when rising in the morning (*although it was by now a few minutes after noon … I keep unusual hours*), but all the while I was thinking about Miles and Dorothy's words and what death means to humans.

I arrived at the TLAS with plans and packages 23 minutes after being woken. I re-tooled the plans within seconds of walking in the door of the shelter. Miles was laying down in the hallway, rheumy eyes following my steps as I walked in; he was surrounded by cats. In past visits, even as recently as the previous week, all of the cats in the shelter would head to high ground when Miles was around; he would snap at any cat that got close (*or even thought about getting close*). Today was different, the ordinarily noisy building (*dogs and cats making their trademarked noises, washers and dryers laundering bedding, people yelling about where stuff was or which dogs/cats needed cleaning*) was more quiet in general, but the space around Miles was palpably, forcefully, silent.

The cats took turns walking up to and around the big, bony, dog — his elbows and feet appearing to stick out everywhere — today he ignored them … his eyes were just for me. His back legs were shaking/trembling as I knelt down on the floor (*dropping my bag on the high front counter first, to avoid distracting him*), and when I patted his shoulder he shuddered and yelped a bit in pain.

"Hello Miles, not feeling so well today?" I said.

A long whip-like tail thwacked on the tired linoleum twice at the sound of my voice. I leaned over from the waist, and buried my nose in his ear to sniff … he still smelt like dog.

"Probably not up to a walk this afternoon, huh?" I asked, trying to keep a happy and friendly tone in my voice (*I've been practicing my human act on dogs for years, and find that they appreciate some level of emotion, as opposed to my unadulterated flat delivery*).

I was aware of Dorothy behind me, the sound of boots and smell of bleach and feel of radiant warmth closer than other shelter people tend to get to me.

"He can walk a couple of steps, but not far. If he'll let you lift him, we could take him to the beach for a bit. He'd like that, I think."

I heard an unaccustomed and medicinal clink and crinkle and clunk from the backpack over her shoulder, and wondered/worried at the nature of this outing.

"We'll manage … what's the worst that can happen?" I heard a little chuckle from Dorothy, as she remembered some of the stuff that's happened with me and her dogs over the years … not even the worst, by far (*I don't tell her the worst things, for fear that she won't let me come back*).

I scooped him up carefully (*he trusted me to pick him up, but it seemed to hurt him everywhere, so I almost needn't have been careful*), "Dot, can you grab that bag I left on the counter?"

We walked slowly out to the TLAS Element, Dorothy mumbling something about me not having to drive on the way back. There was already a nest of fleecy blankets made in the back, and the passenger seats had been removed. I sat on the tailgate and scootched my butt across and into the bunched blankets, and then tilted over, so I didn't have to dump or let go of Miles … after a few seconds of my not moving, Dorothy closed the tailgate behind me, and walked around to the driver's door, got in and drove us away.

The drive to Lake Colby town beach took only a few minutes, but every turn/bump/hill jarred Miles' joints. His scared eyes looked into mine from a distance of a few inches, squeezing in the moments of pain, but never turning, never closing (*I don't know what he was looking for, but*

I hope that he saw it). His breath was rotten, not doggy, rotten … like spoiled meat and turned milk. His tongue slid out to kiss my face, usually a warm and muscular thing, on this day it was like a slice of bologna just out of the fridge.

I carried him down to a sunny spot near the water's edge, and out of the wind. Dorothy ran ahead of me by a few steps, laden with her (*and my*) packages, and an armload of fleece blankets. I set Miles down facing the water.

"Dorothy," I say in a stupidly hushed voice (*Miles doesn't speak English, but if he could, he'd certainly be able to hear better than Dorothy*), "What's going on here? I know some of it, but I can feel it's important (*to her, and to Miles, both*), and I don't want to screw things up," I said.

"Why don't you get out your treats, and we can talk while Miles has a picnic," she said (*she obviously peeked*).

She handed me the bag I'd stopped off for at the in-town (*low-rent*) Grand Union supermarket in Saranac Lake, and I started pulling out things for Miles.

"I got you some yummies, boy," I said, "a pack of hot dogs, some Velveeta, a box of donuts."

I looked at Dorothy for permission. She would normally kick me for giving a dog this kind of junk, but she nodded and smiled … a broken thing that fell off her face after a few seconds (*and she had to look away, out to the water*).

I arranged a few bits of each, broken up into tiny pieces like I would for a puppy, on the fleece blanket; Miles dug in.

"You made a promise to Miles that first day that you walked in all those years ago (*4 years, 6 months, and 3 days, I thought, but didn't correct*). That time, and every time since, that you came and took him out in crappy weather, letting him rip your clothes, giving him McNuggets you thought I didn't know about. All of that was a part of making the promise," she said.

I looked (*and was*) clueless, so she continued.

"Remember that time you helped me hold him down while we cut that broken toenail of his?" she said.

I nodded.

"Once he saw the clipper in your hand, he was so fast, so strong, so slippery … he got away and hid under your desk and barked at us," I said, remembering. "He wanted nothing more than to get away."

I could see the moment perfectly, and it was so far away from this one, today, and I wanted to be back there/then … I reached down to scratch Miles' ears and gave him more of his favorite cheese food (*he burped up at me, fondly I think*).

Dorothy nodded, "Yup, but you catching him, holding him, even hurting him a bit, were all a part of the promise … keeping the promise," she said.

I was starting to see the shape of this discussion, and wanted none of it; I let her continue, now that she had a head of steam up.

"Our promise to these sweet beasts is to love them — stop, don't interrupt me — I know you think you don't, or can't love, or some stupid shit, but you do, in your way, as best you can." She had lost her train of thought getting pre-emptively mad at me.

"Love, and the promise," I prompted, reaching down to scratch the spot under his collar that always itched, and gave Miles another hot dog.

"Besides, the love and the treats," she paused for a moment here, looking over at her backpack, "we have to do the tough stuff, the things our dogs and cats don't want us to do. We have to do it for them, because we know what's best for them. That's the pointy end of the promise,

Tyler," she said.

There were a few Adirondack-tough kids playing at the edge of the water, shrieking now and then when one went in too deep, or splashed the other especially well. We all took a minute to watch them; Miles looked worried that they might come over and ruin our picnic (*but they didn't*).

"What's in the bag, Dorothy?" I asked, reasonably sure that I knew, but not wanting to guess incorrectly.

"Two injections, one a sedative to calm and relax Miles, the other will stop his heart," she said.

"Are you sure that he's had his last good day?" I asked.

"It's possible that he could have an upswing, but likely it gets worse, a lot worse, from here on for Miles. He's had a nice sit in the sun with the only two people on this Earth who love him ... he's watched some kids play in the water on one of the last warm afternoons he'll see. It's all downhill, and steeply, from here, Tyler," she finished.

"Do I have to do it?" I said, terrified that I would, or wouldn't, and feeling, now the tremendous weight of this promise I'd unwittingly made.

Dorothy shook her head, "All you have to do is tell me it's the right thing to do, make the decision. I can do most of the rest."

I split a Freihofer's donut three ways, gave a bit to Dorothy, took one myself, and gave Miles the biggest piece; he chewed and swallowed and licked my fingers clean, giving me a minor 'kiss with teeth' in the process. He reached a paw over and dropped it heavily on mine, and I leaned over to smell it ... like popcorn and grass.

"Do it. How can I help?" I said.

"Distract him is all. Once I find the vein on his leg for the first shot, he'll be dopey and relaxed, and the (*she almost said 'last' but switched to*) other one is easy. Talk to him, look at him, touch him, let him see and feel and hear you."

I got down close in by Miles' face and kissed his muzzle, talking and rubbing his ears the whole time while Dorothy felt around on a once-muscled (*but now bony*) front leg, just above the ankle. He tensed briefly when she eased the needle under the skin, but then I felt all the pain and tension leave him ... it just fell away, maybe blew away in the light breeze.

He was still there, I could see his consciousness in the way he looked at me, but the trembling and little cries and jerks just stopped ... his breathing deepened and strengthened and grew regular (*not quite like that of sleep, but relaxed and peaceful*). I kept talking and rubbing his old-dog belly, burying my nose in his neck, and ... waiting.

"Tyler ..." she said. I nodded, not looking up from the Miles' eyes, but feeling Dorothy move again.

He took two more deep breaths, then part of a third, and it ran out of him as he seemed to deflate and give a little shudder. I kept talking to him until I had felt thirty seconds pass without a heartbeat beneath my fingertips, then I looked up and into Dorothy's eyes.

She was smiling a broken little smile, "That's the promise, Tyler. It's a promise that we never say out loud to them, but we have to keep it anyway. Sometimes in little ways, like the toenail, sometimes like this."

We sat in the weak September sun for a few minutes, remembering stories about Miles over the years, and eventually we all headed back to the TLAS.

I learned about the promise that day, and kept my promise to Miles.

Adirondack Medical Center, Saranac Lake, NY
Tuesday, 1/21/2014, 9:58 a.m.

I drove carefully and slowly, getting used to the feel of
Billy's truck, hearing the gear and guns in back shift and
settle during the 139 minutes that it took me to reach the
hospital parking lot (*139 is both a prime and a happy number ...
this helped me shake off some of the uncharacteristic worry that had
settled on me as I neared the hospital, and circled to find a distant
parking slot*).

There was no reason to suspect that Dorothy had taken
a turn for the worse since I had last seen her, and talked
with her doctor, but 139 made me feel better. I walked
through the entrance and lobby and hallways leading back
and through and into the depths of the hospital, away from
the real light/air/world and into a world of dead colors
and bad smells and hissing sounds and too warm/dry
air ... I dislike hospitals (*as any sentient being should*).

I put my hand on the door to Dorothy's room, resting
my fingertips lightly on the fake wood ... listening with my
hand. I felt no vibrations or movements that I would
associate with either speech or someone walking around,

so I lowered my hand to the knob, turned it and slipped in (*closing the door quietly/ quickly/ firmly after me*).

There was a rasping sound coming from the air vent overhead, a toilet running very slightly behind a door in front of me, and a delicate wafting of the scent of the sick and injured coming from (*my*) Dorothy lying in the shiny metal and starchy white industrial-looking bed. I stepped gingerly over, desperate not to squeak her awake (*I had scuffed most of the snow and water off of my shoes on the way in, but Adirondackers are seldom entirely dry during the winter months*).

"How was camping, how were the woods?" a dry and tiny voice said from somewhere in the bed.

I jumped a bit, not expecting her to be awake.

"Lovely, dark, and deep," I answered, immediately regretting the Robert Frost that was bouncing around inside my head; not wanting Dorothy to connect the dots and figure out what I was planning, or why.

"Sorry you had to come out for this," Dorothy croaked, gesturing at herself, before continuing, "… and Lisa …."

Her mouth was a messy gash, torn and bruising, in a field of white bandages on an oppressively white pillow. One of her teeth was chipped and canted inwards, towards her tongue; it made her lisp slightly in a way that I hadn't noticed when I'd seen her yesterday. She started to speak again, and broke off to cough and wheeze. I handed her one of the weird Styrofoam drink containers hospitals use that was resting on the tray table next to her bed, shaking it first to make certain that it had something in it. She was clumsy and slow-moving, so I aimed the straw for her and held her up with a hand on the small of her back while she took a sip; predictably, she sputtered and coughed some of the water down her hospital robe. She may have been waiting for me to speak, but I had nothing to say (*and was having more than the usual amount of trouble judging expressions, as hers were masked by bruising/swelling/bandages*).

"I'm sorry about Lisa," she said, more clearly this time. "She's angry, and can't lash out in any useful way at any of the people responsible."

"I know ... I understand," I said (*I didn't, and I didn't, but people seem to feel better when I say things like that at times like this, and in my ongoing attempt to convincingly play human, I do what I can*).

She looked at me, seemed about to say something (*probably about to call me a liar*), but shook her head minutely, grimacing an eighth of an inch into the shake due to her injuries.

"Meg must be pushing Frank, and he's shaking every tree, trying to find out what happened, and where, and why. Lisa just clamps her mouth down tight and starts to cry every time he talks to her. I just keep telling him the Tupper story and acting vague and out of it. He's been looking for you, though, and when he finds you, he'll lean on you a bit."

"He won't find me, I'll be leaving town in a few minutes, won't be back for a couple of days, and my credit card's down in Lowville if he takes the time and effort to look," I said.

She looked up when I mentioned Lowville, remembering (*due to her intense dislike of his flavor of hunter even more than ordinary hunters*) Billy, so I pushed on with my next question in the hope of derailing her train of thought.

"Are you going to die?" I asked.

"What? No. Not from this stuff," she said. "What are you up to, Tyler? You can't mess with this, you promised. I mean it!"

"I remember my promise, Dot. I'm not going to do anything but get out of town for a few days to give Frank some time spin his wheels doing something besides looking for me. I just wanted to check in to see how you're doing before I head out."

I started toward the door, and was out before she could say/ask anything else. Walking out to Billy's truck, I saw 17 people that I knew (*by which I mean people I recognized, and who might recognize me*) … I made sure that nobody was near, or even watching, when I climbed into the truck.

Double-U Farm, Union Falls, NY
Tuesday, 1/21/2014, 10:26 a.m.

I left town, heading north and east, forgoing both Dunkin'
Donuts and good Chinese food, cruising past Hope and
John at the farm without slowing, and continued on
towards Plattsburgh on Route 3, making the right turn
onto Alder Brook Park Road, decidedly heading/looking
for trouble.

As soon as I was around the first bend in the road, I
pulled over and rolled down the windows to listen for
traffic or other human noise. Hearing none, I quickly
changed into a mix of some of my fancier/nicer/dressier
clothes along with some costume elements I had borrowed
from Billy: his expensive wristwatch, a sheathed
hunting/skinning knife on my belt, Billy's custom made
boots (*he claims that a hill-tribe of ancient boot makers work all
year high up in the Wind River Range to make 20 pairs of these
boots a year for hunters with too much money ... like him*), and a
waxed cotton hunting coat with blanket lining inside that
has been passed down to menfolk in Billy's family for the
last 150 years. I stomped, and then rolled around in the

snow for a minute before dusting myself off and getting back into the truck, confident of the fit and feel of my moneyed-trophy-hunter costume.

The road is a horror to drive on in the summer (*nearly a jeep trail, except for foot-deep potholes of the sort that only ancient tarmac can support*). In winter the first downhill stretch of it is more like a bobsled run wide enough for 1.58 cars. I was still getting used to the differences between my Honda Element and Billy's serious pickup truck (*mostly more horsepower/torque as far as that goes*), and almost didn't notice the rundown farm on the left at the bottom of the big hill, by the river.

The memories, drawn out by the place, ran over me like a tide coming in.

Double-U Farm, Union Falls, NY
Wednesday, 7/4/2008, 10:47 a.m.

I hadn't heard her steps on the stairs up to the SmartPig office, but her voice and the ferocity of her hammering on the door was unmistakable, even for me, "Tyler, wake up! From my drive-bys, it looks like they left Friday. Today's the day!"

I surprised Dorothy by pulling the door open in front of her clenched fist before she could begin the second round of knocking, "Come in. Grab a Coke. I'll be ready in 113 seconds," I said, turning to the sink for a quick splash before she could say anything.

If I was the kind of person who smiled, I would have been smiling ... 113 is a great number to come up with just out of sleep. It was a reasonable approximation of the time it would actually take me to get ready. It's a prime number (*naturally*). Beyond that, it's a permutable prime (*with the others being 131 and 311*).

Dorothy understands/accepts/tolerates my proclivity/ fondness/need for numbers, especially powerful and precise numbers, in my life. Change of, and deviation from, routine are the things I hate/fear most in the world; I assuage my hate, fear, and discomfort with numbers … preferably prime numbers … preferably interesting prime numbers, when possible. Assigning or finding interesting numbers associated with potentially fear/discomfort-inducing events in my life works something like autohypnosis … allowing me to graft the illusion of control over event and people and things that I have no control over. I have always had a fondness/alacrity for number games and manipulation, and can note through meticulous self-evaluation that I use this crutch less now than when I was six years old (*my habit was a departure from the norm for other six year olds, but I was only mildly aware of other children at the time*), but it still spikes in times of stress … which this morning was.

107 seconds later (*a significantly less interesting prime*), I scooped up my partly filled backpack, threw a trio of Cokes into the open pack on my way to the door, and flipped off the lights … leaving Dorothy to close the door when she caught up.

We didn't speak on the stairs, or crossing the street to get to her car (*a van with all of the rear seats torn out for ease of dog/gear transport*) parked in front of Nori's (*a health-food store that I had still not seen the inside of, despite the fact that they were/are located 75 yards from my front door … when sleeping at SmartPig*). Given that it was still dark, and the fourth of July (*doing all of this on a/the national holiday, when people tend to be busy celebrating, was Dorothy's idea*), we were the only things awake and moving in downtown Saranac Lake. We got underway unseen/unnoticed … which was as it should be, since we were on a secret mission, doing wrong things for the right reasons.

It was just getting light when we turned off of Route 3 onto Alder Brook Park Road, bouncing and jouncing down a lane that had no business calling itself a road (*it felt and looked more like a wide trail that someone had randomly dumped gravel and tarmac on at some point in the distant past*).

"Slow down, nothing good happens if we break your car in one of these potholes before we get there," I said.

"Shut the fuck up! I got this," Dorothy said in a tight, giddy, voice that made me think offering her another pre-dawn caffeinated beverage on the road had been a mistake.

We slowed down at the bottom of the big hill, and looked in through the gate announcing 'Double-U Farm' (*which experience taught me was meant to be either cute or clever, although it seemed neither ... admittedly, I'm not the best judge of that sort of thing ... especially that sort of thing*).

Dorothy slowed the minivan to a crawl and we both peered down the driveway looking for signs of life. I could see an upstairs bedroom lamp shining brightly, presumably on a timer of the type seemingly designed to fool only the dimmest of burglars, and nothing else that signaled occupancy. Fifty yards further down the road, and across the small rusted bridge, there was a turnaround for snowplows that worked just as well for crappy minivans. We used it. Dorothy idled up to the head of the driveway, yanked the shifter into 'P', and rolled down the front windows to listen.

We each cocked our heads out our respective windows, opened our mouths minutely (*I'd shared an article with Dorothy about the efficiency of human hearing being improved when our mouths are open 13 weeks previously, and it had apparently stuck with both of us*), and cupped a hand behind the outside ears to catch as much sound as was possible.

I heard: Dorothy's car engine knocking slightly, the river babbling behind us, wind in the leaves of trees between us and the farm, an ongoing barking and yipping from the closest of the barns, and, for the whole two minutes that we sat there listening, a mechanical whining/whirring/clatter coming from a support building between the house and the dog-barn.

"Nobody's home. That's an overheated pump with a bearing about to go, and it's been running since you parked ... nobody living on a farm ignores that sound for that long without checking/fixing it," I said.

"You're probably right, but let's go in soft anyway. I'll drive up and honk a few times; if anyone comes out, we'll say we're lost and looking for a friend's campsite on Taylor Pond," Dorothy answered.

She dropped the transmission back into 'D' and we rolled slowly down the driveway towards the house. Both of us were looking/feeling for signs of life other than the dogs, who had heard us, and shifted their shrieks to new levels of desperate volume ... Dorothy grimaced each time the cacophony grew in pitch and level and clashed and crashed and echoed around the small clearing that the farm filled. She honked the horn a few times, but we could both sense a lack of human presence (*besides our own*) from the place.

She parked and we both climbed out to get a quick look around, yelling hellos to the house and barns to no effect (*save for driving the dogs inside even more crazy*). I could see a shiny lock holding the double doors of the dog barn closed, walked around to the back of the minivan, selected the correct tool for the job, and 'opened' the door (*a four-foot wrecking bar will pull the hasp from any door on the planet, obviating the need to worry about even the toughest lock ... something people generally overlook*).

The stink from inside the barn literally took my breath away, and brought tears to my eyes (*and stung my nostrils ... and turned my stomach*). Metal cages lined one wall of the barn (*two rows of ten cages*). Two larger pens filled the space at the back and along the opposite side of the barn, with the rest of the space filled with pallets of food and wood-shavings and hoses and rakes and shovels and such. The barking stopped as soon as I stepped inside, and 23 sets of eyes glinted back at me in the light coming in from behind me. The dead and dying dogs and puppies were in the larger pens. I looked around the barn, working out what to do as Dorothy brushed past me. Her headlamp shone everywhere her head turned as she spoke in gentle tones to all the residents of the barn, promising an end to their suffering.

The jury-rigged watering system must have come undone at some point during the weekend (*explaining the dehydrated and dead dogs/puppies, as well as the continually running pump*), presumably after the people living/working on the farm had left. The barn was like a sauna, except for the screaming dogs and overpowering smell of dog shit and rotting meat ... so not really like a sauna at all. We smeared Vick's VapoRub (*that Dorothy had been smart enough to bring*) under our noses and donned blue nitrile gloves (*which still make me think of Firefly*) and started to work as quickly as we could, given the noise/stink/mess/horribleness of the room.

The first order of business was to get fresh/cold water to every living animal in the barn. Once that was done, we gave the living a chance to drink while we dragged the dead out into the hot sun of the farmyard (*which was still dramatically cooler than the inside of the barn*). We had no idea when the owners of the farm would come back, and clearly didn't have time to bury the dead ... but we did it anyway (*Dorothy started digging, and I didn't argue much*). Once the line of small graves was filled and spoken over (*by Dorothy, I could do nothing for the dogs except sweat and cry and vomit and blister, which I had already done*), we started moving the live dogs out to the van. We hosed them down with cold water to both cool them down and wash them off before jamming them into the van.

After the first few dogs, it became clear to Dot that we would not fit all 23 into the van (*it had been clear to me from the moment I made a count of the still living dogs, but I waited for her to get there on her own*). Dorothy drove the van over to a beat-up looking horse trailer, which I helped her attach to the van's trailer hitch … when I raised my eyebrows at this, she said, "Sauce for the goose, Mr. Saavik," in her imitation of Leonard Nimoy as Mr. Spock from Wrath of Khan (*which sounds a lot like her imitation of Sean Connery as Captain Marco Ramius in the Hunt for Red October*).

We jammed the rest of the dogs into the van and trailer within minutes. Dorothy, more nervously now, listened for approaching traffic … an impossibility over the choir of angry/scared/mournful dogs all around our ears. We pulled slowly out onto the rotted/rutted road, the van squealing and protesting at the unaccustomed weight/strain of the trailer and nearly two dozen stolen/freed/rescued dogs.

"We can't bring all of these dogs to the shelter in town," I pointed out, fending off four dogs trying to either climb into my lap or out the window. "You don't have room, and this many new dogs would draw all sorts of attention."

"Yah, I appreciate your super-melon working that out Tyler, but I got this," Dorothy said.

I projected a map of the Adirondack Park up on the inside of my skull, and considered our current situation, "No ferries to Vermont, no Northway, no big cities, not Canada, not through Tupper (*Tupper Lake PD is legend for stopping cars on any pretext*) … how?" I asked.

"Peggy, a friend of mine that fundraises for a bunch of shelters in Vermont is going to meet us on this side of the bridge at Crown Point, then drive back across and disperse the dogs throughout her network," she said.

"Speaking of which," she pulled out a cell phone and dialed the number right in front of me (*my eyes slid down and captured the number, as they do everything that passes in front of them*).

"Hi Peg, Dot. We're on our way, and Peg — 'you're gonna need a bigger boat'," (*she said this in her imitation of Roy Scheider as Martin Brody in Jaws, which sounds a lot like her imitation of Clint Eastwood as Harry Callahan in Dirty Harry*).

"Yah, there's twenty-some ..."

"Twenty-three" I offered.

"Twenty-three dogs, some of 'em in pretty rough shape. Yup, I'll see you at the place we had the picnic that time after the bird-guy," she said.

Peggy met us at the cryptically-appointed place, standing beside a big panel truck with ventilation slats cut throughout its length.

We moved the dogs from our van (*and stolen trailer*) to her truck as quickly as possible, pausing only when we noted that one of the dogs had died between being loaded at the farm and the transfer at Dot's picnic spot. It was a young beagle that had obviously given birth and nursed in the last few months, and she deserved better than life had given her (*many, possibly most dogs and people do, but this one meant a bit more to me somehow*).

While Dorothy and Peggy loaded the rest of the dogs into the Vermont-bound truck, I wrapped the beagle in a towel I'd stashed up front in the van, grabbed Dorothy's wrecking bar (*lacking a shovel*), and headed into the woods with my small bundle.

The dog still felt warm in my arms, but was loose in a way that living flesh isn't; I found a downed log, and rolled it out of the way, as a place to start my grave. The soil under where the log had been was easy enough to tear up with the wrecking bar, and I quickly had a small pile of dirt next to a small hole. Laying the wrapped dog gently into the hole (*the care I took seemed irrational at first, since the dog was beyond pain/suffering, but it had suffered enough*), I covered it with dirt and then piled it over with logs and rocks to protect the corpse from scavengers. When I got back to the picnic spot, Dorothy and Peggy were hugging and looking around for me.

"Thanks ..." both began at once, then laughed nervously.

"We should all get going," I said.

We all nodded, turned, and left.

Central Garage, Union Falls, NY
Tuesday, 1/21/2014, 11:04 a.m.

I continued a few miles down the road, heading towards
Union Falls Pond, looking for the right place to crash
Billy's truck. There was a perfect rocky outcropping at a
sharp left-hand turn in the road, which I slowly cruised by
before turning back around for another, faster, approach. I
placed an imaginary deer in the road at just the right spot,
stamped the brakes while moving at 60 mph, and felt the
back end slide perfectly ... the rear-right tire and quarter
panel slammed into the rock with an impressive basso
crumpling and explosion of metal and rubber. I waited
until the noise stopped (*and the truck stopped rocking and
settling*) before getting out to survey the damage.

The tire was flat ... more than that, it had been
shredded by an impact with the sharp edges of the rock at
that speed. The rim of the wheel had been bent, possibly
cracked, in the crash. More impressively, the wheel was no
longer perpendicular to the road ... the top of the rim had
been pushed in a bit more than four inches relative to the
bottom of the rim, and the rear of the truck was tilted

slightly towards the accident site (*implying some axel or other damage that I couldn't see*).

It was exactly what I had been hoping for, and as such, I had to work even harder than ordinary when I called AAA to paste an anxious and disappointed look on my face to modulate my tones into one of worry and anger (*people listening to me on the phone can, for some reason, tell that I don't feel/emote in the same way that they do so I try method acting for realism*).

While waiting for the tow truck to come from nearby Silver Lake, I organized my gear a bit, ate a half pound of beef jerky, drank a liter of slightly too-sweet iced tea (*which for me is saying something*), and then lay down on the rock to wait. I didn't rest too long before I could hear a heavy truck gearing down nearby. Sitting up and opening my eyes, I took in the tableau before me, and tried to get into character for my first appearance on stage as 'Billy the Gun Guy' (*I didn't anticipate being great at this role, as I'm barely convincing as 'Tyler Cunningham, human', but I had the props and story lined up, so figured that I would give it my best efforts*). I stood up, shook the snow off, and walked over to the truck as its driver was just getting out.

"Thanks for coming so quick! I was messing with the CD-changer, and almost missed the turn altogether (*I don't listen to music as a rule, but felt confident that my version of Billy liked Ted Nugent*). I hope the truck isn't too badly banged up; I'm meeting some friends for a hunt in Vermont day after tomorrow," I said.

Greg (*if I was to take the nametape sewn onto his left breast pocket at face value, which I decided to do*) walked all the way around the truck, climbing the rock I had crashed into to get a full view of the damage before speaking.

"Yah, nope. Tire's no big deal, but the wheel, and maybe the axle are shot. We can do the work, but it won't be quick, or cheap." He leaned on the last three words especially, and looked me up and down.

"If you call it in now, and I pay for overnighting everything, could we be done tomorrow? I'm happy to spend for speed, if you know what I mean (*who wouldn't ... apparently, my version of Billy was something of a moron ... a rich and spoiled moron*)," I said.

The outer edges of Greg mouth tilted upwards a hair, and he said, "Yah, I think we can do that. Hurry things up. Can't guarantee tomorrow though, it might be the next day depending on delivery and availability of parts."

"Whatever you can do, I'll be very grateful," I said.

He nodded and went back to his truck, backing it up to the rear of Billy's (*my*) truck, which he lifted for the tow back to the garage. When he was done hooking things up, he cleared a space on his front seat, and gestured for me to get in ... I did.

On the way back to the garage (*which turned out to be his garage*) he started engaging in small talk ... that human convention the point, and knack, of which totally elude me.

"So, where you from Mr. Dunham?" he said.

"Lowville" I replied.

He then spent a pair of minutes I'll never get back asking if I knew the seven people he knew from that area ... I replied honestly that I didn't (*and hoped fervently that the real Billy didn't either, although it seemed unlikely that it would matter in any case*).

"You said you was going to Vermont, hunting?" he asked.

"Yes." I embraced my natural conversational reticence in this instance, as books I've read seem to indicate that having him pull details out of me would help sell the whole deal.

"I saw some serious hunting gear in the back, but unless they got seasons and critters I ain't heard of, there's no big game seasons on in Vermont," he said. His tone didn't suggest a question at the end of that sentence, but he left it hanging, obviously waiting for me to fill in the blanks.

"Well, I know a guy up in the Kingdom that's got a private game reserve, and he imports all sorts of game for private hunts. His setup, you can hunt whatever, whenever," I said. There were elements of this that were true; I'd talked a bit with Billy about it before stealing/borrowing all of his best gear.

Greg drove in silence until we arrived, and he expertly (*which, since I would be paying for his expertise, I had taken for granted*) backed the conjoined trucks into one of the bays of his garage. He separated our trucks and ran the lift up, so that he could get a worm's eye view of the damage I had done to Billy's truck with a flashlight. He led the way back out of the garage and we went into an office, where he pecked at a dingy computer with his index fingers for a few minutes before turning to me with a face ravaged by poorly concealed (*if even I could see it*) avarice.

"I can get what you need, and get you back on your way, but it's gonna cost you a bunch, and you'll most likely be a day late to your hunt up in the Kingdom," he said. "A couple of the parts won't make it here until tomorrow night, maybe the next morning, even expressing things, and the only way we can get the work done is if we bump other jobs." (*The garage had two empty bays, alongside the one with Billy's truck, but I wasn't going to question any part of this*).

"Okay, assuming you do all of that, how much are we talking about?" I asked.

Greg tipped back in his chair, looking at the ceiling (*or heaven?*), deep in thought for 17 seconds, moving his lips and ticking off fingers the whole time.

"Twenny-five hunnert if we don't run into anything else while we're working," he said.

"Sounds good, will it help get things moving to run this for two grand?" I asked, flipping Billy's credit card onto the table in front of him (*I did this to avoid any money awkwardness between us, and to reinforce his thinking of me as a ready source of money*). "I could pay for some of it in cash if that'd be better, but lots of people nowadays prefer credit to old-fashioned cash."

Greg brightened at the mention of my paying in cash, and sat up/forward/taller a bit. "Cash is fine," he said, pushing the car back towards me. "Let's say a thousand now, for parts and shipping, and you can pay off the rest when we're done with the plastic."

I counted out ten hundreds from my wallet right in front of him, and made sure that he could see that there was more left in it than was now in his hand.

"Why don't you head over to the diner across the road for a spell, and I'll make the calls I need to, to get everything on its way over here, and I'll come and find you in an hour or so to get you caught up when I pick up my lunch," he said.

"Sounds good, Greg. Thanks."

I was content to wait until lunchtime to move forward with the next phase of the plan/idea/scheme.

Deb's Diner, Union Falls, NY
Tuesday, 1/21/2014, 12:23 p.m.

Greg joined me at my table 67 minutes later ... while I
waited for him to give me good/bad news I reached back
in my head and pulled out the (*only marginally interesting facts*)
that 67 was both a lucky prime and one of only nine
Heegner numbers.

"I got through to all my parts guys, and things are
moving, Mr. Dunham," he said.

"Billy, please Greg. Anyone who can help me get out of
this fix and back in business is a friend, and all my friends
call me Billy," I said.

"We're not there yet, but I'll get you to your hunt as
soon as possible. Whaja say you were hunting up in the
Kingdom?" he asked.

"I didn't," I answered, trying to force a little reluctance
into my voice and face ... I'd worked on this during my
drive and wait, based on talking with Billy about how some
people respond to his going on this sort of hunt. "I'll be
there for a few days ... maybe a week, and we'll be going
after a variety of game. Are you a hunter Greg?"

"Yessir. I go out every fall for my buck, and generally get a permit for a doe up at a cabin I share with some friends just south of Potsdam," he said.

I slumped my shoulders down a half inch and continued, "This preserve has a couple of different species of interest to me ... some game birds he brings in special, a few species of wild ram, Russian wild boars, elk, and bison."

I looked up and across at him, as if gauging his response before I kept talking. "If things go well, and my friend and I are having fun, I might bring home one of each. I'd just as soon you kept all this to yourself, as not everything the owner of the preserve does abides by the letter of the law a hundred percent," I finished.

I went back to my Coke and fries, hoping the idea might come to him on his own ... 17 seconds into this, I asked about places to stay in town and grumbled about pay-per-view to try and prime the pump a bit.

Greg flipped the paper placemat at his place over and drew a map (*including the diner and his garage for orientation, which I approved of*) showing me how to get to a few cabins for rent only a few hundred yards from where I sat, "Tim don't have no TVs in his cabins though, sorry to say."

"Argh! Not only am I going to miss the first day of the hunting with my guys, but I'm gonna be stuck here with nothing to do. Maybe I should just get you to arrange a flatbed to bring the truck to Vermont," I said, hoping that I wasn't laying it on too thick ... I'm a poor judge of human emotional interactions, and even worse at pretending to have them.

"Well," Greg interjected quickly ... perhaps anxiously, "there is something that might be fun, or at least interesting to you; if you don't mind keeping it on the down-low. How do you feel about dog fights?" he asked.

"I saw some, cock fights too, in Costa Rica last year … didn't know it happened much in the US. I'm interested. It's around here?" I asked.

"Yup, not right in town, you understand, and not in the same place every time, but if you know the right people, and they can vouch for you, it's easy enough to find."

He seemed relieved that I had expressed an interest, mostly perhaps because he didn't want to lose my business if I decided to spring for getting my (*Billy's*) truck brought all the way over to my imaginary hunting preserve.

"Any going on this afternoon or tonight?" I asked.

"No, but they'll be setting up tomorrow for fights all afternoon and into the night. If you're interested, I can set you up with an invitation, and maybe a loaner car too, to get out there, since we're fixing your ride," he said.

It was a blatant quid pro quo, it met both of our needs (*although for different reasons than he thought*), and I let him see the happiness that Billy (*my version of Billy anyway, the actual Billy thought dog fights abhorrent*) would have felt at this outcome … giving him my #18 smile (*I've been working on a collection of human smiles for nearly three decades, and was up to 26 fairly serviceable ones*), fatuously happy at snatching victory from the jaws of defeat.

"That sounds great Greg, I'd be really grateful if you could set that up for me … it might make this area a worthwhile stopover every time I'm heading over to Vermont or Cow Hampshire," I said. "Oh, while I'm thinking of it, can I borrow that loaner this afternoon to move some of my stuff from your garage to the place I'll be staying tonight?"

"Shouldn't be a problem, Mr. Dunham," he said.

"My friends all call me Billy, Greg," I answered.

He seemed happy at the outcome of our talk as well, and grabbed a bag of burgers and a to-go Coke from the woman behind the counter (*who I assumed was Deb*) and headed back across the street to his garage.

To celebrate my forward progress, I ordered a slice of each of the four pies that Deb was featuring for the day (*blueberry, apple, rhubarb, and pecan, if you were wondering*) ... dismissing her offer of coffee with a wave of my hand, but nodding a clear 'YES' to her query about ice cream.

I followed him back to the garage some 13 minutes later, got a set of keys from Greg, loaded a small number of ridiculously heavy duffel bags into the back of a beat-up Toyota Cressida hatchback Greg showed me to, eschewing his offer of help while trying to make hefting the bags look effortless. My plan was one of those that comes with a 'some assembly required' notice, and I planned to take care of it long after everyone in town was asleep, and there was no chance of a friendly visit to my cabin ... to check on the out-of-towner.

Connor's Country Cabins, Union Falls, NY
Tuesday, 1/21/2014, 5:27 p.m.

I split the afternoon between napping (*in an actual bed … it seems fancy now, after sleeping either outside or on the couch in my office for the past 12 years*) and thinking (*about 'The Plan' and my dog Hope and the concept of biological immortality, as presented by the jellyfish turritopsis dohrnii*) and eating gummy bears (*reflecting as fondly as I am capable about Dorothy's proclivity for biting them in half, or thirds, and making multi-colored bears*) … roughly 47 percent, 39 percent, and 14 percent respectively.

Connor's Country Cabins lacked Wi-Fi, but my semi-smart Tracfone had sufficient bars (*when standing by the door*) to reach out to some essential contacts via text and email. I confirmed plans with Mickey Schwarz for his visit for the Saranac Lake Winter Carnival. Frank had sent numerous emails with updates about Dorothy's state of health, as well as a tersely worded warning against taking any action in retribution … I declined to respond. A series of back and forth emails and texts with John during the course of the afternoon about progress being made on his end of things was encouraging. We worked the problems likely facing me in the upcoming conflict, big and small, back and forth, trying to come up with solutions and to subsequently pick those solutions apart; it was alien to me to share this type of work/thought with another person (*sometimes I talk about my cases with Hope, but she seldom comments*), but both he and Barry had been adamant the previous morning that I would be unable to successfully navigate this flavor of human interaction without their direct help ... and Barry had been conspicuous in his absence since I had left John at Helgafell Farm yesterday.

Eventually I ran out of naps to take, emails/texts/ to send, and gummy bears, so I splashed my face, worked to reassemble my Billy persona/disguise, and walked back down to Deb's Diner to see what she had to offer me for supper.

Central Garage, Union Falls, NY
Wednesday, 1/22/2014, 10:57 a.m.

A bit short of 24 hours after ingratiating myself with Greg through the judicious application of money (*and the promise of more money to come*), I returned to the garage, in theory to check on his progress getting my (*Billy's*) truck roadworthy again, but also to get directions to the dog fight.

"We were able to drive to P'burgh and get some of the parts by yesterday afternoon, more came in this morning, and a few final items should be coming in this afternoon or tomorrow morning. If we keep pushing our other work, we should be able to have you on the road by sometime tomorrow afternoon at about the figure that I quoted you yesterday," Greg said.

"That's just great Greg; I can't thank you and the other guys enough (*although I'd seen other people in his garage, I had no clear/compelling evidence that anyone but him was working on my car, but we all have roles to play*)," I said.

"You still interested in that other thing we talked about?" he asked, lowering his voice, and talking out of the side of his mouth a bit. "The thing going on tonight out at the Old Miller Place?"

"Yessir, but I thought you said it got started in the afternoon?" I asked, not wanting to seem overeager, but balancing that with my desire to check things out (*and set things up*) as much as possible during daylight hours.

"They're prolly out here now setting things up, but people don't start rolling in until late afternoon. It lets them set up parking and the grill ... hell, they'll even get a bar setup by sundown," Greg added.

"Sounds good, but I wouldn't mind getting out there a little beforehand, to check out the dogs that'll be fighting and get a good parking spot ... I wouldn't want your loaner getting stuck in snow or ice or mud or whatever," I said.

It must have sounded good (*or good enough*) to Greg, because he ripped a big piece of blank newsprint that looked like it might have otherwise ended up protecting car floors and seats from greasy boots and overalls, and started drawing a highly detailed map describing the country between his garage and the Old Miller Place. He finished by writing a few words on the back of one of his business cards, signing it, and giving it to me.

"This'll get you in the gate, make sure to bring cash ... these boys don't take plastic or checks," he said, smiling a bit, but also with a serious cast to his eyes that made me think of Dorothy (*I made sure to lock my facial expressions in a knowing and happy grin to avoid slipping into any other, less useful emotive expression*).

I was pretty sure that he'd get a finder's fee for steering money their way, but asked, "What do I owe you for the invite, or vouchsafe, Greg?"

"Nothing, they'll want something for entrance fees, for the grill, bar, and they take a piece of all the action on the fights," he said.

"Nonsense, without your help, I'd be spending the

afternoon and evening watching the walls at Connor's Country Cabins," I said, pressing a pair of twenties into his hand, which he pocketed without examining.

"Thanks Mr. Dunham … Billy," he said when he saw me start to speak, "I hope you enjoy yourself." Greg made one final notation on the highly detailed map he'd drawn and handed it to me.

I folded the map, nodded at Greg, went out and started the car, drove to the Country Cabins, loaded a few more supplies into the back of the car, covered everything with a wool blanket from the second bed in my room, and drove away after consulting the map and orienting the car/myself and grafting Greg's map onto the one already in my head for the area.

Empty driveway near Old Miller Place, Peasleeville, NY
Wednesday, 1/22/2014, 3:23 p.m.

My first stop was at the single gas station in Union Falls,
where I checked fluids, tires, filled up on gas, and loaded
the car with fat/carb heavy food and drinks before heading
off in a generally north-easterly direction, following Greg's
map. I drove by the "X" marked on the map at three
minutes after noon, took a hi-def mental picture of the
setting, and continued past the huge and rusting steel
building, only stopping when I was far beyond being seen
or heard by the small crew already at work setting up for
the evening.

The metal-sided building looked to be 40x60, and 20
feet tall at the roofline; similar to many farm storage
buildings I'd seen in the North County ... generally not a
barn so much as a storage site for vehicles and equipment
and feed and those big round plastic-wrapped things
farmers produced instead of hay bales these days. It looked
to be mostly empty, judging from my brief look through
the tractor-sized open doors in the side of the
building/shed/barn facing the road. There were two

heavy-duty trucks plowing a piece of a field into what I assumed would be parking for as many as 60 cars or more (*I did not have enough 'materials' to manage 60 cars, briefly considered retooling my plan, and then settled on their either being ambitious or my having to make do with what I had*).

Four men had been working inside the barn (*I decided to call it that, rather than the lengthier moniker building/shed/barn, as it seemed the best fit to me*) when I drove by. Two were setting up a fenced ring in the middle of the big space, two were hauling big cages from a container truck pulled mostly into the barn to the far wall. I couldn't see a bar (*not that I wanted a drink, much less an alcoholic one, but I was interested in checking Greg's story for accuracy*), but there was a pair of huge grills set up off to the side of the big doors at the front of the barn.

Six men plus Bronsen made sense to me … I had been expecting five to eight men, given the information Dorothy and Lisa and Greg had given to me about the operation. I noted the color and configuration of the vehicles present … so that I could pay them special attention later. If the plan worked as outlined with John and Barry, it shouldn't matter how many men Bronsen had working with him.

"And if it doesn't, it won't matter either, 'cuz they'll punch your ticket, and throw your body down an old well," Barry said, joining me (*at last*) in the passenger seat … squished and slightly compressed from his actual/remembered size so that his bulk and breadth could actually fit in the tiny space without denting the roof and door outwards.

"Hi Barry," I said. "I suppose this means that some part of me is scared enough about what's coming to activate the adrenal system and whatever corner of my head you live in."

"No se, compadre mio," he said in rough Spanish (*Portugese?*), with an even rougher accent. "I don't make the rules, I just go where they — you — tell me."

I flipped open my cell phone, and saw a full set of bars. "There must be a tower close by ... what if people just call 911?" I asked.

"I don't think they will; they'd have a lot to explain about why they were all the way out here with dead dogs and an illegal bar."

I raised my eyebrows at this ... minutely, but since Barry is a figment of my imagination, he didn't even have to be looking to pick up on it.

"Really, police take that shit seriously; maybe more seriously than the dog stuff ... unlicensed food and beverage places take money out of the state's pockets, and they hate that shit," Barry added.

"Plus, they're set up in the middle of nowhere on purpose ... even if somebody does call, it should take fire and police a while to find their way out here on a Wednesday night in the middle of January," I offered.

"Yup, so as long as you take care of business quick-like, everything should be fine," Barry finished, as I pulled into a plowed but unoccupied driveway.

I went around to the back of the loaner, popped the hatchback, unzipped the two big duffel bags, and started making final preparations/adjustments to my 36 packages (*the walkies came in packages of 4, the Tupperware in groups of 6, and the magnesium-strip enhanced sparklers oddly in boxes of 9 ... Barry was walking up and down the driveway behind me, stamping his feet and muttering something about hot dogs and bun-packages and "OCD pyro-fucking-maniacs"*).

"Whatever, Barry. Thirty-six should be just about the perfect number," I said.

"Have you noticed that your solution to lots of

problems over the years has involved fire?" Barry asked.

"I have, and I sometimes wonder what, if anything it says about me, and the life I've chosen (*although it probably says more about me that I have this sort of conversation with the ghost of a man I murdered and dumped in an abandoned mine*) ... that being said, I think that this way, plus the add-on that you and John helped with, will help me avoid more violent measures. I would prefer not to have to kill anyone ever again," I said, looking in his direction at the end.

"Keep in mind that things seldom go according to plan, and that this plan has lots of moving parts, along with at least seven angry and violent people coming together at the chokepoint; you may end up with a difficult choice if things go south and you want to get home and keep the dog-lady safe. All that being said, I wish that you'd had this respect for life when we had our thing, Tyler," Barry said.

"Me too, Barry," I said. "But it's possible that couldn't have worked out any other way, given all of the variables ... I think about it. Now, let me concentrate on this next bit, and then we'll give John a call."

Barry walked up the driveway, around the corner of a garage, and vanished. He used to disappear from right in front of me, but I once pointed out that it was disconcerting, and now he generally makes use of physical features to go away, rather than simply blink out of existence (*I don't understand what/how/why Barry is, but he's less of a presence in my life than he was immediately after his death — murder — and we continue to work on our relationship, forced as we are to occupy the same skull*).

I focused on the job at hand for another 48 minutes, then zipped everything back up, and went around to the front of the car to get an armload of junk food (*three bottles of Welch's grape soda and a mix of jerky/Twinkies/beer-nuts*) to refuel after the exacting work and concentration of the last hour. Seven minutes later, I threw all of the detritus into the well behind the front seats (*consciously making a decision not to throw it in the front passenger seat/well because ... Barry*).

John picked up his phone on the third ring, "Give me good news, Tyler."

"If I remember the mileage back to the Old Miller Place correctly, and I do, then I should be pulling into the parking area they've cleared just as the odometer on the car I've borrowed turns around to 121,393 miles ... the 27th number in the Fibonacci sequence ... 27 being three to the third ... that's a whole lot of favorable numbers at the outset of a pretty dicey caper," I replied.

"Uh ..." John seemed at a loss for a moment, "I meant do you have good news about the setup of the situation; is it pretty much as we suspected?"

"Oh ... yes, it is," I answered.

"I'm ready to go any time. I made initial contact and have an opening that I can take advantage of, so I can be in position whenever you specify," John said.

"It'll be more impressive in the dark, and my app says sunset is at 4:50, with last light at 5:22, I'll wait until 5:30 to light the fuse, so let's plan on sometime at, or just after, 5:40 p.m.," I said. "Assuming that you can manage it."

I was unsure/unclear/nervous (*as nervous as I get*) about John's side of the plan. It was important — vital, really — to what we were trying to do, and my end of things wouldn't be sufficient if he couldn't deliver.

"No problem, I'll be there, here's the number you should have him call."

As comfortable as I was with the chemical/electrical engineering involved, he seemed equally comfortable with the human engineering that he had signed up for ... it baffled/frightened me, but I was willing to take his word for it that he was ready on his end.

"What time is it down there?" I asked, just to make sure ... not to make sure for myself, but to insure that he got the timing right.

"Don't worry about it, Tyler, I'm an hour behind you, so your 5:40 will be my 4:40; I'll be inside and we'll all be waiting for your call," he answered, with what sounded like a small laugh at my expense in his voice ... it was worth it though, I would trade minor ridicule for timetable certainty any day of the week.

I thanked him, and hung up, looking at my watch as I did so; it was 3:23, which I took as another good sign ... 323 is the sum of nine consecutive primes (*19, 23, 29, 31, 37, 41, 43, 47, and 53*) and the ninth Moztkin number which, among other things, is the number of non-intersecting chords you can draw on a circle between eight points ... 323 is one of the numbers that I used to love as a child when the going got confusing (*generally in dealing with people, or in trying to avoid dealing with people ... I made mistakes in both cases*).

The Old Miller Place, Peasleeville, NY
Wednesday, 1/22/2014, 5:29 p.m.

I drove back to the Old Miller Place by a circuitous route
(*scouting some of the roads leading to/away the site ... thinking
ahead to my exit later, after dark*), hoping to be early-but-not-
first to the festivities; there were a few more cars present
than the last time I had been by, so I pulled in and rolled
(*yes, actually rolled*) down the window to talk to a tall thin
man waiting at the mouth of the plowed parking area.

"I don't know you," he said.

I held out Greg's card, writing side up to the guy, "Greg
told me where to find you."

"Fifty dollars gets you parking and dinner and the dogs.
The bar is pay-as-you-go, and any action you take on the
dogs is done through us. If that sounds good, come on in."

His tone wasn't exactly inviting (*based on years of listening
to, and studying, and judging, invitations to various social
gatherings/outings*), but I passed him a fifty dollar bill and he
waved me past him and into the parking area.

I backed into a spot directly across from the entrance
to, and in a corner of, the parking lot, so that: my car was

close to the barn, I could leave quickly/easily when the time came, I wouldn't have more than one car parked next to mine, and when I got stuff out of the back it wouldn't be out in the open. I made sure that everything in the back was covered with the blanket, locked the car, and wandered casually (*too casually?*) to the barn for a look around.

There were 30 travel-crates against one of the long walls of the barn each one had a Saranac-Lake-Special-looking dog (*the large pit bull/ shepherd/ lab mixes that we seem to generate hundreds of in the Tri-Lakes*). A long wooden bar and a few tables were set up at the back of the barn, along with some big/noisy propane heaters that hadn't yet caught up with the cold in the barn (*although they were doing a good job, and might even get the place warm by the time the fights started and/ or the place filled up with people*). A pair of tables were spaced out along the long wall opposite the dog crates, with piles of Xeroxed sheets of paper and boxes of golf-pencils. Three guys were fiddling with the arrangement of stuff on the tables, two were rat-like and dressed like accountants, the third was Barry-large and sported a wife-beater (*and no jacket*) and an ostentatiously/ridiculously large sidearm in a white leather shoulder-holster that Barry whispered invisibly in my ear, "Must chafe something awful!"

I wandered around and then outside to grab a burger and chicken leg and potato salad from the grill/table/tent set up alongside the barn, looking around as more and more people began arriving. If I was the sort of person who gets/shows surprise, then I would have … they were all here to watch intentional acts of cruelty, and yet they all looked like regular people. It seemed bizarre to me that someone could look as normal as these guys (*mostly guys, there were a few women, but they seemed essentially the exceptions that proved the rule*). I accepted it while finishing my paper plate of dinner and a Coke from a two liter yellow-capped circle-K bottle (*I recently read online that these bottles are Kosher, which also means that the Coke inside them was made with real sugar instead of high-fructose corn syrup*), thinking that I've been able to pass (*mostly*) as human for nearly 30 years.

"First time?" said a man who had just sat down across from me at the table I was using.

I prolonged my chewing to avoid answering until I could try to guess if his question was good or disastrous news for me.

"I could tell because you're looking all around sorta blank-faced," he continued after a few seconds of my silence (*something I've noticed over time that most people will do*) ... I tend to be somewhat blank-faced unless I purposefully arrange my features into my approximation of human expressions, and I hadn't been doing that for the last few minutes, which must have been what this guy picked up on, and mistook for wonderment.

"Yah, when's it start ... you know, the ..." I said, ignoring the grimace Barry made as I delivered my line, and hoping that my dining partner would not be as unforgiving.

"The fights. It's okay, I felt funny talking about it my first time too. I'm Tom," he said holding out his hand.

"Bill Dunham," I said, holding up my barbeque soaked hands and shrugging at him (*I don't enjoy physical contact, especially with strangers, especially with strangers who enjoy participating in the torture of animals, if I don't have to, and in this case I didn't*).

He pulled back his hand, and continued undaunted, "Nice to meet you, Bill. They'll bring out the dogs a couple at a time starting at five, ya know, let us see how they move, how they look. Betting for the first five fights takes a while, and they'll generally start at 5:30 on the nose."

"Cool," I said. "Almost time to get inside to check out the dogs then, I guess (*crap, I may have to move up my timetable, as I want to avoid letting the fights start, if possible)."*

Tom was looking at me, perhaps wondering a bit at the stranger who didn't have any questions, so I wracked my brain, "How do you know which dogs to bet on? What makes them better? Is it being bigger?"

"Nope, the two dogs in each fight will be within five pounds of one another, so size isn't a big deal. I look for how the dog moves. How alert it looks. How scared of the crowd it is, how aggressive it is towards the other dogs when they're moving them in and out of the crates. Lots of little things really, they all work together to give me a picture; I do okay betting, although mostly I like the sport," Tom said.

I nodded, and tried an amalgam of a few of my learned smiles, unsure of how people would react to this discussion, trying not to imagine my dog, Hope, in this situation (*which was surprisingly easy, actually ... she is so old and slow that her two main strengths in a dog fight might well be farting and falling asleep*).

"Thanks Tom," I said, rolling my now empty plate around my chicken bones and plastic fork and napkin, and moving to get up and find the garbage. "I think I'm going to go and check out the dogs in their crates, but I might look for you when it gets closer to get some tips or advice."

"Sure thing, I'll keep an eye out for you," Tom said. (*I hoped not ... hoped that was just something people say*).

I wandered inside, stopping to top up on the excellent Coke on my way, and did a slow oval walk of the entire barn. The dogs all looked sad/scared/angry/stressed to me, and since nobody else was talking to them, neither did I. I picked up one of the sheets from a table, and looked at the lineup of the 15 fights slated for this evening; the odds for each dog in each fight were listed, they were all big dogs, mostly under three years old (*and all under five years old*), most of them had a successful history of fights (*I didn't think too long about what happened to dogs that lost their fights in this 'sport', not wanting to throw up my tasty supper*).

"No old dogs in this crowd either," said Barry in my ear; I didn't turn to see if he was there, threading his way through the crowd in an impossible manner ... it was so crowded in here now that it would force my brain to scale him down to a manageable size, which seemed somehow rude.

The Barry-analog was leaning back against the wall behind and between the two betting tables, keeping an eye on everything in the barn, but especially the tables in front of him. There were some people already filling out betting tickets in exchange for little marked chits from the two guys taking money.

I tried not to be obvious about trying to take in everything around the room, and felt that made me more obvious than ever about trying to take in everything around the room ... I suddenly didn't know/remember how normal people position their hands while walking, and had to look at the people around me to re-learn it. Despite the cold (*although noticeable warmer now*) air in the barn, I was lightly sweating, as the time got closer and everything (*myself included*) got tighter. Everything seemed to get louder and hotter around me for a few moments, and then it all backed off again, and I felt my control come rolling back in ... both the nervousness and the returning control, along with the feelings that they evoke, were things that I've only talked with Barry about (*since he knows everything that I know, it would be silly/crazy/pointless to try and keep things from him*). When I'm talking honestly and openly about why I do what I do, with Barry or with Hope, this is one of the top five reasons (*number three currently, although sometimes it slips back to numbers four or five*) ... the feeling of power or strength or control of helplessness or walking a knife's edge. A part of me (*maybe the human part*) loves it ... the gambling ... taking a chance ... betting against the numbers and the strong guys, betting on me being smarter/quicker/ruthlesser (*I know, it's not a word, but it should be ... I think*).

I suddenly felt as though I was getting more oxygen with every breath, standing an inch taller, walking more efficiently, able to see and hear with more effective discrimination. I could see and feel patterns of movement and sound in the crowd, and turned to the dog crates before the others around me did, sensing the change before it actually happened.

A middle-aged man moved through the crowd, parting them as he approached by something ... force of will maybe. He had to be Bronsen; about my size, but a little more triangular in shape (*broad shoulders sloping down to a narrow waist, as opposed to my narrow shoulders, which went straight down to comfy, if not flabby, hips*), black hair shot through with grey, and wearing new/clean/unscuffed Carhartts and work boots like a uniform as though trying to blend in. I got the feeling that he too was getting more oxygen with every breath, standing an inch taller, walking more efficiently, able to see and hear with more effective discrimination; I had a momentary concern that he would feel my eyes on him, and know my mind, my desire, my plan. I turned away to tie my shoe, and let him arrive at the wall of crates.

Someone tapped two short blasts on an air-horn and the room quieted.

"Good evening folks! I'm glad to see so many familiar faces, as well as some new ones here tonight. We've got some great dogs, some great fights, lined up for tonight, and we're all lucky to be here for some of the matches we'll be seeing later tonight. For now, we're going to show you the first five pairs of dogs, and get this party started. Have fun," Bronsen said, in the manner of a ringmaster, and then passed the megaphone he'd been holding to a smaller man who held a card to read off the information about the first ten dogs to the assembled crowd.

I'd seen a porta-potty outside the barn on my way in, and I asked the guy pouring drinks where the bathroom was, so I could reasonably slip outside while everyone's attention was focused on what was going on inside the barn.

I went directly through the growing darkness to my car, popped the back open, unzipped the duffels, and flipped each package to the on position briefly ... checking the battery level and the channel of each walkie before flipping it back off. I walked down the line of cars, starting a few from mine, and put one of the small packages on every other car, skipping the ones I'd noted earlier in the day as belonging to Bronsen's guys. As I placed each package, I turned the walkie attached to it to the on position and move along the line of cars. When I reached the end of the parking lot, having zigged and zagged my way up and down the rows, I had eight of the packages left, so I picked cars/trucks at random on my way back down the line, listening all the while to the voices in the barn. Nobody was watching, nobody noticed me ... either they weren't expecting trouble, or they weren't expecting it until later. I put the empty duffels back in the car, grabbed the master-walkie and walked back into the barn to rejoin the crowd, just as the last pair of dogs were put back in their cages.

I saw Tom, the man I had spoken to earlier, over supper, and he waved me over, "Hey Bill, what'd you think? Some good looking dogs, huh?"

I nodded, and thought back to our earlier discussion,

"Which ones did you like best? Are you going to be betting?"

He answered, in more detail than was probably necessary, and urged me to join one of the lines to place my bets, as there were only a few minutes before the first fight was due to begin.

"Excuse me, I have to take this," I said, pulling the walkie out of my pocket ... it's been my experience that if people expect to see a cell phone, they'll see one, regardless of what small black item you take out of your pocket.

I walked away from Tom, and generally over towards the dog crates by way of the bar, while turning on the master-walkie and selecting the proper channel and code setting (*to reach out to all of the packages in the parking lot*). When I was about as far from the parking lot as I could be while not actually standing in a corner, I pushed the send button.

Nothing happened.

Thirteen seconds later I started to hear some noises from the door/open end of the barn ... people and other less distinct sounds (*and light*) from outside the barn, in the direction of the parking lot.

Eight seconds after that, I heard the first small deflagrations (*witnesses would later incorrectly call them explosions ... a forgivable error*) as the thermite from my packages ignited gas in carburetors, oil in engine blocks, and in the case of a few cars, gas-lines and eventually gas-tanks.

Less than a minute after I had pushed the button, activating the thermite charges placed over the engine blocks of 36 cars and trucks in the parking lot, many of them were burning ... a significant fraction (*roughly half to my eye, as I walked over to my car along with the panicking throng*) had burned straight through the engine block without catching the cars/trucks on fire; these vehicles were still effectively rendered really big paperweights by virtue of the fact that the internal combustion engines had been destructively remodeled at 2500 degrees Fahrenheit.

When the first sounds of cars burning and exploding began to filter through the walls and into the minds of the spectators inside the barn, I heard a low, then growing, hubbub and excited panic from within ... followed moments later by the first trickles of an eventual flood of people leaving the huge barn to check on the noises and flee the scene. I grabbed a smaller duffel and headed back around the side of the barn to wait for the next stage to begin.

The Old Miller Place, Peasleeville, NY
Wednesday, 1/22/2014, 5:43 p.m.

The sounds and sights and smells from the parking lots
were better than I could have hoped for … crackling
flames and shattering glass and gut-thumping booms and
loud/angry/scared car horns and shouts and cries; from
everywhere the licking lights of flames and wildly swinging
lights of cars madly trying to flee the inferno, either seen
or reflected in snow or glass or against the distant trees in
the dark of night; the thick stench/smoke of burning cars
and oil and tires and upholstery … taken together it was
nearly overwhelming for me, and I had been expecting it.

The people working at, as well as those paying to see,
the dog fights were panicked and flowed in and around the
parking lot like a combination of angered bees and
popping corn … bouncing and changing direction and
humming with a nervous and terrifying energy. It was
noisy, it was frightful, it was chaos … it was perfect.

As predicted by both John and Barry during our
planning session just a few days ago, Bronsen's guys
immediately packed up the money as soon as the

disruption began. They all took off in separate vehicles (*including the container truck, leaving all the dogs*) before the crowd of dog fighting enthusiasts had fully begun to panic. I had skipped enough cars in the parking lot to insure that those people whose cars were bricked could get home by bumming rides (*I didn't want anyone to freeze to death walking home*). I imagined them explaining the damage done to their cars, along with the location and circumstances, to their insurance companies, and felt badly for them for approximately three microseconds.

In the slightly less frenzied moments after the first fires started and were noticed, I had slid around the side of the barn and thrown a number of empty boxes in front of, and behind, the car that I had seen Bronsen park behind the container truck (*now gone*) that had hauled the dogs to the site. I was relieved to see Bronsen storming towards his car alone, feeling his pockets for his keys (*my plan had allowed for his having a driver/minion, but it was much easier to manage without*). He saw the boxes blocking his car and cursed, not softly, under his breath; it was when he bent over to grab the first box that I stepped out from the shadows and called his name. He straightened up and registered the shotgun in my arms just as I shot him in the chest.

The loud report was lost in the chaos already surrounding us, and he fell back in the snow next to his car; he rolled roughly to one side and seemed to be trying to rise/crawl upright using the car as a prop, so I shot him again, aiming generally for the area where I pictured his kidneys residing. He arched backwards for a moment, and then his head slammed forward into the side-panel of his car, after which he remained motionless. I looked around and counted to five (*waiting for someone to point at me or scream or anything, but everyone else had other things going on at the moment*).

301

I cautiously moved towards Bronsen's limp form, ready to fire again if needed (*having seen lots of 'scary movies' with Dorothy over the years, I was always ready for the bad guy to rise against all reason*). I found the keys to his car in the pocket he had been patting when I interrupted him. I unlocked the car, opened the front door, hit the hood release, and went around to open the hood. I went back to Bronsen, dragged him over to the hood, hauled him partway up and draped him over the engine, using first cable-ties and then duct-tape (*when it comes to restraining the monsters of this world, I'm a 'belt and suspenders' kind of guy*) to secure him to the solid parts of the car. From a distance it might have looked like we were trying to get his car started. I likely wouldn't need to fool anyone (*if the police or firefighters came before I was done, my plan was just to walk into the darkness and wait until I could circle back to get Greg's car*). Headlights from a steady stream of fleeing cars and trucks gave me an ongoing, if not steady amount of light by which to work. As I finished securing him, he started to roll around a bit, limited in his field of motion by the ties/tape.

"Bronsen. Can you hear me?" I said.

"Mrrrrph!" Bronsen said.

I leaned back against the building to wait a bit, and ran through the next few minutes in my head once more, just to be sure.

"Bronsen!" I said, reaching out to tap his forehead with the barrel of the shotgun a couple of times to try and get his attention.

"Stop ... stop! I'm awake," he said. "What the fuck did you do?"

"I shot you — twice — with beanbag rounds (*less than lethal rounds, which actually/thankfully lived up to their name ... I had/have every intent of Bronsen's getting through this night essentially unharmed, or at least, alive*). You may have some broken ribs and/or some blood in your pee for a few days, but you're not cooling towards the ambient temperature and making a blood-colored snow cone, so it's a win for both of us."

He turned his head and looked at me, "Chicken-shit bastard, in any kind of standup fight, I'd demolish you."

"That seems a perfect explanation/reason for why I didn't/don't fight fair," I replied, noting that my speech was regressing in humanness a bit (*perhaps nerves or tension, although I felt okay*). I'd long been a proponent of fighting dirty every chance I got for exactly his reason.

"He's got a point," Barry said from beside me. I wasn't sure if he was replying to me or Bronsen, but since he was my imaginary friend, I chose to think he was supporting me, and ignored him (*mostly so that Bronsen wouldn't get distracted by wondering who/what I was speaking to*).

"So you didn't kill me. Why? Whadya want?" he asked. "I don't see your angle, here."

"You will, assuming you're half-smart and as awake as you seem," I said, stooping to grab a handful of snow and throw it in his face to try and make sure that he was fully awake.

"What the fuck?!? What's it like in the world where you live? Do you imagine us making some deal where I don't cut out your fucking heart and eat it?" he asked.

"I do, and I hope that in a few minutes you will too," I answered.

"What the fuck do you want, and how do you think that any of this is going to get it for you?" Bronsen asked, essentially reiterating his question of only moments ago, so I looked at my watch and figured that I should get going.

"I'll start with the broad strokes, Mr. Bronsen, if that's okay with you, and then we can circle back to work out the finer details as you need … sound good?" I asked.

"Fucking go ahead ... whatever. By morning one of us will be dead. You've got me, I'll admit it, but lots of guys have thought that before and they're all gone, and I'm still here," he said.

"Okay ... here it is. The thing you had up here, the dog fights, that's done."

He started to talk, and I channeled Barry for a moment (*seeing his appreciative nod out of the corner of my eye*), "Shut up and let me talk, or I'll warm up your car for a bit with you tied to the engine."

He settled back against the car and I continued, "Thank you! So, your dog fight thing is done. There's thirty or forty cars trashed out there, and even if the people you took money from tonight aren't angry with you, the police will get involved now, and someone will mention your name. Say 'yup' if you heard me so far."

Barry grinned at me from across the open hood.

"Yup," said Bronsen in a flat and angry voice.

"I'm betting that you've got money set aside and can just go away somewhere and set up a new life for yourself ... hopefully something a bit more wholesome, but I've got no interest in policing the planet ... I just want you gone from my corner of it. Say 'yup' again."

"Yup."

"I don't care what you do, or where you do it ... you just can't do it here. I've set up conditions that will reinforce my request/demand. When we're done here, you'll get in this car and drive until you're outside the Adirondack Park. Say 'yup'."

"Yup," Bronsen said again, only this time I thought that I could hear a smile in the single syllable.

"My friends told me that even though this deal makes perfect sense to me, that a guy like you won't let himself get pushed around by a guy like me. Is that right? I hope not, because this can end pretty well for both of us in just a few minutes if my friends misjudged you," I said.

"Your friends are right. You made so much effort to save those fucking dogs, and not kill me ... you don't want to kill me ... prolly don't have the stones for it."

He paused for a moment, and craned his head around to look at Barry and me (*more likely just me*), "Wait, is this about that shelter chick? It is. I'm going to throw her and her girlfriend (*wife, I mentally corrected*) in the front door of that rat-hole shelter and burn it to ash, and then piss on the ashes. I'm gonna do that, and make you watch, just cause I can. Say 'yup' if you unnerstand me, fuckwit," he said, this time with a note of savage glee in his voice.

"Yup," I said. "I'm glad that I've learned the limits of my understanding of human behavior, and trusted my friends. They convinced me to come up with a second component of the deal to sweeten the pot in a way that you'd understand. Are you familiar with the term 'Standover Man'?"

Bronsen was silent for a few seconds (*which was all the answer either of us really needed*) before replying, "What? How do you think you're going to stand over me? Besides killing me, which you're not gonna do, you got nothing I need and nothing that can intimidate me."

"I'm going to free one of your hands in a minute and ask you to dial a phone number, and talk to whoever's there, okay?" I said.

"Yup," he answered after a few seconds, although I hadn't prompted him to do so.

I reached carefully around him, waggling the shotgun (*probably*) gratuitously in front of his face, "I'm going to cut your left hand loose now, but please remember that I have dozens of beanbag rounds left (*really I only had four, but I was pretty sure that it would be enough*). Nod if you understand me."

He nodded.

I put the phone next to his left hand before cutting it mostly free (*I cut the cable-tie and most of the way through the duct-tape*), The number you're going to dial is 504-566-5003," I said, and waited for him to process, look shocked for a moment, and then dial.

"When you get through to your mother or sister at their house in New Orleans, they will have a visitor with them, a new neighbor, or so they think. My guy found your family in a couple of hours in five different ways; if you move them, he can find them again ... just as quick," I said.

Bronsen dialed the phone, apparently never even thinking of throwing it at me or trying to grab me, or any other stupid stunt. He waited for a few seconds while the connection was made.

"Hey Ma," he said. "How are you and Mel? Everything okay?"

Her answer took a couple of seconds ... he looked pained (*maybe she was talking about the weather in Louisiana, people wasting time talking about weather always made me feel like he looked right now*).

"You got company? Hmmm, nice guy? Can you put him on for a second? No, nothing, just put him on, I wanna see what he thinks of the condo."

He waited a second before continuing, "Who's this? If you touch my Ma or sister, I'll ... yup."

He deflated while he listened to John on the other end of the phone, then seemed to struggle to rally, "Yeah Ma, he seems like a nice guy, I hope he sticks around to take you two to a Saints or a Pelicans game sometime. I gotta go, talk to you later, okay?"

Bronsen sagged against the frame of the car, and remained silent for a 23 seconds, perhaps thinking about Standover men (*a term applied to a sub-class of criminals who extort money or valuables, often from other criminals ... in this case it applied to John, down visiting the Pelican State*) before speaking (*with enough less swagger in his voice that I could hear it, and I'm not a good listener for that sort of thing*), "Okay, what do you want?"

"Same deal as before, nothing, except for you to leave ... tonight, and never come back to this part of the world. I'd like your promise that you'll stop hurting dogs and people, but I wouldn't believe you, and can't be bothered to follow you around for the rest of your life," I said.

He started to speak, and I cut him off, riding over his opening reasonable tones.

"You leave, and you leave us alone ... me, Dorothy, Lisa, the dogs in the barn behind you, everyone. If you come back or hurt me or hurt them, or one of us gets hurt crossing the street or struck by lightning or dies of cancer, my friend John, who you spoke to a minute ago will find your mom and sister and ... do bad things."

"Sissy, you should have told him that John would skin them, or some shit," Barry interjected, not too helpfully (*although again, mercifully, I was able to ignore him*).

I waited, watching him think and try to find a gap ... he couldn't ... there wasn't one.

"It's a good deal, so long as you won't miss the Adirondack winters. You can have the rest of the planet ... sound okay?" I asked.

After another pause, he replied, "Yes. Fuck this place and fuck the cold, and fuck you."

"Good, I was hoping you'd feel that way, although I could do without the gratuitous bad language," I said. "That's the good news ... the bad news is that there's one more thing ... just a small thing before I let you go. You'll need a more lasting — physical — reminder of our deal."

By this point in our conversation, I was nervously looking up and down the road adjacent to the barn for lights of approaching emergency services vehicles, feeling that my time had certainly just about run out.

He stiffened, as he worked out what this other shoe dropping might mean to him, and I tried to put soothing tones in my voice.

"Relax, you put her in the hospital, and she'll be there for weeks. If I were to do that to you tonight, how could you retire to Boise, or wherever?" I said.

"Okay, so, what?" Bronsen asked, putting a little attitude in his reply, which Barry seemed to admire/respect.

I dug into the duffle bag hung around my shoulder/waist, and pulled out the big cast-iron frying pan that I'd given Dorothy and Lisa for Christmas two years ago (*we'd made biscuits in it Christmas morning, and cooked with it lots of times since, but Lisa had ordered me to take it when I'd picked up Hope a few days ago*), "Make a fist with your left hand, please."

Bronsen looked up at me, waited a beat, and then nodded (*either seeing my logic, or giving in to the fact that he had no other option at this point in the game*). He let go of the phone (*which I reached in to grab off of the engine housing before it could get broken or lost ... I had another call or two to make before I chucked it*) and curled the fingers of his left hand into a fist.

I raised the heavy frying pan and brought it down in a fast and brutal arc smashing his hand between it and the unyielding ridges of his car's engine. I could hear and feel bones breaking. I repeated my swing twice more. He screamed each time and tears ran down his cheeks when he looked up at me as I put the pan back into the duffel and made ready to release him.

"I'm going to cut you free in a second, but I need to make sure that you're not going to get stupid all of a sudden. If I don't call John in the next twenty minutes, telling him that I'm away, he'll gut your family. Do you understand me? Are you in control, Mr. Bronsen? You're about to walk away from all of the atrocious things that you've done with your money and your freedom ... count this as a win. Okay?" I asked, waiting for his nod. "I want you to remember tonight, and why you were smart to leave, five years from now ... ten ... when you flex your left hand and feel the pain from those broken bones; remember, Bronsen."

I cut through the cable tie and tape holding his right hand, turned around, and walked away from him, walking backwards at first ... waiting for stupid anger to overtake reason and fear, but in this case, it did not. He didn't say anything else, and neither did I ... there was nothing left to say.

I got in my borrowed car, started it up, and drove away, passing the first fire trucks on the road a mile from the Old Miller Place ... I didn't see a police car until I turned off of Peasleeville Road onto Strackville Road, and then it was simply flashers in my rearview mirror. Once I was ten miles away, I called John to tell him that I was okay, and thank him for saving my bacon, again (*which made me think of bacon, and I asked him to set a slab aside for me when he got back to the farm*).

After finishing up my call with John, I dialed a number from memory (*from more than five years ago*), "Hi Peg, you might not remember me, but we met five years ago through Dorothy and those dogs in the truck on the fourth of July."

"I remember you, the odd boy," she said.

"That's me. Anyway, something similar's come up. I heard about thirty dogs abandoned in crates in an old barn in Peasleeville ... let me give you directions," I said.

"Wait, wait, wait!" she screamed into the phone. "What

dogs, why, where, how?"

"All excellent questions, none of which I can answer. I just heard about this from a guy I know, and it's important that both he and I are left out of it. You need to know that these dogs were part of a dog fighting thing that Dorothy got involved in, and it'd be great if you could find someone to help these dogs, if you can't help them yourself," I said.

"Okay, I get it. I'll start making calls and get someone there tonight if you give me the directions," she said. I did, and then hung up.

Adirondack Medical Center, Saranac Lake, NY
Thursday, 1/23/2014, 5:18 p.m.

I made it back to Union Falls that night and slept in the bathtub with all of the furniture piled in front of the door and windows (*just in case Bronsen rethought his position on our deal ... he didn't*).

In the morning I was waiting on the steps of Deb's Diner when she arrived at a bit before six, and helped her open up the place (*I had biscuits and gravy ... twice, and six glasses of milk, and three slices of yesterday's pie*). I was waiting on the curb outside of the Central Garage when Greg arrived at a bit before eight, and with the promise of overpayment, and a pointed lack of questions about the dog fight, he had me on the road by ten-thirty.

I made it to Billy's place by two in the afternoon, switched cars with him, and headed back out again after a quick bathroom break and face splash. I rolled into the parking lot of the hospital in Saranac Lake at 4:32 p.m., and found my way through the smells and friendly old ladies in the front of the house, such that my hand was on the doorknob to Dorothy's room three minutes later. I breathed in and out, turned the handle, and walked in.

Dorothy was sleeping in the bed with tubes directing input and output and festooned with sensors and leads that connected her to machines that go 'BING'; she was covered by a sloppily rendered quilt that I assumed was from their home (*Lisa had started quilting last winter, and I kept hearing about quilts and quilting and patterns and how mathematic it was, all the time, from Dorothy*). I started to retrace my steps, and back out of the room when Dorothy cracked open an eye, and spoke.

"I wondered if I'd see you today or tomorrow," she said. "Frank was in a couple of times earlier today; it seems like you've been busy, despite what you told me and Lisa and Frank."

The stern tone was ruined by a tiny smile that lit up her bruised and broken face.

"I have no idea what you're talking about, I've been camping for a couple of days down near Utica to get away from the worry," I replied.

"Frank was positive you'd say something like that, and I wouldn't have taken a bet against it, no matter the odds offered," she said, smiling a bit more now … enough to hurt bits of her face apparently.

"Well," I said, "I had a promise to keep."

I wasn't going to say anymore, either way, but two seconds later, she started a clumsy clapping and giggled.

"I'm your dog … I'm Miles," she said, with delight.

"Not exactly … not yet, anyway," I added.

She gestured me in closer, and reached out to give me a pat on the arm (*I made sure to stay out of kissing range, as that's what she does when in this sort of mood*). "You did what you had to do, even though I didn't want it, for my own good. You love me like a dog!"

At this juncture, she actually teared up and the tears

started leaking down her face.

My face was hot and I felt a bit cornered, so I asked her if she needed anything, and then made good my escape; out of her room and down the seemingly endless halls towards the eventual exit, hoping to escape before Frank circled back. I was nearly to the door when Lisa came out of the gift shop with a balloon tied to the arm of an enormous stuffed bear that looked more like a panda than the polar bear I think it was aiming for (*which naturally made me think about the apparent evolutionary fitness differences between the species, and some research that I'd left incomplete on the subject*) ... I had somewhat lost myself in thought, and tried to avoid her seeing me, but failed to make good my escape.

"Tyler!" she called. "Stop for a minute."

"Hello Lisa," I said, turning around and sitting down on one of the surprisingly uncomfortable couches the hospital had scattered around the entrance/waiting-room.

"I was just going to stop in and see if Dot's awake, would you like to come with me?" she asked, with a tone at the end that I didn't recognize.

"I was just there," I answered.

"... and you probably wouldn't want to come in with me after the way I treated you the other day. I completely understand. You must think I'm horrible," she said.

"Not at all, Lisa, you were upset, and I wasn't able to give you what you wanted/needed in a time of crisis," I said.

She tilted her head, like dogs/cats/birds do when they hear a strange sound.

"Regardless, Tyler, I feel terrible about the way I screamed at you," she said, vigorously/excitedly digging a Coke out of her duffel-sized purse. "I was hoping that I might see you."

I ducked minutely when she initially brandished the

Coke can, and she looked (*in quick succession*) shocked, surprised, sad, and then amused, which she landed on … laughing a bit, snorting once.

"I'm not gonna throw this one at you. It's a peace offering, and a thank you for — you know — what you did," she said.

"I don't know what you think I did, or why you think I did it, but I hope that when you see Frank you'll tell him what I'm going to tell you now. I was down camping near Lowville for the past few days, and just heard about some disturbance up north and east of here." I had no trouble keeping a straight face as I said this, as that's my default setting, and it takes considerable effort to arrange it in any other configuration.

"Ha! Whatever, I'm just grateful that you got that sonovabitch, and that he can't hurt my Dorothy, or any dogs, ever again (*I wondered briefly what she thought I did to/with Bronsen*)." She was smiling with me as the target for the first time in (*my perfect*) memory. "Do Dorothy and I need to go into hiding?"

"Again, I don't know what you're talking about … and, no," I answered, trying out a slightly modified #3 smile, friendly/helpful/sincere (*with a bit of rascal thrown in at the end*).

"Why don't you go get that nasty dog of yours, bring her over, and we'll have some supper while I visit with the cats for a while, and you can tell me all about your camping trip. Dorothy is stable, and may even be a bit better today; I know that this thing being over and done will be a burden lifted from her."

She gathered herself together and took a deep breath, as if she had made up her mind about something.

"Thank you, Tyler," she said quietly, as she reached over and gave my hand a squeeze, then she looked up and apologized. "Sorry, I know you don't like touches, but it's how I relate ... how I love."

"It's what Dorothy loves most about you, the touching and wild gestures you have to use when talking," I said. "But, on the other thing, I didn't do it for the reasons you wanted, or because you demanded it, or slapped me ... if I did anything, which I didn't," I quickly added.

"It doesn't matter why you did it, or for whom, just that it got done. I'll see you and that nasty dog in a half hour. I'll call the order in, can you pick up the food from the good Chinese place on your way back from the farm?"

I could, and I did ... it was spicy and fatty and greasy and wonderful, and we shared bits of food with Hope and the cats (*who still hated/hate me*), and it was nearly as though Lisa and I were friends, or friendly, for the first time.

Dorothy grew better/stronger/healthier a bit at a time, and was out of the hospital ahead of predictions. Frank never pushed as hard or as pointedly as he could have on where I went for those few days, and what happened while I was gone; he didn't really want to know.

Lisa and I grew closer, as closer as I was likely to grow with her given all the complex givens of a relationship based on sharing parts of a third person centrally important to the other two, a big part of our warmer relationship based on her perception of my having avenged Dot ... which I didn't. I like my world the way it is, and Dorothy (*and the TLAS*) is a big part of my new world (*up here in the Adirondacks, as opposed to my old world down in Manhattan and the surrounding boroughs*) ... if I let her get beaten up or killed or chased away, or the shelter burned down, that would present/represent an unacceptable level of change/imbalance to the world that I've built up here. I did what I had to do — no more, no less — to keep

Dorothy and the dogs (*and the cats, who got my help despite our mutual antipathy*) safe and sound. Telling that to anyone besides my internal monolog would result in odd stares and possibly anger, which wouldn't improve things ... thus, as is often the case, it's much better to let people assume what they will about my motives and motivations (*or, ideally, to languish in complete ignorance of my actions*) rather than explain or defend my actions.

I will likely tell Dot some version of what happened, accentuating the frying pan aspect of the story (*which is the only part of the events that makes me a bit uncomfortable ... it feels a bit revenge-y to me, but somehow seemed necessary ... I don't always understand why I do what I do*). Hope knows the truth, the whole truth, and nothing but the truth, and I've purchased absolution/indulgence with food far too spicy for her aged and delicate belly (*from the good Chinese place*).

Frank knows what he knows, and is happy not being able, or having, to prove any of it; we don't talk about the events of those few days, and it's working so far...

ACKNOWLEDGMENTS

The Tri-Lakes Humane Society (TLHS) is a massive force for good in the Adirondack Park, and an inspiration to me as a writer and a human being. The Tri-Lakes Animal Shelter (TLAS) in my books is loosely based on the TLHS … everything good about it is true, the illegal activities were (of course) entirely made up. We've brought four dogs home from the TLHS to live with us, and all of them have been instrumental in helping me write the books in one way or another.

The students that I have had the opportunity to work with, and learn from, over the years at Lake Placid Middle/High School have helped me to celebrate our differences, and explore some of the various ways that there are to see, and experience, the world.

Friends and family have inspired and supported me throughout the writing and editing process, and I can't thank them enough. My parents (Jim and Jill Sheffield), sister (Sarah Sheffield), wonderful son (Ben), and wife (Gail Gibson Sheffield) all gave me the time and space and loving support that I needed to follow this dream, and their love gave me the courage to try, again. Rick Schott, Bryce Fortran, Derek Murawsky, Kevin Curdgel, and Stephen Carvalho have helped me expand my map of the world through their friendship while camping in all seasons. Countless other friends have also offered encouragement, especially Jonathan Webber and Gail Bennett Schott who have given me unending support and positive vibes during the writing and editing process over the last few years.

Over the past three years I have an incredible outpouring of support from readers of "Here Be Monsters" and "Caretakers," as well as the novellas, published as e-books in the Tyler Cunningham series. It is one thing to put creative ideas on paper, a completely different thing to know those ideas are being read and accepted by people all over the world. It is that acceptance and encouragement that moved me from being someone who writes, to being a writer. That is what made all of the writing possible, thank you all for that.

A big shout out to the entire staff at SmartPig Publishing for their tireless efforts throughout the process ... thanks Gail and Randy! Randy Lewis joined the SmartPig team last fall as Copy Editor, and her work to polish was more appreciated than she knew. We miss, and will miss, Randy's help and love and support for the rest of our lives, and are grateful for the time that we had with her.

While I couldn't have done it without any of you, any errors or omissions are all mine.

ABOUT THE AUTHOR

Jamie Sheffield lives in the Adirondack Park with his wife and son and two dogs, Miles and Puck. When he's not writing mysteries, he's probably camping or exploring the last great wilderness in the Northeast. He has been a Special Education Teacher in the Lake Placid Central School District for 15 years. Besides writing, Jamie loves cooking and reading and dogs and all manner of outdoor pursuits.

To read his novels:

"Here Be Monsters"
and
"Caretakers"

And other works by the author.

Visit Jamie Sheffield's website:

http://www.jamiesheffield.com

and at his Amazon Author Page.